## By Gayle Callen

THE GROOM WORE PLAID
THE WRONG BRIDE
REDEMPTION OF THE DUKE
SURRENDER TO THE EARL
RETURN OF THE VISCOUNT
EVERY SCANDALOUS SECRET
A MOST SCANDALOUS ENGAGEMENT
IN PURSUIT OF A SCANDALOUS LADY
NEVER MARRY A STRANGER
NEVER DARE A DUKE
NEVER TRUST A SCOUNDREL
THE VISCOUNT IN HER BEDROOM
THE DUKE IN DISGUISE
THE LORD NEXT DOOR
A WOMAN'S INNOCENCE
THE BEAUTY AND THE SPY
NO ORDINARY GROOM
HIS BRIDE
HIS SCANDAL
HIS BETROTHED
MY LADY'S GUARDIAN
A KNIGHT'S VOW
THE DARKEST KNIGHT

# GAYLE CALLEN

# THE GROOM WORE PLAID

## Highland Weddings

AVONBOOKS
*An Imprint of HarperCollinsPublishers*

This is a work of fiction. Names, characters, places, and incidents are products of the author's imagination or are used fictitiously and are not to be construed as real. Any resemblance to actual events, locales, organizations, or persons, living or dead, is entirely coincidental.

AVON BOOKS
*An Imprint of* HarperCollins*Publishers*
195 Broadway
New York, New York 10007

Copyright © 2016 by Gayle Kloecker Callen
ISBN 978-0-06-226800-6
**www.avonromance.com**

First Avon Books mass market printing: March 2016

Avon Trademark Reg. U.S. Pat. Off. and in Other Countries, Marca Registrada, Hecho en U.S.A.
Avon, Avon Books, and the Avon logo are trademarks of HarperCollins Publishers.
HarperCollins® is a registered trademark of HarperCollins Publishers.

Printed in the U.S.A.

10 9 8 7 6 5 4 3 2 1

*To my patient editor, Erika Tsang, who steered me into the world of Scotland, opening up new ideas and lots of fun research. Your help was invaluable in making this book the best it could be. Thank you!*

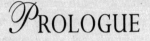

# PROLOGUE

*Scotland, 1717*

Maggie McCallum was only sixteen and Owen Duff eighteen the autumn their families spent in Edinburgh. Her mother had said she was too young for courtship, but Maggie secretly scoffed at that. Men looked at her now, and she was finally allowing herself to give a flirtatious look back.

And then at a dancing assembly, she saw Owen, Viscount Duncraggan, heir to the earldom of Aberfoyle. She'd met him only once before, at a dinner with their parents. She'd been twelve, he fourteen, and he'd ignored her. Now a friend giggled and pointed him out.

"He's from the Duff clan," the girl said. "Even I ken

that the McCallums and the Duffs have always despised each other."

Maggie nodded without really listening. She was staring at Owen with wide, curious eyes. He did not wear a belted plaid as so many of her family did, but an expensive tailored coat and waistcoat over knee breeches, and the polished sword at his hip sparkled in the candlelight when he strode across the dance floor to bow to a blushing girl. He had a thin face and bony shoulders that hinted at the broad strength of the man he would become. His sandy hair was gathered in a haphazard queue on his neck, loose strands brushing his cheeks as if he were too busy to be bothered fastening it more securely.

"Isn't your brother to marry his sister? Ye'll be practically family."

Family or not, Maggie knew better than to be the McCallum who approached a Duff in public, right in front of her mother. She thought of her brother's misery at marrying a woman he didn't know or love, the way he'd done foolish, reckless things in anger when he'd first discovered his fate at thirteen. Maggie had pitied him, and felt guilty that she was secretly glad it wasn't *she* forced to marry a Duff.

Her next meeting with Owen wasn't auspicious—she merely passed him on the stairs outside her flat on High Street, as dusk settled in dark waves on Edinburgh. The tall building with a dozen floors housed all manner of people, from the chimney sweep in the cellar to the dancing master in the garret. The best floors were reserved for noblemen, and though her father didn't have a title, he was the chief of the Clan McCallum. Her mother had leased the flat to be near the earl's family, since her son was marrying into them, but she did not want her daughter involved beyond what civility expected.

Upon seeing Maggie, Owen came to a stop on the stairs and grinned that grin that lived in her dreams for many years to come. His warm brown eyes made her think of the chocolate English ladies favored for their morning drink, and as they took her in, skimming her form, she felt as suitably overheated as that cup she'd only once clutched in her hands on a cold winter morning in the Highlands.

She wanted to scold him for his bold gaze but then she saw the round tube he carried.

"Is that a telescope?" she demanded.

Those eyes now brightened with more than warmth. "Aye, I'm heading out to gaze upon the stars. Have ye looked through one before?"

She shook her head. She'd done nothing more intellectual than read passages from the Bible—she hadn't been allowed more, had no access to other books. Knowing there was a whole world of knowledge out there made her ache with regret and frustration.

He held out a hand. "I'm Owen. Do ye want to come?"

She hesitated, realizing he didn't recognize her. In

that long moment she thought of her grandparents already preparing for bed, the fact that she'd just seen her mother into a sedan chair to meet with friends, and that her brother lived in his own flat near the university. She was alone.

Owen stood a couple stairs below her, and that put them at just about the same height. She stared into his eyes again, and the admiration and curiosity made her unfurl like a blossom in springtime.

But she had to be honest. Taking a deep breath, she said, "I'm Maggie McCallum. 'Tis my brother who's to marry your sister."

He looked at her for a long moment, and the first feelings of regret and resignation washed through her.

But Owen didn't rush away, only extended his hand closer to her. "Nice to meet ye, Maggie. Do ye still want to come with a dreaded Duff?"

She bit her lip to keep from giggling like a foolish girl. She was sixteen, a woman now. He obviously didn't remember her from four years before. Maybe that was for the best. Putting her hand in his, she let him lead her out into the twilight.

During the next few weeks, Owen was the excitement in days that were once dreary and repetitive. Sneaking away to ride down to the shore at the Firth of Forth, boating, exploring the grounds of Edinburgh Castle, or even meandering through shops seemed like wild adventures when she was at Owen's side.

Rather than deter her, the very forbiddance of a

friendship between them caused her to be far too reckless. He was so very different from the men she knew. He discussed physics and chemistry and astronomy as if she was as smart as he. She saw his wonder in the world, but when she asked if he would be a scientist, his expression turned hard as he said his father had forbidden it. He was the heir to an earldom, and would be educated as such. If he didn't study the classics, his father would refuse him attendance at university next year.

Maggie sympathized, and distracted him from his sad and angry thoughts, but she could not stop dwelling on her own confusion. Every moment she spent in his company, Owen seemed more and more familiar to her, as if they'd met much earlier in their childhood, though he swore they had not. Sometimes it was as if a ghost of a dream teased her from just beyond the shadows, and she shivered.

Her dreams were nothing to make light of. More than once, she'd dreamed something that eventually came true. The family of a little boy in her clan had thought him drowned and were about to give up the search, when a dream led her to the bedraggled boy huddled beneath a cliff. Another dream foretold the suicide of a young woman whom Maggie's father had abused. Maggie hadn't understood what she was seeing until it had actually come true, which was often the case. And then it had been too late to help the girl. Maggie's mother had taken her away from Larig

Castle and back to Edinburgh, to keep her safe from her father.

But Owen? Could he have been part of a dream she couldn't remember? The puzzle of it flooded her mind when she was separated from him, but the hours they were together were full of happy laughter, insightful discussion, and endless moments where she stared into his face when he wasn't looking and imagined herself married to him. Maybe her mind was simply trying to tell her that he was her destiny, that they were meant to be together. She wanted him to kiss her, but he was ever the gentleman—or maybe he assumed that the centuries-old feud between their clans meant they could never share a more intimate relationship. It seemed to be a forbidden topic between them.

But he touched her, and each time she could have surely melted with delight. He would take her hand running across a field, guide her by grasping her elbow, put his hand gently on her waist when they stood watching the sun set amid beautiful orange and pink clouds adorning it like trailing scarves.

Two weeks into their friendship, they were carrying a luncheon basket along the river, Water of Leith, on a particularly sunny autumn day, when Owen suggested they look for mussels and Scottish pearls. This was no mere meandering in ankle-deep water, and soon they were both dripping wet, pearl-less, shivering as they crawled back up the grassy bank, laughing.

Owen lay down in the sun, and feeling reckless, she

did the same, eyeing him boldly since his own eyes were closed. His queue had come undone, and long strands of his hair, dark brown with water, covered his cheeks. Without thinking, she came up on her elbow and used a trembling finger to move the locks away from his face.

His eyes snapped open, and she expected him to laugh up at her, but he seemed to concentrate intently on her face just above his. Everything external seemed to go silent as they shared a hot, meaningful gaze. She was focused on the rough sound of her breathing, the moisture beaded on his skin, the way she could feel his heart pounding in his chest when she rested her trembling hand there.

And then he cupped her head and brought her down for a kiss. His lips were cool from the water, yet softer than she imagined a man's would be. Such boldness made her dizzy—or was it simply near-ness to Owen? Her hand still on his chest, she lifted her head and stared down at him uncertainly, but he only brought their mouths together again. He parted his lips, and the shock of his tongue sliding between hers made her start with surprise and wonder. Her cool, wet skin seemed to heat, the warmth spreading out from her mouth and down her chest. Her trembling was no longer from the cold, but she didn't know why her limbs seemed so restless. She wanted to be touched—needed it with a desperation new to her. But she was afraid to do more than brace herself against his chest as he explored her mouth and taught her to explore his.

The world shifted as he rolled her onto her back. It was his turn to rise above her, his intense face framed by blue sky and towering autumn-hued trees. She had no time to think as he kissed her again and began to touch her. His hand on her body was a hot, welcome presence, and with each touch she felt more and more as if she couldn't lie still. His caresses journeyed across her wet clothes from her hip and upward. And when at last he touched her breast, pushed upward by her stays, she moaned against his lips and shuddered with each delicate strum across her nipple, as if he made her an instrument of desire.

Their shared world of passion was suddenly overwhelming, and she pushed against him before it was too late to stop. Owen lifted his head and stared down at her, his breathing as erratic as hers.

"We cannot do this," she said with a trembling voice. Not that she regretted any of it, she realized, staring at his mouth and wishing to feel again the pleasure he'd given her.

Owen was looking at her mouth, too, and he practically growled, "I knew ye'd find out. Forgive me. I didn't ken how to tell ye."

"Find out what?" she demanded.

He grimaced.

"Owen Duff, ye have to tell me now."

"My father betrothed me some years ago to the daughter of a Lowland clan. Even now, they journey here for us to meet."

The last warmth from their kiss deserted Maggie. Shivering, she sat up and scooted away from him, covering her chest as if it was bared to him.

"Why did ye never tell me this?" she demanded. She'd let herself get lost in the fairy tale of their friendship, and the romance she'd thought had been blossoming. Now she knew she was simply a fool.

Owen tucked his hair back into the queue, as if he needed something to do with his hands. He didn't look at her, and his face was as red as hers felt, but she didn't feel any sympathy for him.

His words came out slowly at first, before tumbling over each other as fast as the rippling water behind him. "At first, I thought we were simply friends, and to know ye were a McCallum made it daring. But the need to kiss ye has been dominating my thoughts more and more."

He met her gaze at last, and she felt like she'd never forget the heat she saw there, the passion he was showing just for her. But he was betrothed, and a lump rose high up into her throat, shutting off any words.

She scrambled to her feet and backed away from him before she would embarrass herself more by crying. "I—I have to go."

"Let me walk ye back," Owen said.

He didn't try to change her mind, or promise to end the betrothal. The first tear fell down her cheek and she angrily wiped it away.

She held up a hand. "Nay, I—I don't want to see ye again, Owen."

His expression twisted with pain, and she knew she'd hurt him. She didn't trust easily, not with a drunkard for a father, and she felt the worst kind of fool for trusting a stranger—a Duff. They'd exchanged so much about their lives these last few weeks, but not the most important detail of all, at least in a woman's eyes.

She barely remembered the journey home, for she ran part of it, and even tripped on her skirts and bruised and bloodied her palms. She avoided supper with her mother by claiming a headache, then curled up in her bed and cried like she hadn't allowed herself to all day. Her last conscious thought was how foolish she'd been. She wasn't sure if she was crying over the loss of the friendship more than a romance, because she knew she couldn't trust him again.

As if the floodgate of her emotions had opened up a deeper place inside her, she dreamed that night, one of the vivid dreams that felt so real to her. She saw Owen, but he wasn't looking at her. Instead, there was another girl at his side, red-haired and freckled and lovely. They were being presented to each other. Light reflected strangely off a ring, and it seemed to pierce Maggie's eyes as she looked at it.

Then the scene disappeared and Maggie saw the

redhead again, staring at her with intent. But the girl's face was waxen, her clothing soaked, and water puddled around her.

Maggie awoke with a start, gasping for breath. Her whole body shuddered with chills, as if she, too, were soaked and freezing. She knew what the dream predicted—Owen's betrothed would drown. Covering her face, Maggie rocked in the bed, telling herself she was being ridiculous—but this was not the first time she'd dreamed of a death before it happened. The first time, she'd been uncertain and afraid, and had watched in horror as it had all come true. This time, this time she wouldn't bury the blatant warning.

After a restless night, she slipped out of their flat at dawn and went outside. She couldn't knock on Owen's door, but she could wait for him, and by mid-morning, he appeared, thankfully alone. She caught up with him by the end of the block.

"Owen!"

He turned around with a start and simply stared at her, his expression impassive, not glad, yet not uncomfortable either. She was so confused that she didn't know what she wanted him to feel. Maybe sorrow, because that was what she felt.

She twisted her hands together as she faced him, not having realized how difficult it would be to reveal her secret, to risk his derision, or even his pity. She almost turned away—until she remembered the dream girl's waxen face and aggrieved eyes.

"I—I didn't want to approach you," she said, "after—after everything that happened yesterday."

He gave her a formal nod as if they were strangers. "I don't blame ye. I didn't think to tell ye a truth that still doesn't seem real to me."

"What is her name?"

He frowned.

"The girl ye're to marry. What is her name?"

"I don't see why it should matter, but she's Emily."

Maggie nodded, because hearing the name made Emily seem more real. "Can I speak with ye in private about her?"

Owen hesitated, and now he finally did look uncomfortable. "Maggie, what is there to say? I should have told, ye, aye, but—"

She waved away his words. "It's not that. It's—" She looked around, feeling as if everyone stared at them. "I cannot say it here, not like this." She pointed down the wynd, the narrow lane that led between the town houses. "Come with me, away from prying eyes. Please, Owen."

To her relief, he didn't protest again. They walked silently until they'd left behind the fenced close at the rear of the town house, and out into a lane that led into the countryside.

At last she stopped beneath a tall larch tree. She was nervous now, and his air of impatience wasn't helping. She'd been angry he hadn't told her about his betrothal, but then again, she hadn't told him about her dreams. But how did one confide such a thing and not be thought crazy? Scotland had always had its seers, but she did not wish anyone to believe she was such an outcast. And the whispers of "witch" could be a woman's end.

Could she trust her secret to a man who'd already been proven untrustworthy? But she didn't have a choice.

Maggie stared into his chest, at the embroidered waistcoat of a viscount. It reminded her that they were very different. "I—it's hard for me to say this. I don't tell many people, but . . ." She trailed off, her throat closing up as she realized she was risking her future.

"Maggie, just say it," he said with exasperation.

As if he was already done with her and wished to be gone.

She took a shuddering breath. "I . . . dream things, and when they're vivid and real to me, they . . . come true."

She met his gaze at last, and he eyed her with growing amusement.

"Och, Maggie, ye had me going with nerves there," he said, shaking his head. "I spent all night wondering how to apologize to ye."

"Owen, this has nothing to do with apologies!" she cried. "I'm not telling tales. I had a terrible dream last night, and your Emily was in it."

His brown eyes narrowed. "Ye can't have seen her. They haven't arrived yet."

With a groan, she flung her arms wide. "I haven't seen her, Owen, not in truth. But in my dreams I saw her presented to ye. I saw a ring."

"There's always a ring—why are ye doing this to us, Maggie? Hurting us both for no reason."

"I don't want anyone to be hurt and that's the point. I didn't just see her with ye, Owen, but I saw her wet, puddles of water around her, her face cast white as death. And she was staring at me, as if she needed me to do . . . something about it."

He crossed his arms over his chest. "Ye're making no sense."

She winced, feeling his disbelief like the cold chill of a late summer evening, the breath of approaching winter. Her voice grew rough. "When I see a person wet, Owen, it means they're going to die by drowning."

He said nothing at first. She could hear chickens in the distance, the low of a cow, but no human voices. No one was overhearing them to understand her secret—only Owen. And he looked at her now with pity, and even a little disgust. She closed her eyes so she didn't have to see it.

"This isn't worthy of ye, Maggie," he said. "I didn't think ye'd let jealousy make ye tell lies."

"This isn't jealousy! Owen, please, ye must believe me, for Emily's sake." Her voice faded into a whisper, because she knew it was too late. He didn't believe her; he thought her a pathetic liar and a fool.

"Good-bye, Maggie." He turned and walked back down the wynd toward High Street.

"Owen, warn her, please," she cried, taking several steps as if to follow him before halting, unable to embarrass herself further.

He didn't look back at her; he didn't stop. She hugged herself, feeling more alone than she ever had in her life.

Two weeks passed, and Maggie never saw Owen on the stairs again. He lived in the same building, but he might has well have been in London. At another assembly, she saw him dancing, but not with the red-head from her dreams. Maggie prayed that she'd been mistaken, that no one would die.

He never looked her way. And the anger she'd kept buried finally rose up, and it took everything in her to remain calm. She hadn't deserved any of his treatment of her.

And then she heard the gossip at the dressmaker's shop before any announcement made the newspaper. Lady Emily Douglas had been boating with her family and drowned in the firth.

# 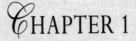HAPTER 1

*Ten years later . . .*

$O$wen Duff, newly the Earl of Aberfoyle, escorted the
woman he'd reluctantly offered to marry into Castle
Kinlochard. He dutifully took her slender arm, felt
her stiffen, but she didn't fight him, not openly. She'd
agreed to the marriage, after all, though making no
secret of her reluctance. It was ironic, considering how
many women over the years, both Scottish and English, had flattered and flirted for the chance to be his
bride. And he'd thought he'd have his choice of them,
had been taking his time. It was all for naught.

It was long past supper, and a handful of servants
were clearing the tables and talking among themselves. His sister, Catriona, trailed behind him, tired,

but still able to give him a warning look when they both saw their uncle, Harold Duff, standing beside the giant hearth beneath a display of claymores and targes that practically announced his status as war chief. Yawning, Cat waved in sympathy and headed up to bed.

Seeing Owen's party, Harold slowly lowered the tankard he'd been about to drink.

No time like the present, Owen thought. As he brought his future bride forward, the formality of the gesture was not lost on the servants, who all grew quiet and wide-eyed, awaiting what Owen would say. Harold, a broad-shouldered man with a heavy beard, eyed Owen expectantly.

"Uncle, may I introduce my betrothed, Mistress Margaret McCallum."

A gasp and murmurs rippled away from them throughout the great hall as the servants reacted to her surname. The Duffs and the McCallums were ancient enemies.

Owen said, "Maggie, this is my uncle, Harold Duff, war chief for the Clan Duff."

Owen watched Harold and Maggie eye each other and, as usual, Maggie didn't appear bashful or intimidated. That hadn't changed in these ten years. Owen had thought of her occasionally, the laughing girl who'd once listened raptly as he rambled on about his obsession with science. That autumn, he'd willfully ignored his future, the one with duties and responsibilities, as if wishing that a different life was within his grasp.

It had been easy to enjoy Maggie, innocent and bold, eager to discuss and debate and learn. Her eyes were still arresting, one blue, one green, and used to study him so solemnly, so eagerly, making him feel important, even if only just to her. Maturity had added dignity and wisdom to the beauty of her face. Her dark hair was drawn to the back of her head, emphasizing her heart-shaped face, her lips full and kissable, as he well remembered.

Harold cleared his throat and bowed his head. "Mistress McCallum."

"Ye may call me Maggie, sir," she said.

She spoke with her typical cool politeness. She'd been showing little reaction at all, these last few days since their betrothal. His sister, Cat, had nervously, brightly monopolized Maggie, as if sensing that things might not go smoothly.

Harold's shrewd gaze shifted back to Owen. "And how did such a betrothal come about?"

Maggie studied Owen, too, her eyes alight with mischief, as if she was curious to hear what he'd say.

"It's a long story," Owen said. "Perhaps, Maggie, you'd rather wash before supper?"

She looked about. "We've missed supper, and if I delay, we might miss any meal altogether. Nay, the servants can bring me a basin to wash. I'm far too hungry to wait more than that."

"As you wish."

Owen gestured to the housekeeper, Mrs. Robertson, who was waiting for his signal. Soon he and Maggie were side by side on the dais. His bodyguard, Fergus Balliol, stood just behind, one hand resting on his sword and the other on his pistol, as if the empty hall posed a threat.

Maggie broke into a freshly baked bannock, closed her eyes, and inhaled with satisfaction. To Owen's surprise, such an intense look brought a tightening of anticipation inside him, but he forced it back. It was good to be attracted to the woman one had to marry, after all. Or at least, that's what he'd been telling himself. He'd fought a hard battle against his father to win the right to choose his own bride—only to lose that right because of the McCallums.

When the worst of his hunger had been assuaged, Owen took a sip of whisky.

Maggie studied him with those affecting eyes. "Is that the whisky ye've made from our lands?"

He arched a brow. "Your lands?"

"Aye, my family's lands. The marriage contract between our families permitted ye to share in its bounty, not own the land itself."

Owen knew there was no point launching into a deeper discussion of the contract. The decision had been made, and there was no going back. "This whisky is from—"

"Never mind my question," she said. "I'll tell ye if my guess is right."

And Maggie plucked the glass out of his hand and took a sip. She didn't cough or wheeze or even make a distorted face, as so many women did trying the Water of Life.

"I assume you don't imbibe regularly," Owen said dryly.

Ignoring him, she narrowed her eyes as she considered the taste on her tongue. "Aye, this is from our land. But ye've done something . . . different."

"Have we."

As if she hadn't heard him, she studied the glass. "Ye've changed the proportion of the peat, I believe. The smoke of the peat fire is used to dry the malt."

Her voice was a tad slow, as if explaining to a simpleton.

Maggie sighed, then spoke with satisfied pride. "Och, well, ye had to alter it somehow, or everyone would have thought it was ours. We do distill the best in the Highlands."

"You did."

She swished the liquid in the glass and sniffed. "Believe what ye'd like, my lord."

He took the drink back. "You called me Owen not too long ago."

"Ten years is a long time—Owen," she said brusquely.

After the wary distance she'd shown him during her brother's wedding celebration, he found himself relieved for the renewal of her spirit. He didn't want to be married to a martyr.

"Ye seem familiar with each other already," Harold interrupted. "Is that why ye decided to marry?"

"Nay, no familiarity involved there," Maggie said with a dry tone in her voice. "At least none that mattered. I do believe he offered for me because it was the only *honorable* thing to do to keep the peace."

Owen stiffened. "Honorable? You cannot possibly question *me* about that after what your brother did."

Her smile faded and they looked at each other intently.

In a mild voice, Harold said, "Shall I play the role of arbiter, as well as war chief?"

"That won't be necessary, Uncle," Owen said. "You asked me to explain what happened and I shall. You knew that Maggie's brother Hugh was engaged to my sister since her birth. It was our fathers' attempt to bring peace to the clan, to offer a dowry to the McCallums, and to share the land where they distilled their whisky. After Hugh became chief, he came to collect his bride, and my father behaved dishonorably by secreting her away and putting our cousin Riona in her place."

Harold stiffened, but his expression remained impassive. He well knew the cruelty his brother had often practiced.

"Hugh took the wrong bride and fell in love with her," Owen finished.

Maggie's gaze shot to his face, and she didn't hide her surprise. Had she thought he'd continue to berate her brother's choices, the way the man had kidnapped Riona and wouldn't believe the truth? Hugh's mistakes were in the past, and after all, Owen's father had played his own part. But the earl was dead, and it was up to Owen to make things right. His father managed to control him in the end, even from beyond the grave.

"So the marriage contract was broken," Harold said slowly.

"Maggie and I decided to set it aright," Owen answered. "We will marry and seal the bond between our clans. I don't want animosity to ever erupt again."

Harold looked from him to Maggie and back again. Maggie was simply pushing her food about her plate, her expression pensive, perhaps even sad.

They'd been forced into a marriage they didn't want because of poorly planned actions on both sides. Owen was doing his best—she damned well better try just as hard.

"When will this marriage take place?" Harold asked.

The sooner the better, Owen thought. What would be the point of delaying the inevitable? "Four weeks. That is enough time for Maggie to settle in at Castle Kinlochard and have the banns read."

Maggie stood up, pushing back her chair with force.

"I'd like to retire now. Mrs. Robertson, will ye show me to my bedroom?"

And without looking back, Maggie left the great hall. Owen watched her until she'd gone, anger and frustration warring within him.

"Take heart, lad," Harold said. "Many a marriage has started worse."

"Says the man who never found the right woman to marry," Owen shot back.

Harold gave a rare grin. "Didn't say which of us was the smartest, now did I?"

Owen exhaled swiftly. "Before I find my bed, tell me what has happened since I've been gone."

They spoke for another hour before Owen said good night and departed, after insisting Fergus find his own bed. Another level up in the towerhouse, Owen strode down the hall, passing the chamber Maggie had been assigned without slowing down—until he heard a high, frightened, piercing cry from within.

MAGGIE struggled to return to consciousness, the weight of hands holding her down. She felt mindless with fear at the vividness of the dream, for it had been years since one stole so completely into her mind and soul. She was locked in the terror and reality of Owen lying bloody and near death on their wedding day.

"Maggie! Maggie, lass, wake up."

She thrashed to escape, to stay in the dream and find out the truth of what might happen to him, to know if being married to her meant his death, but the insistent voice kept calling to her, and large hands seemed to drag her from the depths of a deep pool.

She opened her eyes wide and saw Owen, and the night shadows cast by the moon looked like blood upon his face.

She screamed again, then grabbed ahold of his coat and pulled him even closer. "Are you well? There's so much blood!" She spread his coat, then felt frantically across his chest, looking for the hot, sticky wetness. Nothing except the strong beat of his heart. She touched his stubbled face, and the back of her hand became a part of the mottled shadows, not blood.

He took both her hands in his and spoke firmly. "Maggie, it was a nightmare. You're awake now."

She took a deep, shuddering breath. He was too close, hovering over her, powerful and intimidating. She yanked away from him and sat up, leaning back into the headboard of the four-poster and pulling the counterpane to her chin as if for protection from the evil she'd just witnessed. She couldn't forget the image of his bloody face, and she covered her eyes and moaned.

"Are you well?" he asked. "Should I fetch a doctor?"

She shuddered. His cultured voice had lost the Gaelic rhythm and accent of their people, making him seem even more a stranger.

"I'm fine, I'm fine. Is there water in the pitcher? I'm parched."

He went to pour her a glass, and it was a relief to have him not staring at her. She had to get herself under control, to push the dream away—for now. Because certainly, she would have no choice but to dissect it when she was alone.

Owen brought her the water, and to her dismay, she was shaking, and had to hold the glass with both hands. She took a long drink, then let it rest in her lap while she willed herself to cease trembling.

His brows were lowered in a frown of concern. "Are you truly well?"

"'Twas just a nightmare," she said, boldly meeting his eyes and daring him to disagree.

She hadn't had a vivid dream portending the future in ten long years. After the shock of Emily's death and Owen's derisive disbelief, she hadn't ever wanted to experience such a dream again. The few times she'd felt one become too real, she'd learned to wake up until, gradually she'd molded herself into a normal woman who faced each day hopeful for the future, unaware of how things would truly turn out. She no longer had fears that people would find out and call her a witch or keep their children away from her. Yet . . . she never felt whole, but as if a part of her was missing.

But tonight a dream had swept over her like an ocean wave, more powerful for the long restraint, battering her emotions against the crumbling rocks of stability she'd erected to protect herself. Seeing Owen near death . . . would he really die?

His derision and Emily's death had forced her to change everything about herself. The happy girl who'd known there were exciting mysteries in the world had been replaced by a woman who wanted to forget such things existed.

But a dream had happened again, and she was back to being the outsider. She had no one to confide in, because she'd insisted Hugh and Riona needed to celebrate their marriage, not accompany her to the Duff stronghold like she was a child. Maggie had probably hurt her mother by making her stay behind, too.

"Are you feeling better?" Owen asked, his voice low and cool.

Maggie jerked and looked up at him. Her anger toward him had never dissipated after how he'd caused her to hate a part of herself and then forgot she existed. But she nodded her answer to his question.

"You don't look better."

He went to the hearth and, using a taper, lit several candles about the room, including the one at her bedside. The shadows receded, making her feel a little calmer, and giving her a clearer view of him. It had still been a shock to see how much Owen had changed in ten years—and yet how little, as well. Had she expected him to grow ugly and deformed? She'd been almost angry enough to wish for it. His face was still lean and handsome, with prominent cheekbones, and a bold square jaw. His light brown hair was drawn back into a queue rather than hidden beneath a wig.

There was a maturity to him now, a heaviness to his shoulders and upper body that said he had not been simply dancing and paying court to ladies so far away in London all these years. But it wasn't just his physical appearance that still consumed her—it was his very presence, an attraction that she hadn't imagined could still exist after everything he'd done—yet it seemed to have grown stronger through the passage of time.

So when he'd offered to wed her only moments after seeing each other again . . . she'd been so stunned and affronted and full of a dawning futility that she couldn't decide which one she was supposed to feel.

"What are you doing here?" she finally asked. "Was my scream so very loud?"

"Yes, it was." He rocked back on his heels and considered her. "I was passing by on my way to bed when I heard you. I thought you were being attacked."

"So you rushed in to save me," she said coolly.

With a shrug, he leaned against the bedpost, arms folded across his chest in a way that seemed so masculine, so aware of himself and her as a couple who were supposed to marry.

She shuddered at the sudden memory of herself in her bridal gown with his blood spattered across it.

Owen frowned. "You're shaking with the cold. There has to be another blanket here somewhere." He bent over one of the chests that lined the wall.

"Nay, 'tis all right—"

But he ignored her, spreading a wool blanket across

the counterpane. He was leaning over her, and when he met her gaze, it was as if he touched her.

"Better?" he asked, his voice suddenly gone husky.

"Aye," she answered quickly, wishing he'd move away.

She did feel warmer. Perhaps it was a blush, or another memory of his kiss and his hands bringing her body to life before she'd made him stop that day in the grass. Since then there were lonely nights when her guard was down and she wished she'd have dared to go farther with him, just to know what it felt like to be with a man. Her body aching with memories, it had been difficult to remember that he'd derided her for telling him the truth about her dreams, told her she acted out of jealousy. He hadn't trusted her; she couldn't let an inconvenient attraction make her forget what he really thought of her.

And now she was betrothed to him to end the feud that had cost so many lives—and he might meet his death if they went through with the wedding.

"This is the first time we've been alone since the betrothal," Owen said.

The calmness in his voice suddenly seemed for show, as if there were deep things beneath the surface. She stopped breathing, caught in the smoldering intensity of his brown eyes. She'd forgotten their power over her—perhaps deliberately forgotten in her anger—but now those eyes forced her to remember the newness of passion, the excitement of sharing it.

But they'd been little more than children, with no understanding of the world and the responsibilities they owed their clans.

Huskily, Owen said, "There is much we should discuss."

She gathered her wits and spoke coolly. "Ye didn't discuss it with me when it mattered. Ye didn't ask for my hand. Ye said ye'd have me to satisfy the contract, an easy replacement, like a spare wheel to fit on a cart. Not very flattering. Ye've become a practical man, I can see."

"Did you expect to be wooed in such a tense moment?" he asked with faint sarcasm.

"Ye mean since you and my brother were about to fight to the death without having a rational discussion. Ye conveniently left that out with your uncle."

Owen moved as if to sit upon the bed.

"Nay, I'll not be having that," she said sharply. "If someone else heard my scream and comes in to find ye so close . . ."

"They could think *I* was the reason you screamed, and then force me to marry you," he said dryly.

"Very funny," she said with her own sarcasm, then frowned. "Just go, Owen. I'm exhausted, and surely ye must be, too."

He leaned over her, and she stiffened when he touched the side of her face. His hand was warm, when she felt so very cold.

"We could have a decent marriage, Maggie. I'll make you glad you're mine."

Her mouth dropped open at his arrogance, but he didn't wait around for her response. After he closed the door behind him, she jumped out of the bed and ran to press her ear against it. She heard his footsteps receding down the hall.

Blankly, she stared about at the wainscoted walls with the beautiful landscapes, which the McCallums had seldom been able to afford. Everywhere in this manor was proof that the Duffs were wealthy, from the elegant, upholstered furniture to the silver candlesticks on the mantel. Owen was an earl, with a title and estates, even several in England. And now she was betrothed to him.

At the thought of marriage, she began to relive the dream and then stopped herself. She indulged in a moment of self-pity, wondering why she'd been cursed with something some might call a gift, when she knew it to be anything but. Once upon a time, she'd thought it made her different, special—but Owen had showed her otherwise.

She'd never felt so completely alone, though a castle full of people surrounded her. But they were Duffs, and her father's drunken railing against his enemy clan echoed through her memory. She remembered stories of warfare across centuries, castle raids, cattle thieving, fires set in stables and cottages alike. Over a hundred years before, the McCallum and his wife were killed when accepting the hospitality of the Duff. But since she hadn't been able to trust her father, some part of her had always put these stories aside and been intrigued by the hated enemies of her clan—which explained her forbidden fascination with Owen ten years before.

She might be alone, but she could not be a coward. At last, she had to let the dream take hold of her mind again, and she watched in growing horror as the brief scene unfolded. All she could see was herself rushing to Owen's side, his face pale, blood pooling beneath him, her own gown stained as she grabbed and held him, screaming. What was terrible and frustrating was that she had no idea what had led to such a tragedy. Try as she might, nothing else came to her, no glimpse of a clue she'd missed. It was just her and Owen in a dark room, and his imminent death.

She paced for long hours, too wide awake to sleep. She didn't know what she was supposed to do with the information fate had granted her. Her family, her entire clan, was dependent on her to make this marriage work, or they would lose the land they cherished, and be unable to produce the whisky that helped them survive the lean years. Not to mention the resumption of a feud that had caused too many deaths over the centuries.

But how could she marry Owen if it would cost him his life? Yet she wasn't even certain he *would* die, and confusion and fear chased each other around in her mind.

She was simply going to have to tell him the truth.

She started second-guessing herself almost immediately, because she well remembered his mocking disbelief the last time she'd told him about her dream. But she couldn't tell him that she wouldn't marry without offering a plausible reason. She would be honest and convince him that there had to be another way to satisfy the contract, because she wasn't going to marry him and be responsible for his death.

At last she crawled back into bed and huddled there. Her eyes wouldn't close, and at dawn she gave up and went to sit in the window seat, watching the courtyard as it came to life.

Feeling like she needed to be close to those she loved, she sat down at the delicate writing desk and began to compose a letter to her family. She wrote it to Hugh, knowing he'd share it with the others. She told superficial stories of her first view of the castle, of how polite and considerate Owen had been, and how the castle residents seemed friendly. Silently, she wondered how friendly they'd be if they knew she dreamed things that came true.

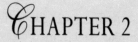

# CHAPTER 2

As if used to aristocratic ladies who rose late, the housekeeper did not arrive with a tray of bannocks and chocolate until several hours later. Maggie felt weak with hunger, exhausted, and worried about her coming discussion with Owen. She had to find the right time to speak with him—as if there was a right time, she thought grimly.

Mrs. Robertson was tall and thin, with a long gray braid wrapped about her head like a crown and topped with a lace cap. The crown idea wasn't far off; she was a reserved woman who took her position as head of the household staff with the seriousness reserved for a head of state surveying her kingdom. After a double look at Maggie's different colored eyes, Mrs. Robertson served her with silent efficiency, but Maggie sensed a faint whiff of disapproval that Mrs. Robertson would never deign to admit out loud. Hospitality was important to Scotsmen, and it was part of Mrs. Robertson's position. But Maggie was a McCallum, after all.

Once Maggie had been taken away from the oppression and constant fear of her father's household, she'd discovered the joy of being around people who knew her only by what she showed the world. She'd been happy, lighthearted, pretending that she was like any other girl. Owen and the heartache that had followed had changed her, made her realize she might never have a normal life. But she'd vowed to find her own way, wouldn't allow herself to wallow in regrets. She'd changed from a girl into a woman who'd understood caution. And then Owen had returned, stirring up her anger all over again.

"Will there be anything else, Mistress McCallum?" Mrs. Robertson asked, when the items from her tray were neatly arranged on a small table.

Maggie had many questions, but none she thought the housekeeper the right person to ask. "Nay, ye've taken good care of me, Mrs. Robertson."

There was a knock on the door, so hesitant that Maggie knew it wasn't Owen.

"That'll be Kathleen, your lady's maid," Mrs. Robertson said.

"I've been assigned a maid?" Maggie asked in surprise. She'd never had a maid just for herself.

"Of course. Ye're to be the new countess, after all."

*Countess.* Maggie struggled to keep a pleasant, neutral expression, when she wanted to wince.

Mrs. Robertson opened the door, and a parade of young men entered, carrying Maggie's trunks, the ones she'd brought with her from Edinburgh. It wasn't everything she owned, but it made her feel better to know she'd soon be surrounded by her own things.

The last through the door was a young woman with a round-faced chubbiness that was unusual in the Highlands, especially for a servant. Kathleen had blond hair tinged with red beneath her cap, and a happy smile.

"Mistress McCallum, what a pleasure to meet ye!" Kathleen bobbed a quick curtsy. "Mrs. Robertson was kind enough to give me the opportunity to serve ye. I've brought yer trunks and cannot wait to go through them with ye."

Mrs. Robertson's eyes narrowed, as if Kathleen's effusiveness was improper, but Maggie couldn't help giving an encouraging smile.

"Thank ye, Kathleen. I do feel a need for a bath and a change of clothing."

She swallowed several bites of the oatcakes while Kathleen bustled about, shaking out gowns and admiring them as she hung them in the wardrobe. Maggie thought she was simply being polite, for her wardrobe would be unusually plain for a countess.

"I think ye'll like it here, mistress," Kathleen said, pouring another cup of chocolate for Maggie. "I'm new here, but I've been made welcome."

"New here?" Maggie echoed. "Ye mean new to the castle?"

"Aye, and new to everything with the clan. Me brother and I recently returned from the American colonies, where our parents took us when I was a wee babe. So I'm sympathizing with yer feeling like ye don't know anyone. Ye know me now!"

Kathleen smiled, and Maggie couldn't help smiling back at her.

"How was America?" Maggie asked.

Kathleen went back to the trunks, but said over her shoulder, "Me parents thought life would be different there, but it wasn't, not really. The same family but in a new place. They worked hard and we survived, but it wasn't easy. And when at last it was just me brother and me, we decided to come back. I've heard stories all my life of Duff lands and our clan. I'm glad to be here."

Maggie nodded. Her maid was far more talkative than most servants, but she was comforted by the chatter. Kathleen was right; it made Maggie feel less alone to know someone else was a stranger here as well.

But Kathleen wanted to become a part of the Duffs, to get to know her relatives and fellow clansmen; Maggie could only think that for herself, being here was a terrible mistake. By agreeing to Owen's proposal, she'd set in motion a destiny that would change all their lives.

AFTER a morning spent in the stables, going over the horseflesh with the marshal of horses, Owen was looking forward to a more sedate luncheon that he could share with Maggie. Ten years ago, they'd shared dinner from a basket one or the other of them had taken from their family kitchen. Occasionally they'd even bought something from a shop. They'd been dangerously alone, while he'd fought against the desire he shouldn't have been feeling when there'd been another woman he was supposed to marry.

Not that they'd be alone at Castle Kinlochard, of course. They'd be sharing meals in the communal great hall of his ancestors. His father had put too much stock in living like an English earl, where one ate only with family or friends of the same Society. Here in the Highlands, one shared the day with one's clan. He was on display, as everyone measured him against the—admittedly low—standard his father had set. He was determined to be a different chief, one who spent more time with his people when he was home. He would do his duty and serve in the House of Lords for several months each year, but when he was home, he would be a Highlander.

He was wearing his belted plaid for the first time in a long while, and he'd seen the way the stable grooms, even the marshal, had eyed him. No one showed outright skepticism, but he sensed it, there beneath the surface. There was no way to undo the damage his father had done to the chiefdom, except to lead by example and to prove his worth.

And then Maggie arrived in the hall, radiant in a rose-colored gown that set off her creamy skin, her hair a dark, silky cloud about her head. Owen was standing before he even realized it. Several tables were full of clansmen, and they, too, noticed her, as all conversations died. No one else stood at first, and Owen was about to rake them all with a deadly gaze, until an elderly lady rose to her feet, leaning heavily on a cane. With reluctance, more followed, and he saw Maggie blush as she stood in the doorway, an ethereal sprite amid uncouth Highlanders. He would have to introduce her to his clan in an elaborate way, so that they'd begin to accept her.

He strode to escort her the rest of the way, and saw her eyes dip to his garments and then widen.

"Ye're pretending to be a Highlander now, are ye?" she asked.

"Pretending? I don't have to pretend what I've earned from my ancestors." He had also donned a black armband for his father, but Maggie didn't comment on that. She wasn't wearing mourning for her own father. From what he remembered of her stories when they were young, he didn't blame her.

"Ye just look different, as if ye want everyone to forget ye're an earl."

"I am a *Scottish* earl. And remember, I'm not an earl to you, Maggie, but a bridegroom."

With an impudent toss of her head, she looked away. He glanced down her body, seeing the way she had more curves than he remembered. She had lush breasts shown off to perfection by her stays, and her gown flowed out from her narrow waist, hinting at a curve of hip that made him want to test it with his hands.

He put out his arm, and her cool hesitation before taking it made him grind his teeth. He saw her into her chair and then sat beside her. Trays of roasted venison, mutton, and hares; bowls of turnips, leeks, and cabbage were displayed before them both. She filled up her plate, then set to eating as if she could ignore him that way. She kept her eyes downcast, but more than once, when she raised them to a servant, their own eyes widened at her different-colored eyes, and they crossed themselves. That had to be an annoying reaction. He would speak to Mrs. Robertson about it.

"Did you have a pleasant morning?" he asked.

"Mrs. Robertson gave me a tour of the castle," she said.

Boldly she looked about, since many were staring and not doing a good job of hiding it. Owen arched an eyebrow as he glanced pointedly at the clan, and most immediately returned to their meal.

"What did you think of your new home?" he asked.

"'Tis an adequate fortress."

She wasn't going to give an inch. "The clan has several, but I thought you'd be most comfortable here, nearer your kin."

"We have several castles as well. We're not competing over this, are we?"

"Of course not," he said impassively.

He let her return to eating silently for several minutes, but he found it was difficult to keep quiet when he still had questions. "What did you like about Castle Kinlochard? It's to be your home, after all."

She considered him with narrowed eyes, as if he was trying to trap her.

"I like your library," she said at last. "My father did not believe in books for their own sake, just what was needed for the estates. Whereas ye have so many."

"Surely you remembered my focus on educating myself," he said. Alluding to their aborted time together in Edinburgh was a risky move.

Anger flashed in those amazing eyes, but she kept her voice level. "I remember *many* things. But I imagine ye don't want them discussed here."

"Do you plan to make this more difficult than it has to be?" he asked quietly, coldly.

"Do ye like your women so meek and accepting, *Owen*?" She emphasized his name. "If we're not to discuss *difficult* things, we won't have much of a marriage."

"I will discuss anything you wish, but I'd prefer to be more subtle and private about it."

"So we can only discuss things the way *you'd* like to."

"I'm trying to know you better, Maggie. Why are you angry with me when you agreed to this marriage?"

Her eyes widened, and she looked him up and down with barely concealed scorn. "If ye cannot remember how we parted ten years ago, then for a man who reads history, ye seem good at deluding yourself about it. Aye, I agreed to this marriage—I didn't say I was happy about it."

They regarded each other in tense silence, and many people gave them curious glances. At last, Maggie seemed to notice them.

"Very well," she said, "ye'd like me to be as polite and vapid as callers are in an Edinburgh parlor. Aye, ye were focused on an education—one denied women, by the way. Did ye take up the classics like your father wanted, or the sciences?"

"My father and I agreed to an arrangement," he said coolly. "I would study what he wished, the classics, as long as I could choose my own bride."

"And it took ye so long that ye're settling for me at last?" she asked with sarcasm. "Och, forgive me, I couldn't resist my baser nature. Ye've met no other women ye like?" Her skepticism was obvious.

"A woman I would willingly marry? No." He leaned closer to murmur the last words. "Until you."

Her eyes narrowed. "Ye didn't offer to marry me willingly, now did ye. Let's not pretend otherwise with false flattery." She regally turned her head away, giving him the back of her dark brown hair, caught in a chignon at her nape. He thought she shivered, but he couldn't be certain of his interpretation. He wanted her to be aroused, but was she hiding behind a wall of indignation?

He was so near he could inhale the scent of her, a hint of lavender and springtime. It was heady and enthralling, and if they could just put the anger behind them . . .

She glanced at him again and her lips were far too close, reminding him of the kisses she'd once offered with eager naiveté.

"Lord Aberfoyle, your nearness is embarrassing me before your clan."

He didn't believe that; the attraction between them surely had her rattled. He wanted her to feel off balance; he wanted clues as to how to deal with her; he wanted to remind her of pleasure. "Does the telescope in the library bring back memories of nights beneath the stars?"

Frustrated nights, when he'd thought of kissing her, but had known he wasn't free to offer more. Then came the day he could restrain himself no longer. He'd regretted his impatience, and had striven hard to control his emotions ever since.

Those unusual eyes narrowed, and she silently studied him, as if looking for a trap. "The telescope is of little interest to me," she said.

That was a direct rebuff, and he reluctantly admired her for it.

"But the books are another matter," she continued, then asked stiffly, "Might I read through them?"

As if it was difficult to ask him for anything. She was a proud woman.

"As my wife, you're welcome to anything I have."

It was her turn to arch a brow. "But I'm not yet your

wife. Blackmail, is it? Will ye withhold books from me until the deed is done?"

Her wariness made him irritable. She actually thought he'd keep knowledge of the world from her? "I'd not withhold anything from you, Maggie. The books are yours to read as you wish."

She nodded and went back to her meal. Winning her would not be as easy as simply offering to wed her. Perhaps he'd been more swayed by his father's bragging about the sanctity of their title than he'd imagined. It obviously didn't impress Maggie. Regardless, he knew what to do to win a woman's favor. He'd done it once with Maggie—he could do it again, using very slow, passionate methods. He was looking forward to it. Not that he was going to make her fall in love with him; then she would only be hurt when he didn't return those feelings. He wasn't going to love her; he wasn't going to give a McCallum—or any woman—that much power over him.

"I wrote a letter this morning to my brothers," Maggie suddenly said. "Who should I ask to post it for me?"

"I'll send a man to deliver it, and bring back any reply."

"Thank you."

He suddenly frowned. "You said 'brothers.'"

"Aye, Hugh and I have a half brother. He's only ten years old. I guess ye didn't meet him during the wedding." She bit into a forkful of mutton and chewed thoughtfully.

"Are you going to leave me with so little of the story?"

She took a deep breath, and he thought she would refuse.

Instead she lowered her voice. "Brendan is my father's child by a village girl. She died giving birth to him. Many people thought he was Hugh's, but he's not."

Pain darkened her eyes, and Owen knew there was far more to the story than she was saying. "Why did people think Hugh was the father?"

"Because he'd offered to marry the girl, Agnes, to protect her after what our father had done. But Father refused to permit the marriage, since Hugh was already betrothed to your sister."

What their father had done. There was an ugliness behind those simple words. He'd known her father was a drunkard, and pitied her for it, but if he'd hurt young women, too . . . Those thoughts took him to a darker place.

"Did your mother take you away from Larig Castle because of your father's behavior?" he demanded. "Did he hurt you?"

She set her jaw stubbornly. "I was not hurt. But this is none of your concern, Owen."

"Not my concern? You're to be my wife."

She opened her mouth, and he realized she was going to counter him, but then didn't. What was she thinking? They were betrothed, and denying that would catapult their clans back into the distrust no one wanted. He'd thought she was simply upset that she hadn't had the romantic courting other women did, that he'd lied to her when he'd been young and foolish. Now he wasn't so sure.

The double doors at the far end of the great hall were suddenly thrown open by the guards, and in walked his mother, Edith Duff, Countess of Aberfoyle, and his sister, Cat. They were dressed in bonnets and shawls, which along with their gowns, were dyed black in mourning for his father. Each carried a basket on her arm, which reminded him they'd walked to the village that morn. It was Cat who'd asked if she could invite Maggie, and though Owen had appreciated the gesture, he'd thought it best to let Maggie sleep as long as she needed.

He remembered Lady Aberfoyle's unspoken disapproval of Cat's invitation, a reminder that he would be smoothing the way between his mother and Maggie for a long while yet. Lady Aberfoyle had been shocked and distressed this morning upon hearing that he'd offered to marry a "poverty-stricken McCallum"—her words. He'd explained that Maggie had a dowry, and his mother had countered that it was nothing compared to what an English bride would have brought to the family. He'd asked if she wanted another war with the McCallums and the loss of even more innocent lives. She'd had nothing to say to that, but he could see now that she still wasn't going to welcome Maggie into the family with ease. The whole conversation had felt . . . off to him. They didn't need a large dowry, and to focus on that seemed disingenuous.

After Lady Aberfoyle walked down the center aisle between the tables, nodding to the clansmen who bowed in her direction, she came to a stop when she spied Maggie, as if she'd forgotten her. Owen watched the two women eye each other.

Owen rose. "Mother, allow me to introduce my future wife, Margaret."

"Maggie McCallum," Maggie said pointedly, rising to curtsy from behind the table. "Good day, Lady Aberfoyle, Lady Catriona."

Lady Aberfoyle bowed regally, almost imperceptibly, but said nothing.

Lest his mother think this a temporary situation she could alter, he added, "Please congratulate us. We shall be married four weeks from yesterday."

Maggie's eyes narrowed, but she said nothing.

"That is far too soon for an earl to marry!" Lady Aberfoyle said indignantly. "You should be married in Edinburgh, or perhaps London as befits your—"

"We will be married in the chapel here," Owen interrupted, "in the ancient stronghold of our clan. It will also enable Maggie's family to easily attend."

He thought he was proving his concern to Maggie,

instead, it made his mother glare at her, as if the marriage was all her fault.

Owen ignored it and turned to include his sister. "Will you ladies be joining us for dinner?"

Cat's furrowed brow smoothed out as she smiled at Maggie. "We'd love to. I have so many questions about your brother, now married to my favorite cousin."

Cat removed her bonnet and came around the table to sit beside Maggie, leaving their mother to sit on Owen's left. As the servants brought trays of meat and vegetables for the ladies to choose from, Owen forced himself to attend to his mother, while listening to Maggie and Cat.

Maggie was surprised at her own hearty appetite after such an awkward introduction. Luckily, Lady Aberfoyle was on Owen's other side and perhaps she wouldn't have to speak with her. Maggie had no respect for the countess, who hadn't protected Riona from the old earl's manipulations and now sulked that she couldn't control her son.

Of course, if there was no wedding at all, maybe Lady Aberfoyle would thank her, Maggie thought wryly.

Lady Catriona was far easier to deal with. Maggie was grateful for the woman's kindness toward Hugh.

"You must call me Cat, and I'll call you Maggie," Cat said.

Like her brother's, her Scottish burr seemed sub-

dued after she'd spent most of every year in England.
Maggie wondered if either of them even spoke Gaelic.

"We're practically related already," Cat continued,
"with my cousin marrying your brother. And soon we
shall be sisters."

*Sisters.* That probably wouldn't happen, not if
Maggie could help it. But she made herself smile politely. "Riona has spoken so much about ye, as if ye're
her own sister, too."

"We practically are. We spent much of our childhood together, and then as adults, we attended the
same Society events." She hesitated, then lowered her
voice. "I hope you do not feel awkward around me. I
didn't want to marry your brother—and it wasn't because he was a McCallum," she hastened to add. "He
was simply . . . a stranger. I'd hoped to choose my own
husband, and . . ." Her voice trailed off and she covered her mouth with her hand. Faintly, she said, "Oh,
forgive me. That was terribly insensitive. You volun-
teered to marry a stranger and I'm going on about my
luck escaping the same fate."

"Nay, do not worry. And your brother wasn't a
stranger. Surely he told ye about our encounter ten
years ago." Maggie couldn't resist taunting Owen,
knowing he was listening.

Cat's gaze searched hers. "No, he never did."

"That is because it's none of her concern," Owen interrupted.

Cat leaned forward, the better to see her brother. "How like a man to think the details don't matter."

Maggie's gaze clashed with Owen's. She could tell his sister he'd nearly betrayed his first betrothed, but . . . that would be revenge, rather than honest anger. "He simply asked if I liked to look at the stars. We struck up a friendship that only lasted a few weeks before he had to leave."

"That does not exactly capture the imagination," Cat teased.

"Which is why it was so forgettable," Maggie said brightly.

Owen narrowed his eyes

Cat sighed. "But . . . it is only through luck that you knew each other at all before you both agreed to do such a brave thing."

Brave? Maggie thought. Nay, it was with a desperation born of having no other choices. Owen seemed contemplative as he continued to eat. She knew he didn't think she was brave—he thought she was being ridiculous holding on to her anger. If only he knew how brave she was trying to be right now, holding herself together when it looked as if her uncertain future was even more complicated than he knew.

Not that he'd think anything to do with her dreams was brave, only foolish or childish. With that attitude, how was she possibly going to make him believe her?

But Cat was still speaking. "What is hardest for me to understand about this whole"—she waved a hand to encompass them both—"dilemma is that my own father tried to break the contract he'd agreed to. It was such a dishonorable thing to do. He—he didn't care that Riona might be kidnapped, that our clans could end up at war again. I think . . . I think the strain of his actions led to his death."

"You give him too much credit," Owen scoffed. "He chose to behave dishonorably, and I'm not all that certain it weighed on his conscience."

Cat looked past Maggie at her brother. "Owen, you didn't have the kind of relationship where you saw a softer side to him. I, on the other hand—"

"—was his favorite."

Though Owen seemed to speak without amusement, he must be teasing, for as Maggie looked from one to the other, Cat smiled. Then the woman's eyes took on a sheen. However mixed Cat's feelings were in regards to the earl, he'd still been her father, and he'd died of a fever less than a month before.

"So tell me about Hugh," Cat said, obviously rallying herself to appear happy. "He's married to my cousin now, so I want to know everything about him."

"I don't exactly know what to say. He's my older brother, and has spent his life taking care of me. He's a loyal man, even went off at eighteen to fight the British and the Scottish Hanoverians during the Fifteen."

Cat suddenly shot a concerned gaze at her brother. Owen continued to eat at a measured pace, but Maggie sensed a new tension between them. Though she wasn't going to ask, unwelcome curiosity kept her brain calculating. Owen had been only sixteen during the Jacobite uprising of 1715, hardly of age to fight. Maggie already knew the Duffs weren't Royalists like the Campbells and other clans, so they must have sent men into battle on the same side as the McCallums. She imagined a sixteen-year-old boy would be upset to be left behind. Nay, she wasn't going to ask.

For several minutes, they all ate in silence. Cat wanted to be her sister, and liking the woman only made Maggie's muddled thoughts even more confused. How appalled would Cat be if Maggie didn't prevent Owen's death when she had the chance?

As if she'd ever been able to prevent any of her dreams from coming true, Maggie thought. But she reminded herself that this sort of dream was different, that she hadn't married Owen yet—if only she could make him believe the truth.

Time to change the subject. How better than to address the countess head-on, force her to acknowledge Maggie and see what her husband's manipulations had wrought? Maggie said, "Lady Aberfoyle, thank ye for assigning a maid to me. Kathleen is very cheerful and efficient."

"Kathleen?" Lady Aberfoyle narrowed her eyes.

"You might not remember Kathleen Duff and her brother Gregor," Owen said. "They're distant cousins whose parents took them to live in the colonies over twenty years ago. Times were hard there for them, and they've returned home to start over. Gregor is working in the smithy."

"Kathleen and Gregor," Lady Aberfoyle mused, as if concentrating on the names. "I do not remember their story. But then after all, seldom did members of *our* clan have to escape poverty for a dangerous journey to the colonies."

Maggie barely held on to a pleasant expression when the woman was proving that nobility did not mean civility or manners. Maggie could have said she'd never heard of any of *her* clan departing for the colonies, but she'd only be rising to the countess's bait. Owen gave his mother a warning frown on Maggie's behalf.

He seemed protective of Maggie, but what did that matter? The proof would be how he handled her confession.

# CHAPTER 3

After dinner, Maggie slipped away from the great hall, and then the towerhouse. She just needed to clear her head and breathe fresh air and not have any expectations. She would wait until the evening to have a private conversation with Owen.

She wandered from workshops to stables to barracks, and everywhere she went, strangers stared at her. Everyone knew she was a McCallum, and certainly, they would be curious about her. Only a few crossed themselves if they thought she wasn't looking, frightened by her eyes. Though she was here to stop a feud, two centuries' worth of bitterness weren't going to end immediately.

As she walked past the smithy, she could feel the heat of the fire the blacksmiths worked over all day long. She paused near the wide entrance and watched as a burly, aproned man, his face red and perspiring, used tongs to hold a glowing piece of metal in the fire.

"Eh, you, what are ye doin'?"

Startled, Maggie turned to find another man bearing down on her. He, too, wore an apron over his barrel chest, and his curly hair was almost as red as his perspiring face.

"I'm simply watching," she said, taking a step away from the door.

"Ye could get hurt lingerin' here," he said. He came to a stop and eyed her suspiciously. "I've not seen ye before."

"I'm Maggie McCallum," she said, using her surname deliberately. She wasn't going to hide who she was.

His brows lowered. "McCallum. Ye're to marry Himself."

He brazenly looked down her body with skepticism.

"Ye're being very rude," she said.

"And ye're a McCallum."

As if the two things equated.

"My sister told me about ye," he continued.

"Your—" She broke off, suddenly seeing the resemblance to another in his short stature and red hair. "Ah, your sister Kathleen," she said with surprise. Kathleen had been so polite and sunny, as opposite her brother as possible. "Ye must be Gregor. Ye're practically as new here as I am."

He took a step toward her, fists on his hips, and spoke with angry defensiveness. "My family's blood is in this very soil. I was born here."

"Ye're right, of course," she said. Starting her own mini-feud wasn't going to help. "I didn't mean to offend."

"Ye've offended just by bein' here," he grumbled.

"Then I won't bother ye again."

She turned away and began to walk, feeling his angry stare as if it were a dirk piercing the middle of her back. And suddenly, she couldn't stay in the courtyard, where escaping the dozens of censorious looks would prove impossible. How could one marriage possibly undo centuries' worth of hatred?

She passed a training yard where men fought with swords. She'd seen no firearms and she knew why—the British government had passed a Disarming Act after the uprising, and continued to pass more, attempting to remove all firearms from the Highlands. But many clans had imported rusty old weapons from the Continent and turned those in for the money, while hiding their own in case they had to defend their land against the British. Certainly they weren't going to display their weapons in front of a McCallum.

And with that thought, she headed through the gatehouse under the watchful, skeptical eyes of the guards, wrapped in their Duff plaid and their Duff righteousness. She felt like she could breathe again away from the high walls of the courtyard that had seemed to trap the air. The water near the arched bridge was still, covered in large oval leaves that floated around white lilies, as befitted a moat that seemed more like a pond. The sky was overcast, but didn't threaten rain as she left the bridge for the dirt-packed road.

She started across a grassy field that sloped up the side of a mountain in the distance. Heather grew in abundance, scattered between boulders and through the fields, and in just a few more weeks it would decorate these meadows in purple blossoms. Maggie felt some of the tension ease away as she took one deep breath after another.

But she couldn't avoid thinking about her problems for long. As if she'd conjured the scene, she could suddenly see herself screaming, her beautiful gown spattered with blood, and Owen lying on the floor, barely breathing, his face waxen, his eyelids fluttering.

Her breath came in pants and she collapsed onto a boulder, light-headed. She forced her mind to stay in the scene, examining it, looking for evidence of what happened next. She tried to push herself forward in the dream until her head ached, but nothing else happened beyond Owen lying wounded, near death.

For the first time in years, she let herself go back farther, to other dreams she'd had, the last being when Owen's first betrothed, Emily, had appeared to her, solemn and dripping wet, foretelling her drowning. There was nothing in that dream that she could have warned the woman about except to stay away from water, but even a bathing tub could have caused her death. Regardless, Maggie had been guilt-ridden that she hadn't found Emily herself and warned her, though she would have looked a fool doing it.

The guilt had never quite gone away, even though she'd had to move on with her life. Owen had never contacted her after she'd warned him. Seeing him again, she realized that the sting of his disbelief and disappointment in her had never truly dissipated. She'd always thought holding a grudge was pointless, but it seemed she couldn't take her own advice. His abandonment of her had been a sign that she was better off without him, that they never would have suited. All that seemed to be left was anger and disappointment and a physical awareness that was awkward and uncomfortable and yet . . . arousing.

With determination, she returned to her dreams, going farther back, past Emily. They rose up in her mind as if coming out of water, surfacing intact, practically bobbing, ready for her to pick from them. She saw the little boy shivering under the cliff, the girl who'd killed herself after Maggie's father had abused her, then back farther still, to her childhood, when she hadn't understood that her dreams were something that might come true.

With a gasp, she remembered the little boy who'd come to her occasionally in those dreams, her secret friend, she used to call him. It was as if she'd looked through a window into his life, saw when he scraped a knee, when he'd hidden from his father's wrath, when he escaped the castle to—

And suddenly she turned her head and stared hard at Castle Kinlochard—the same castle as in her dreams. The little boy had lighter hair then Owen's sandy color, but many children's hair darkened through the years.

Was it possible she'd been connected to Owen throughout her life?

Guards paced along the battlements, and horse-drawn carts rattled over the bridge. Clouds scudded across the sky, giving the building a forbidding yet vibrant backdrop, as if framed in reality as it was framed in her mind.

What was she supposed to make of this new twist? When she'd been hiding from her drunken father, thoughts of her dream friend had consoled her. When she'd watched her brother take a beating in her place, memories of her dreams were what she'd retreated to.

As she'd grown, so had the little boy, and she'd seen him less and less. Her dreams had become scarcer, and only truly powerful ones appeared to her, like the girl who'd killed herself. She'd told herself that she'd simply outgrown the need for a make-believe friend in her dreams, but there'd always been a part of her who'd missed him.

And as if her thoughts had conjured him, she saw the Duff chief himself striding through the heather, his blue and green plaid swaying above his bare knees.

And in that moment, she remembered what it was like to be with him when she was a young woman, the excitement building as he came toward her, the breathless wonder of being in his company, basking in his humor, admiring his dedication to learning, something she knew was forbidden to her. It was still so thrilling to be the focus of his intense gaze, to feel a clenching deep in the pit of her stomach that made her feel weak, betrayed by her own body.

As she sat upon the rock, his eyes swept over her as if he could see beneath her skirts. She kept her legs tightly together, though she wanted to lean back, languid with longing, brazen enough to display herself for him.

"I wondered where you'd disappeared to," he said.

"Ye didn't confine me to the castle, now did ye?" To her relief, she sounded almost normal.

"I would not do that. This is your home now."

*Home.* Just the thought shocked her back to her life, but instead of the truth she knew she had to say, she mused, "I've never been sure where home was."

She quickly looked away from him, back to the beautiful picture of the double arches of stone over the calm moat waters, the castle rising up behind like a solitary mountain. She shouldn't be talking to him about this, but the words had just . . . spilled out.

"Because your father had so many estates?"

She shook her head. "Larig Castle was the home

of my childhood, and although it means much to my clan, it has sad, frightening memories for me."

He came to stand beside the rock she sat upon, gazing where she did, at the castle. It was a relief that he wasn't intently studying her.

"I think I was too shy to tell ye the details when we were younger, but my mother took Hugh and me away to Edinburgh to live with her family," Maggie said slowly. Since she was about to tell him of her dream, she wanted him to know something about her, to understand what formed her.

"I remember you telling me your father was a drunkard."

"Aye, and that was the main reason. But she also wanted to take Hugh away from the friends he'd gotten into trouble with. Edinburgh was a good place for us. Ye remember our tenement—there were so many people to meet. But . . . was it home? Nay, it never seemed like it, though I've mostly lived there these last ten years." She sighed. "Part of me longed for the mountains that cradled Loch Voil and seemed to rim my world."

"You're back in the Highlands now," Owen said. "Soon you will feel at home here."

She stiffened, knowing he'd given her the perfect opening. She stood up, speaking with cool determination. "I won't ever be at home here, Owen. I cannot marry ye."

She faced him head on, but he was still looking at the castle. For a long minute neither of them said a thing. Then at last he turned and squared off against her, folding his arms across his chest and regarding her with narrowed brown eyes.

"You've changed your mind already? You give fickle women a bad name, Maggie."

She took a deep, steadying breath and resisted the urge to insult him back. "I thought I could marry ye. Though I was angry about everything that had happened between us, and having to fix everyone else's mistakes, I accepted my role in all of this. But last night changed everything."

"Last night," he echoed with sarcasm.

"Owen, I dreamed a terrible dream."

He simply blinked at her as if confused.

"Don't tell me ye don't remember." As anger rose up inside her, hot enough to make her ears burn, she pushed at his chest and he barely moved. "Ye don't *want* to remember. I have dreams, Owen, vivid haunting dreams that come true. I've never known them *not* to come true. I had dreams of ye when ye were just a laddie. You were the secret friend of my childhood."

She was spilling it all and he was just regarding her as if she were a new species of plant life. And that made her even more furious.

"I've spent my life hiding what I am from people," she continued, words flowing fast, "knowing I could be accused of being a witch. It kept me from deep friendships, from being myself. And then after everything that happened with ye ten years ago, I pushed it all down inside me, learning how to force myself not to dream, even learning to wake myself up if I felt it happening. Getting a decent night's sleep took a long time to achieve. I thought I was over this curse—until ye told me ye'd have me to wife. And then I dreamed." She shuddered and wrapped her arms around herself, and the dream unfolded in her mind as if it had been waiting to spring up and terrorize her. "When I screamed, ye woke me from the dream of our wedding day." Her voice became rough. "I'm in my wedding clothes, and ye're covered in blood, lying on the floor, white with impending death. I fall on ye and my gown becomes spattered with your blood . . ." She couldn't breathe, she couldn't think, might never feel warm again. The terror of it was so real, overwhelming, incapacitating.

And then she came back to herself to find him shaking her.

"Maggie." He looked exasperated and angry. "This is why you won't marry me? You're allowing a foolish nightmare to upset you?"

Her head jerked away from him as if he'd slapped her, and he let her go.

"And *now* ye see why I hesitated to tell ye," she said. "Ten years ago ye reacted even worse. Ye don't have to take my word for it. Ye can ask my brother, my mother—oh, silly me, they're not here to confirm my story, don't ye ken." His disbelief had haunted her all these years, and it was there again. "Aye, *you* try to tell the mother whose child is thought drowned that I don't have dreams that come true. I was the only one who never gave up; I saw where he was, led them right there. Do ye ken how often my dreams saved Hugh and me from terrible beatings?" All the emotion pouring out of her left her drained, and she regarded him with an exhaustion that seemed older than time. "Ye haven't changed one bit, Owen Duff. Ye still think ye ken all there is in the world. But ye didn't ken enough to save Lady Emily when I warned ye to."

"I cannot believe you're bringing up that tragedy," he scoffed.

"At least ye didn't remind me what a jealous liar I am."

He shot her a look. "I did not—"

"Ye did. And when my dream came true, and the poor lassie died, ye never acknowledged it, did ye."

"I don't acknowledge coincidences."

"Is that what ye told yourself? How ye slept at night? I never got over the guilt that I trusted *you* to do something to help her, when I should have gone to her myself."

He clenched his jaw. "I don't know what you want me to say."

"That ye'll help me find a way to salvage this marriage contract between our clans."

He stared down at her. She well remembered when they'd been together in their youth, when they'd hunched over a snake for an hour, and she'd thought Owen would take notes, he was so intent. She felt that way now, except *she* was his science experiment.

"You will mention this foolishness to no one," he commanded.

She was disappointed by his attitude, but for once they were in agreement. "Aye, ye think I want to be called a witch? But what are we going to *do*, Owen?"

"Do? We're going to marry, of course."

She groaned. "Do ye *want* to die?"

"I won't die, and I'm disappointed you think such a foolish thing will dissuade me. Do you doubt my intelligence?"

"How can I doubt what ye never let anyone forget?" she shot back.

A corner of his mouth turned up, as if he found her amusing.

"Don't make light of me, Owen, or this curse I've had to live with my whole life. I'm trying to help ye."

"Are you? Or are you somehow trying to help your clan? Was this your brother's idea?"

She took a step away. "Of course not! He was the one who tried to make the contract work when your father schemed to break it. Ye think I'd invent a story to avoid my responsibilities?"

"It looks like it. Although I wouldn't have believed it of you, it seems these last ten years have changed you."

"And they haven't changed *you* at all!"

They faced one another down, and Maggie realized

she might never convince him of the truth. She was alone in this.

"I don't know what you thought you'd achieve with such a tale," he said, "but it will not work. You agreed to marry me, and I'm holding you to it."

"Even if it means your death," she said, feeling older, sadder, frustrated.

"Threats, Maggie?" he asked softly.

"I'm not going to kill ye! I don't ken who tries—I didn't see that part of the dream." But perhaps that's what she had to discover, if ever she was to convince him.

"I'm not going to risk my clan's future on your foolish whim."

"Is this guilt over the part your father played or determination to be nothing like him?" she demanded coldly.

"Enough, Maggie. We will marry. And then I will spend my nights making you glad for it."

He spoke with promise, his voice husky, his eyes intense.

He was going to die, and all he cared about was having his pleasure. She whirled away and began to march back toward the castle, feeling him fall into step at her side, though she refused to look his way.

"August is the month for lovers in Scotland," he continued.

She stared at him, infuriated. He was going to ignore her warnings—again.

"This is the month that the harvest approaches, that

trial marriages begin," he continued, lecturing her. "It's a new season for many things—and it will be for us, too."

He gave another one of those faint smiles that looked as if he didn't remember how to laugh; he certainly hadn't been so closed off as a young man.

He was so firm in his beliefs about the world. One would have thought a man who fancied himself a scientist would accept that there were things he couldn't yet prove. Or did a frustrated scientist cling even more firmly to only what the logic of science could tell him?

Being with Himself as she walked through the courtyard was a different experience. She saw how his people nodded respectfully to him, how the men training with their swords seemed to show off their parries and thrusts.

But she was still thinking about Owen and how he'd changed. She remembered him in her childhood dreams. Had that been fate's way of allowing her to know him from the beginning? She'd been granted rare insight to the stubborn boy with a passion for learning, who also adored the outdoors and his Highlands.

He was still stubborn, but he had the power of a chiefdom, an earldom, behind him now. He could try to force her to wed, and though she would resist, she had to be prepared to fight him with the truth. She had to determine how the dream ended. She could not take lightly that she'd been connected to him her entire life—perhaps it had all been so that she could save him, fool that he was.

# CHAPTER 4

Owen knew the moment his bodyguard fell into step behind him in the courtyard. As the daughter of a chief, Maggie probably took it for granted, because she only bid Owen a good afternoon, then headed for the towerhouse. Owen stood still a moment, watching her walk away. The sway of her hips was an age-old siren song to a man, especially to a man who knew he would be married to her.

But not if she had her way.

He gave a frustrated sigh. What the hell was she thinking? He knew as well as she did that their sort of marriage was not one of love. He'd once thought her a practical girl and had hoped she didn't expect unreasonable and blind devotion from a husband. When he'd offered for her, he'd been remembering the laughing girl who'd explored Edinburgh at his side, who could carry on an intelligent conversation, who'd lain with him in the grass and kissed him with an innocent passion. Even her recent guardedness and suspicion were understandable. He knew women wanted romance and undying love, something seldom found when marrying to beget heirs for titles or unite warring clans.

But her reaction was beyond the pale. Refusing to marry him? Pretending some sort of nightmare was a portent of the future? Had she not matured in ten years? It didn't bode well for the peacefulness of their marriage.

Or was it as he'd accused her, part of a plot concocted with her brother to get Owen to break the contract, so they'd have their whisky land back? Once he wouldn't have believed it of her, but their friendship had been too brief for him to assume he knew her.

But if she was the sort to punish him for forcing her into marriage, she could have told his sister the details of how he'd let himself kiss her when he'd been betrothed, honor-bound, to another woman. But Maggie hadn't. She'd kept their arguments between them. He could respect her for that, at least.

He'd keep this argument between them as well, while he figured out what she was up to. Because although he could believe her fickle, or afraid, or part of a conspiracy, he could not believe her daft.

Behind him, Fergus, his bodyguard, cleared his throat, and Owen realized he was standing stock-still in the courtyard, watching the door through which Maggie had already disappeared. Owen started walking.

Fergus importantly swept past him, eyeing everyone with narrowed eyes and a lowered brow, as if he'd
never seen the members of his own clan before. Owen
had seen more than one man snicker behind Fergus's
overly serious back. Owen could only hope that Fergus
struck fear into other clans, because he struck no fear in
his own, at least with his behavior. He'd been assigned
his duties by the war chief—Owen's father's war chief.
Owen wasn't ready to start countermanding orders just
because he'd recently inherited the chiefdom.

Fergus followed him up through the castle to the
chief's solar, where his father had kept to himself
often. Fergus took up his station outside the door, his
back to the ancient stone walls, and faced the wall opposite as if he could stare there all day.

Standing in the doorway, Owen eyed Fergus. "You
know you don't have to spend your afternoon here."

"'Tis my place, my lord, and proud I am to be man-
ning it."

"And grateful am I, of course, but when you need to
rest, you have my permission to leave."

Fergus just stood at attention, hand on his pistol just
in case he had to draw it quickly and use it on whoever
came up the circular stairs.

Shaking his head, Owen entered the solar. Fergus
pulled the door shut for him, regardless of what Owen
wanted. But he was beginning to understand the need
to have a place to be alone. He'd spent part of each
year in London, while his father served in the House

of Lords. He'd found being a bachelor viscount in the city satisfying enough. He could attend the occasional dinner or musicale when he wished the companionship of young ladies, but during the day, he was more often than not to be found at the Royal Society of London for Improving Natural Knowledge—a longwinded title for scientific fellows who gave lectures or witnessed experiments. He liked his time to think, or to write his thoughts about the topics explored. Constant closeness with all his clansmen always took some time to get used to.

It took a moment before he realized that he wasn't alone. Seated in a chair beside the empty hearth was his uncle Harold. Unlike Owen's father and another uncle, this brother was the one who'd stayed behind to oversee the clan holdings. True, he had factors and tacksmen to deal with the land and the rents, but Harold was the de facto chief, on guard against McCallum or Campbell incursions. He was the man the clan had looked to for guidance and protection, not the late earl. Gruff and deliberate, Harold spoke only when he had something to say.

Owen felt his uncle watching him, evaluating him, waiting to see the kind of chief he'd be. And since he'd barely cracked a smile in Owen's direction, he guessed his uncle wasn't all that impressed yet. Owen wasn't about to tell him that he'd arranged his own marriage to a woman desperate to get out of it.

"Uncle Harold," Owen said, nodding a greeting as

he moved past and went to his desk. "Did I forget an appointment?" he asked.

Harold harrumphed. "Ye ken ye didn't, lad."

"Lad" made Owen feel like he was ten again, when his uncle had caught him using a magnifying glass to start a dry leaf on fire, and his protest that he was only studying the lens hadn't mattered.

"I've received word from the foreman of your coal mine near Stirling. He said ye've been exchanging letters about a fancy mechanical thing?"

"A Newcomen engine," Owen said with satisfaction.

"The foreman seems a mite suspicious."

"The engine is a new way to remove water from a wet mine, Uncle. When it arrives, we'll all have a demonstration of the power of steam. The machine calls for water heated in a cylinder to produce steam and . . ." Owen trailed off when he noticed his uncle's bushy brows lower with disinterest and impatience. "Thank you for the message. I'll answer the foreman. Is there something else you wish?"

Harold eyed him skeptically. "Is there anything else ye need to tell me about taking the McCallum girl to wife? I ken ye used to battle with your father over the right to choose your own bride, so I never expected this."

"Neither did I," Owen said dryly. "I never wanted to be forced to marry, and I was not. It was my choice to honor the contract between our families."

"But will ye be happy?" Harold asked softly.

Owen stared at him for a long moment, then admitted with a trace of bitterness, "My happiness doesn't matter, Uncle. I cannot allow innocent people to suffer when it was my father who proved so dishonorable where this marriage contract was concerned." He forced down his anger. "At least she is not a stranger." He deliberately opened an account book and looked at a column of numbers without really seeing them. His uncle was too good at reading the eyes of men.

"And that is all ye hoped for in a bride, that ye'd met her?" Harold asked shrewdly.

Owen didn't answer.

"And is that same requirement enough for her?"

"What does it matter?" Owen asked bitterly.

Harold sighed. "Sorry I am that your father forced ye into this. He was always more concerned for himself than anyone else, even his children."

Sympathy was not something Owen needed. "Is there anything else, Uncle?"

Harold let out a breath. "When will ye be returning to London?"

Owen leaned back in the leather upholstered chair and regarded his war chief. "Not until January at the earliest, whenever Parliament is in session. Why?"

"Ye'll be here that long?"

"I said I would," Owen answered dryly. "I can understand why you might not believe me, since my father preferred England to Scotland. Much as I see the appeal of the country to our south, I prefer the Highlands and will remain here as much as I can."

Harold gave another harrumph as he slapped his hands to his thighs and pushed to his feet. His plaid swung from his shoulder, where it was gathered with a brooch. But instead of leaving, he went to the wall of bookshelves that Owen had had built. The library alone hadn't been large enough to house everything, so Owen kept his favorites in the solar. It made him content to know he was never without a book he might need to refer to.

"These are strange titles," Harold said. "*Mathematical Principles of Natural Philosophy.* Why would this be of any help to a clan chief?"

Owen remained seated at his desk, a ledger open before him. "They'll help keep this clan chief sane. I cannot always be dealing with business, Uncle."

"All the estates in both England and Scotland must surely take up your time."

"Aye, they do. But I have many men to help with them, including you and my tanist."

His tanist—his heir if he did not have a son—who'd been elected to the position after Owen's father died, had his own estate and was away tending it.

"And since you're right that the estates take up much of my time," Owen continued, "allow me to return to the correspondence dealing with them."

Harold nodded and walked toward the door, his gait altered by a strange hitch from an old wound. Not that it inconvenienced him in any way in battle. Owen had practiced with a sword against the old man, and probably only now *might* be able to defeat him.

When Harold had gone, Fergus leaned in. "Expecting any more visitors I should look out for, my lord?"

"Nay, Fergus."

Only when the door closed did Owen put his head back, close his eyes, and try to find his equilibrium again. He'd been telling himself it would take everyone time to adjust to a new chief, but Maggie had complicated everything.

MAGGIE spent several hours alone in her bedroom, writing another letter, this time to her mother. Each letter was harder than the last, for she had to concentrate to keep certain things hidden. Her family knew she used to have dreams that revealed the future, but she wasn't about to reveal she'd had another after all these years—and one that affected the future of so many people, Owen most of all.

Not that he believed her, she thought bitterly—and not that she was surprised, after everything that had happened between them. He thought so little of her that he accused her of being dishonorable enough to avoid the marriage on a whim. Or that it was a plot concocted with her brother.

She gritted her teeth and held back a curse. For two weeks long ago, she'd told him everything, revealed parts of herself she'd never shown another outside her family—and he thought her capable of such dishonor.

And they were supposed to have a decent marriage after that?

But she forced herself to write to her mother about the castle, the people, anything but the truth.

Before supper, Kathleen arrived to help her prepare for the meal, and she glowed with exuberance as she showed Maggie the selection of gowns she'd pressed for her to choose from. It was a momentary relief to be distracted from her worries.

"Kathleen, this was too much work," Maggie said, amazed at how many gowns had been prepared for the evening. "Ye should have just chosen one and given it to me."

Kathleen looked aghast. "Nay, mistress, such a decision isn't up to me. And the gowns were so lovely that I couldn't have chosen if they were me own."

Maggie felt uneasy as she imagined Kathleen's life in the colonies, where things must have been so difficult if they'd felt the need to return to the Highlands after they'd been gone so many years. Gregor was certainly bitter about what they'd experienced. Had there been more family besides their parents?

But she couldn't ask, not now, when Kathleen looked at the gowns as if Maggie were a princess.

"Kathleen, you choose," she finally said, and soon she was clothed in the most elegant gown she owned, green silk with an embroidered square décolletage, and pleated fabric that hung from her shoulders down her back to the floor in a small train. She'd worn it to a ball in Edinburgh, but she wasn't certain it was proper for a supper in the Highlands.

And then Owen appeared at her door, and by the admiring look on his face, it would seem Kathleen had chosen well. The maid slipped out behind the frozen Owen, her eyes dancing as she gave Maggie a little wave and disappeared.

Maggie felt exasperated and defensive. *She* hadn't chosen this gown to entice him, but he appeared enticed, even after their argument. Men and their base ways. But an embarrassing blush spread down her neck to her cleavage, the top of which was too on display.

"You look lovely," Owen said, then stepped all the way inside and closed the door.

Maggie barely resisted rolling her eyes. Flattery meant nothing when it was contrived. She took a deep fortifying breath—and saw where his gaze settled. "I reject you, and the first thing ye do is stare at my softer bits?"

"The softer bits make your tart tongue easier to accept."

"Ye don't have to worry about my tart tongue. I don't plan to offer it to ye in any permanent fashion."

He gave an exaggerated sigh. "Not this again."

"Ye thought my refusal to marry ye a temporary protest? Oh, that's right, ye don't ken me well at all."

"But I'll learn, though it takes me a lifetime. Now come to supper—or are you trying to avoid that, too?"

She stared at him, hiding her dismay. She'd known he wouldn't suddenly change his mind about everything she'd confided in him, but it was now clear that the truth alone wasn't going deter his intention to marry her. While she tried to figure out the end of the dream, maybe she would have to give him reasons to end the betrothal himself.

In the hall, the same young man bristling with weapons fell into place right behind them.

"Maggie, this is Fergus," he said.

Fergus bowed his head. "My lady."

"I'm not your lady yet, Fergus. Just call me Maggie."

Owen eyed Fergus over his shoulder, but said nothing. Owen obviously meant to tolerate this particular clan tradition of protection. It was expected by the people, who wanted their chief to be a powerful man so important that he needed to be guarded. It was a mark of pride.

They arrived in the great hall, where every torch was lit, illuminating even the most shadowy of corners. Light from the setting sun still shone through the tall windows and onto the beautiful tapestries, reflecting off displays of targes and swords.

"My lord?"

The intimidating Harold Duff stood against the wall as if he'd been waiting for them.

"A word in private, my lord?"

Owen made an exasperated sound. "Uncle, call me Owen. You've known me since I was a lad."

"And how am I supposed to know what to call ye when your father preferred me to call him that?"

"I'm not my father, and I don't intend to be. Now what can I help you with, Uncle?"

Harold hesitated, glancing at Maggie.

"You may speak in front of my betrothed," Owen said.

She could start her campaign against the marriage right now, telling his uncle she'd refused the "honor." But making Owen out to be a fool before his clan would not get her what she wanted.

Harold narrowed his eyes. "Aye. I've received word of a cow byre gone up in flames this afternoon."

Owen dropped her arm to face his uncle. "Was anyone injured?"

"Nay. And the cows were grazing in their shieling up on the mountain," he added.

He spoke directly at Maggie as if she didn't know where cows grazed in the summer. She gave him her sweetest smile. He blinked beneath his bushy gray brows and turned back to his nephew.

"Was it an accident?" Owen asked.

"We cannot know that. A man was seen running away, but no one recognized him or caught him."

"Could he have been going for help?" Maggie asked.

"Help was sought from our nearest village, and did not come from the direction he ran," Harold said.

"There is concern that another clan could be testing ye, as the new chief."

"The Campbells?"

"Perhaps," Harold answered, shrugging.

Maggie let out the breath she hadn't realized she'd been holding, as if she thought Owen would accuse her brother.

Frowning, Owen asked, "How bad was the damage?"

"The roof and the hay, of course. The stone remained intact, so the byre can be rebuilt."

"I'll order it done, Uncle. If anyone comes forward with new details, let me know."

Harold nodded and strode away. Maggie watched clansmen respectfully make way for him.

Owen led her to the dais and the servants remained along the walls with their platters, awaiting his word. Fergus took up his position behind the dais, frowning at everyone even as he put one hand on his sword hilt and the other on his pistol. Clansmen had brought their wives and children; the hall was at least two hundred people strong.

And all of them stared at her. She was dressed far more regally, more expensively, than anyone else there. Even Lady Aberfoyle looked at Maggie's gown and arched a cool brow of disapproval. Maggie had only one ball gown, a gift from her mother's sister, but wearing it tonight made it seem like she wanted to put on a show, to remind people that she, a McCallum, was better than they were.

And it suddenly gave her the most perfect idea. If Owen wouldn't believe the truth about his future, she would convince him that a future with her would make him miserable. She would show him that she would be a terrible wife and an incompetent manager of his homes.

Owen did not take her directly to the dais, but began to wander among the tables, introducing her and even introducing himself to those he didn't know. Maggie knew courtesy and hospitality were important in the Highlands, and she could see by the expressions of his people that he was impressing them. She caught a few sideways glances, some of jealousy, some of disdain, some even with pity.

She told herself she could embarrass him by acting bored, but in the end, she couldn't do it. He was already complicating his acceptance by his people because she was a McCallum.

When they approached the dais, Lady Aberfoyle and Cat were already there, wearing the black of mourning, making Maggie feel even more out of place in her ostentatious gown. Maybe Owen's mother would berate him in private for marrying an insensitive woman. Maggie could hope for that. Lady Aberfoyle's expression was cool and remote—at least the disapproval was hidden from her son—whereas Cat studied Owen and Maggie with interest.

"Maggie, I hear you went for a walk today," Cat said, smiling. "If you'd like company, please let me know."

"Neither of you will be walking alone outside the

castle," Owen said, his expression serious. "Someone set fire to a byre outside the village today."

Cat gasped.

"No one was hurt," Owen added, "and I imagine it was simply a prank. But things are unsettled, with me becoming the new earl—"

"And bringing a McCallum into the household," Lady Aberfoyle said, giving Maggie an unreadable look.

There was an awkward pause, where Maggie wondered if the countess's hostility would help her end the marriage or make Owen dig in his heels. And then there was Cat's sympathetic concern. It would be so easy to like her, to confide in her. But Maggie would resist. She wanted Cat to support the ending of the betrothal, not talk Owen out of it.

"We will not assume Maggie is the problem," Owen said, cutting a piece of meat. "It could very well be me."

Lady Aberfoyle scoffed and changed the subject by drawing her daughter into a discussion about a family in the village who needed their support.

Maggie eyed Owen and spoke reluctantly. "Ye surely cannot believe your own people are against ye."

"They don't know me as well as perhaps they should."

"Your father kept ye in England."

"At first. But I, too, was lured by that country, but not for the reasons—Society, prestige—he was."

"Science," she said matter-of-factly. "I remember

things about ye, Owen, when ye've stubbornly resisted doing the same for me."

His jaw clenched but he ignored the provocation. "The work was important to me. I thought I'd find ways to improve what our estates already have, and in a way I've begun. In the last few years, an engine was developed using steam and a piston to raise water from the depths of a coal mine. I own several mines. I'm bringing the engine here, although of course the mine foreman is skeptical."

"Of course ye'll demonstrate it and convince him," she said, taking a bite of roasted lamb.

"And can you *predict* that?"

She heard the emphasis on "predict" and knew he was taunting her. "I don't need to. Ye can make a person believe anything. Ye made me believe ye were an open-minded scholar, did ye not?"

He chuckled, obviously making light of the words she'd meant in truth.

She rolled her eyes. "Don't assume ye can lure us all under your spell. Introducing me to your people one at a time? 'Twas an idea that won't work."

"I had more than one purpose."

"And so I assumed."

He gave her a sharp look. "You don't think I could simply want to make you feel at ease?"

"I already ken ye want that. 'Twill make everything easier for ye. Ye're trying to reintroduce yourself, especially to the men."

"True. And I have a way to begin to cement their loyalty."

"No one will be pledging fealty to the Campbells on your watch, eh?" But she had to admit that she was curious.

"I'm not worried about that. We all know that the Campbells are greedy and loyal to the Crown rather than Scotland. But my people know I've spent a lot of time in England, and they might think I was too friendly at a dinner party with a redcoat or two. But this isn't England. The Fifteen wasn't that long ago. My people must learn that while I'm in London seeing to their interests, it doesn't mean they don't have my absolute loyalty. And the only way to do that is to be among them, training with them, competing with them. As the noblest and best young men of the clan, they will try to excel at everything, to prove themselves, just as I once did."

"Ye make yourself sound ancient," she said dryly.

"To a twenty-year-old, I am."

His plan had merit—and for herself, too. It would keep him busy while she tried to figure out the dream and prove herself a poor bride, but he didn't need to know that. If he would contribute nothing to saving himself, then at least he needed to stay out of her way.

He suddenly leaned too close. "And such competition will inspire my Highland bride to wish that our wedding night was not so far away."

They looked at each other for a long moment, and Maggie knew she'd never see real admiration in his gaze. He wouldn't admire her, not that real person she was deep inside, the one who was cursed with dreams of the future. Nay, *that* Maggie he disdained. But that didn't affect his lust for her. And sadly, she still felt the same lust for him; a sin, any priest would tell her. Apparently, she wasn't very discriminating where men were concerned.

His gaze on her body was as physical as a caress, even here, in front of all his people, in front of his family. And the worst thing was that he seemed to sense her reciprocal desire. The quirk of his mouth said he was aware of her desperation to keep it at bay.

Let him be amused, she thought furiously, forcing herself to stop looking at his lips. She knew what she had to do. Tonight she'd return to her dreams and see if she could bring forth the one she needed to see the most.

Voices at a nearby table grew loud, and a woman shushed someone.

"I don't care *what* she thinks."

This voice belonged to an older man, bald head gleaming in the torchlight, whose broad shoulders still spoke of hard work.

"I don't care what Himself thinks either," the man continued. "He should know what we *all* think."

"Da!" A young woman at his side glanced at the dais with mortification.

"She's a McCallum," the old man sputtered. "She shouldn't be here! Why are we standin' for it?"

Maggie felt a cold shiver of fear over the tenuousness of the peace between their clans, reminding her of how carefully she had to navigate this business of ending their betrothal. If people died because of renewed violence, she'd never be able to forgive herself.

Owen rose to his feet. "Are you speaking of my betrothed, Martin Hepburn?" he demanded.

The young woman gasped, as if she hadn't thought Owen would know the name—as if she'd lived in fear over the trouble her father would bring their way.

Martin rose slowly to his feet, and Maggie stared back at him impassively. Hatred narrowed the man's eyes and put a sneer on his face.

"Aye, my lord," Martin said. "I never believed what the old chief tried to do—peace! With the McCallums!"

The entire hall had gone silent now as the old man's ringing voice echoed up to the cavernous beamed ceiling.

Martin raised a fist. "None of 'em are worth lowerin' ourselves. I bided me time, but I always thought ye'd see the truth and refuse this foolhardy plan. But here she is, a McCallum, and ye cannot take yer eyes from her, when there are plenty of good lasses from yer clan, like me own daughter."

"Da!" The woman practically screeched now, and took her father's arm and began to pull. "I'm beggin' your pardon, my lord," she beseeched Owen. "He's addled with drink. Let me get him home, please."

"Take him and go," Owen ordered.

He nodded at the guards near the door who strode forward, sword sheaths jingling against their belts. Martin looked briefly surprised at the escort, but he said nothing else, only shot a bitter glower over his shoulder at the dais, before his daughter pulled him down the side aisle.

Whispers became conversation soon enough, as neighbors leaned toward each other to talk. Maggie remained still, chin raised in defiance against each curious glance from members of the clan.

# CHAPTER 5

$O$wen stared hard as the doors closed behind Martin Hepburn, then turned an angry glare over the whole hall. Dozens of pairs of eyes focused on their own plates, and the conversation sounded closer to normal rather than salaciously whispered.

He looked at Maggie, whose face was pale, though her eyes glared at him with defiance. He was surprised at the urge to pull her into his arms and promise to keep her safe. It was an emotional response, not a practical one. But he couldn't promise such a thing, not when she was a McCallum on Duff lands. She wouldn't want his help anyway. She was a woman who preferred to stand on her own, to defy the promise they'd just made for the benefit of their clans. She confused him and irritated him and enraged him—all emotions he hadn't allowed himself to feel in a long time.

But he never allowed emotions to interfere with his decisions, especially where his clan was concerned.

Maggie changing her mind and now this act of arson occurring at the same time made him suspicious. His concern about her brother's involvement only increased. He would send someone to Stirling to look into the McCallum finances and dealings, to see if they were more desperate than he knew.

He sat down and glanced to each side of him, where his mother gave him an arched brow that silently said, *You should have known this was going to happen.* His sister's glance was sympathetic, her eyes shining with tears she tried to blink away.

Owen leaned toward Maggie and spoke quietly. "Ignore the old man. He grew up on hatred, whereas we grew up knowing that peace was at hand. We're going to change things between our clans."

She spoke in a murmur. "We will, but not the way you think."

"Maggie," he began irritably.

"'Tis strange to be the object of someone's hatred."

Her change of subject made him grit his teeth. "He has a stubborn need to cling to the past. Having someone to hate doesn't have to be a reason to live."

Maggie eyed him and lowered her voice even more. "If he hates me, Owen, could he have started the fire?"

Owen frowned. "I cannot believe he'd damage clan property in a fit of anger—he's spent his life right here in the village. But I'll look into it."

They were silent as they were served oysters in a butter sauce. Owen insisted on filling Maggie's plate for her, and she didn't object. He didn't mistake her passivity for surrender.

What he'd meant to portray, a celebration of his betrothal, now felt subdued and darkened by both Martin and Maggie's new rebellion. Pipers and harpists played merry songs, and when the whisky flowed, people even danced. But Maggie kept surveying the crowd, as if wondering who harbored the same ugly feelings as Martin did.

Later that evening, he walked at her side after forcing Fergus to go back to the hall.

"'Twill be difficult to rid yourself of your shadow whenever ye want," Maggie said.

"Fergus and I will have to come to an understanding."

He steered Maggie past her own door.

"Where are we going?" she asked warily.

"I'd like you to see something—and it's not in my room."

He led her up several levels by the circular staircase and eventually out on the walkway behind the battlements. Though a chill wind blew, she shrugged off his attempt to put his arm around her shoulder. Moonlight etched her creamy skin with shadows.

They walked to the edge and looked down to the courtyard below. Torches rimmed the interior of the walls, and a line of lanterns showed where the last stragglers headed for the village. Across the courtyard, the barracks housing clansmen still had lights in many windows. Off in the west, the sky glowed with the faint gray above the mountains, the last bit of light before darkness shrouded them all.

"It's peaceful up here," he said. "I come to stare out over the land that has been in our clan for centuries. I wanted to show you that I don't take my place here for granted; I don't take *anything* for granted. I made the choice to take you as my bride, and you will not be able to dissuade me. I choose to look upon this marriage as a destiny that began when we were young."

"Destiny?" she shot back. "Ye believe in something as untenable as fate, but ye won't believe when I speak the truth."

Her fiery refusal to acquiesce both infuriated and drew him. She was upsetting all his plans, but she also presented a challenge. She was no meek maiden to do her duty blindly. Admiring her for it was ridiculous on his part. She was trying to have her own way, risking the peace that had only just begun to take hold over these last years since the original marriage contract.

But then, with his face just above her hair, he could smell the faint hint of perfume or soap—lavender, floral and mysterious. An awareness of her now unfurled inside him, blotting out everything but the alluring warmth of her, the lavender scent of her, the knowledge that he would make her his forever. It was primal, this drive to take her, to bend her to his will, to force her to surrender.

He touched her chin, lifted her face to his. Inside

him passion heated and bubbled like within a cauldron, and it took infinite control not to crush her to him, but he still took her mouth hungrily. Whether she was surprised or overpowered, she let him part her lips with his tongue, but did nothing to either meet him or to push him away. She tasted of wine and warmth, but her unresponsive mouth finally bothered him. He lifted his head and frowned down at her, remembering the girl who'd once shared innocent kisses eagerly.

"Forgive me, I've been told I'm not very good at that," she said.

"And how many men have you kissed?"

"Several." But she didn't quite meet his eyes.

"You've kissed *me*, and I remember things differently."

"You have a poor memory," she said, sounding cool and remote.

"With so little practice, you've proven yourself a highly desirable, innocent bride, one I can mold to my own preferences."

"As if I'm a piece of clay?" she scoffed. "Your kisses won't persuade me to marry ye; I've been shown a sign that it's not meant to be."

"Your stubbornness isn't helping."

"Neither is yours," she countered. "But ye seem to think your kisses will. I'm not the same young girl ye fooled with false sincerity. Ye dallied with me, lied to me, then abandoned me."

"Abandoned—I was betrothed. Aye, I shouldn't

have let things go so far, but I'd never met Emily. She didn't seem real to me."

"She was so unreal she wasn't worth saving," Maggie said bitterly.

"Stop this attempt to make me think you were some kind of seer," he shot back. "You were a girl I hurt, who lashed out and thought she was devising a way to hurt me back."

"Because everything revolves around ye," she scoffed. "This contract between our clans is worth saving, aye, and to swell your head, I agree that even your life is worth saving. And I'll find a way to do all of it, with or without ye."

Then she turned and marched back the way they'd come.

MAGGIE'S emotions, held with such difficulty, now burst forth and she found herself shaking, both with anger at his refusal to believe in her, and at the way he thought he could use her foolish attraction to his benefit. She was so busy fuming that she briefly got lost on the way back. Every torchlit stone corridor looked the same. She silently cursed herself for not paying attention when Owen had guided her to the battlements. When at last she found her room, she closed the door hard behind her and leaned against it, breathing heavily.

Kathleen arose from the window seat with a start. "Mistress McCallum, ye look flushed. I do hope that's a good sign," she added, smiling as if they shared a secret.

Maggie gave her a lame smile in return.

"Himself must have enjoyed looking at ye in that gown all night," Kathleen continued, coming to help her unfasten it.

He enjoyed it too much, Maggie thought.

Kathleen seemed to study her closely. "I've . . . I've prepared ye a bath."

Maggie gave a pleased sigh as she glanced toward the hearth, where the bathing tub was resting on a towel. "Ye read my mind, Kathleen. Thank ye so much."

After Kathleen had helped her disrobe down to her chemise, Maggie said, "Go find your bed now. I'm used to helping myself. The tub can be removed in the morning—unless someone else needs it."

Kathleen shook her head. "Nay, mistress, enjoy it. A good night to ye."

Maggie followed the girl's progress until she left the room, then sighed, relieved to be alone, without the need to put up a false face. She had work to do this night and should be using her bath to relax and ease her way into her dreams. But all she could think about was that damned kiss and how difficult it had been not to respond. From the moment she'd met Owen, he'd been able to appeal to her on a physical level, and even his lies and betrayal hadn't changed her basic flaw: that he could manipulate her emotions and responses, that every touch, every kiss, threatened to sweep away her determination and indignation. Though it had been a struggle, she'd held her response back. Pretending not to respond to his kisses—or maybe to be a poor kisser—was a way to prove to him she'd make a terrible wife.

But tonight she had to put aside those plans and focus on her dream. After the bath, she donned her nightshift, blew out the candles, and climbed into bed. Lying back, she could see nothing but varying shades of black as her eyes adjusted to the darkness. A warm glow of embers from the smoldering peat seemed to pulse. With a sigh, Maggie closed her eyes and thought back to the dream of Owen lying near death. Though it disturbed her, made her nervous and uneasy, soon she was asleep, the bath having worked its magic.

Dreams came eventually, but nothing with that vivid quality. They never took her back to the one she needed to see. She surfaced to consciousness more than once, trying to force herself back into that blood-spattered gown, but all she ended up doing was tossing and turning. She saw Owen in her dreams, but he was Owen the suitor, not Owen the bridegroom. He was kissing her, and she gave herself up to the pleasure, losing herself in him the way she refused to do when she was awake.

At dawn, she finally gave up, lying with her head turned toward the sunrise as it slowly brightened her room. She'd never been able to force a dream before, and apparently she still didn't have the talent. But she wasn't going to give up.

She was already dressed by the time Kathleen arrived with breakfast on a tray.

Startled, the maid slowly smiled. "Ye're makin' things easy on me, mistress. I'll have little to do."

After setting down her tray, Kathleen glanced at the writing desk, where Maggie had scattered letters in various stages to her family and even a few Edinburgh friends. It was a bit of a mess.

"Never mind, I can see ye'll always keep me busy," Kathleen added, shaking her head even as she smiled.

Maggie glanced at her desk. "Nay, ye can leave the desk to me, Kathleen. I may be messy, but I have my own organization."

Kathleen bowed her head in understanding, but Maggie was left wondering whether she'd hurt the girl unintentionally. Having a maid was an intimate, confusing thing.

Maggie planned to explore the library that morning, hoping to find some legal books on contracts. She only got to the next floor when she realized she'd forgotten her shawl. She well knew how thick stone walls held in the cold.

She returned to open her door—then stopped in surprise. Kathleen was bent over Maggie's breakfast tray, eating the scraps she'd left behind.

Kathleen's eyes became stricken, her complexion

paled, and she swallowed. "Oh, mistress," she said faintly.

Maggie closed the door behind her. "Kathleen, don't be alarmed."

The maid couldn't meet her eyes, just stared at the floor while her fingers twisted together over and over.

"I was finished," Maggie continued. "I don't mind but . . . are ye not getting plenty to eat here in the castle?"

Kathleen nodded her head. "I am, mistress, I am, it's just . . . we never had so much food in our house in the colonies. I feel like . . . I'm hungry all the time."

Maggie wished she could give the poor woman a hug, but knew Kathleen didn't want her pity.

"I didn't know things had been so bad," Maggie said cautiously. "Ye can tell me about it, ye know."

"There's nothin' to tell," Kathleen said.

Her voice was so quiet and full of long suffering that Maggie's heart twisted in sympathy for her.

And then words rushed forth as Kathleen said, "Gregor's blacksmith shop failed, and he finally listened to me, that it was time to come home. We had nothin' there."

"Ye've both got positions in the castle. Things will get better." Now Maggie understood why the maid was plump—she must have been starving in the colonies, and some part of her still feared she'd be without food again.

Kathleen shrugged, still staring as if the carpet

design fascinated her. "Gregor is unhappy, mistress. He owned his own smithy, but he cannot afford to here. I tell him 'twill take time."

"I think ye're advising him well," Maggie said with encouragement, even as she wondered what had happened in America.

"Thank ye, mistress. I promise, I'll never . . ." Her voice faded away, and she quickly took the tray and departed.

Maggie wanted to follow her, to comfort her, but she stopped herself, knowing Kathleen would only be embarrassed further. It was true that things would eventually be better for the siblings. They'd returned to the Duff lands, ruled by an earl far wealthier than most chiefs in the Highlands. Her own clan had been desperate enough for stability for its people that her father had brokered this alliance by marriage with the Duffs. Nay, Kathleen and her brother would realize and accept that they'd made the right choice.

Picking up her shawl, Maggie made her way to the library, nodding to the occasional servant passing by. If she received a smile, it was a forced one, and by the time she closed the library door behind her, she was glad to be alone.

Two walls of the room had bookshelves to the ceiling, and Maggie felt a shiver of happiness work through her gloom. She might have an unwanted marriage looming over her, and the fear of a terrible dream, but the knowledge available in these books brought her a moment of clarity and appreciation. Where would she even start?

She browsed the titles with awe. *The Monadology* by Descartes, *Nova Methodus pro Maximis et Minimis* by Leibniz. She eventually noticed they were grouped by subject such as astronomy, mathematics, natural philosophy. She picked up one on astronomy, thinking she liked to look at the night sky, but she was surprised at the level of mathematics involved, and how ignorant she felt.

She finally found several books on the law, but they might as well have been written in a foreign language, for how little she understood. But she worked several long hours, looking up unfamiliar words, trying to find a legal way out of her contract. Nothing seemed to help, reinforcing her idea that getting Owen to break off the marriage might be the only way she could succeed in saving his life—not that she was finished trying to figure out her dream or decipher the book.

After a while, she went to the window and stared out at the countryside. It was raining, a dreary drizzle against gray skies, a sight she was well used to. The rain wasn't restricting her indoors so much as Owen's edict after the arson. It was difficult to be confined after so many years of freedom in Edinburgh. At first, though she'd been away from her father's influence there, he'd never been far from her thoughts, affecting every decision she made. Eventually, when she realized he seldom came to Edinburgh, she'd known true freedom, with no fear for the ugliness of his drunken behavior, or the worry about whom he'd next harm.

But that part of her life was over. Her mother had always promised she'd have a say in her future, and it had come true, Maggie thought wryly. It had been her own choice to accept Owen's proposal. She'd thought she was doing the right thing, desperate to help both her clan and her brother find happiness.

She'd be much happier if that damned dream had come back to her last night.

"There you are!"

Maggie's head came up, smacking hard into the open window.

Owen's sister, Cat, gasped. "I'm so sorry. Are you well?"

Maggie nodded, closing the book she'd only been daydreaming over. She wanted to rub her head, but knew that would only make Cat feel worse.

Cat walked over and stared at the cover. "*Micrographia*? What is that even about?"

"I don't know," Maggie said heavily. "We didn't have many books growing up, and this seemed like the perfect opportunity . . ." *To avoid Owen.*

"I won't keep you if you're busy," Cat said, "but I thought you might be interested in the competition going on right now."

"Competition?"

"The men are swimming the loch. Ye didn't know?"

"They're racing?"

"Yes. It's all in fun, of course, but I imagine the winner will think it more than that. And Owen is planning to lead the pack. Come enjoy the day with me."

So Owen had followed through on his plan. Maggie knew she should refuse, should play the disinterested bride, but Cat was drawing her by the arm, leading her outside to the stables.

"Let's ride," Cat said, "in case the rain starts again."

At the stables, two horses were already saddled, and a clansman straightened up when he saw them, bowing deeply.

Cat laughed and nudged his shoulder with her own. "Ivor here often accompanied me on journeys. He's trustworthy."

The skinny young man went scarlet, and then nodded at Maggie without exactly meeting her eyes. Maggie hoped it was just shyness, rather than another Duff who despised McCallums. She hated feeling so suspicious all the time. She couldn't trust Owen's motives—how could she trust anyone else's?

The ride to the narrows of Loch Ard was peaceful, and when they reached open water, they could see the view of the bare craggy summit of Ben Lomond, the tallest mountain in the southern Highlands, rising high in the distance. It was a distant backdrop to her own hills, and it made her feel achingly closer to home.

Many villagers and clansmen were gathered on the rocky shore of the loch, and Cat giggled at the men throwing off their coats, plaids, stockings, and boots.

They stood wearing naught but their shirts, reaching to their hairy knees, good-naturedly boasting of their prowess to each other.

Maggie remembered what it was like to laugh aloud at such a sight, to cheer on the men, and when she was younger, she sometimes joined the race herself. It had been a long time since she let herself wholeheartedly enjoy something. Suppressing one part of herself had made her cautious of anything that caused her to lose control.

Maggie saw Owen almost at once, one of the taller clansmen, set apart as if the rest of his gentlemen didn't want to crowd him. He didn't see Maggie and Cat, and Maggie was able to study him from afar. He joined the men as if he truly believed himself one of them, regardless of the aristocratic title that should have set him apart. His confidence was far too attractive.

All the men lunged awkwardly into the water, walking like teetering giants until they got past the rocky shore. And then they started swimming, and she could see their war chief, Harold, standing on the shore as if checking for fairness. Arms folded across his barrel chest, he didn't seem happy or disturbed or—anything, by the youthful race.

When the cheering faded a bit since the splashing men could no longer hear it, Cat turned to eye Maggie. "I do believe you've set me thinking about what it's like being a McCallum in a Duff household."

Maggie blinked at her. "Why?"

"I've seen how difficult it's been for you in only a few days, but you've got Owen to look out for you."

Maggie didn't say anything to that.

"But my cousin Riona, on the other hand . . ." Cat trailed off, frown lines etched across her forehead.

"She has Hugh," Maggie pointed out, defensive on her brother's behalf. "I've never seen a man so in love as he is." And probably never would again.

When Maggie was near the two of them, she could feel their devotion and tenderness. Even when their eyes met, there was a connection so deep, no one else mattered to them.

Cat gave a wistful smile. "Well, I'm thinking it's good to hear how much your brother loves Riona, of course, and I did enjoy their wedding, but . . . what now? How is she? A letter will find me soon, I hope, but . . . I'd feel better seeing things for myself. I think I'll go visit for a week or two. I'd like to be part of the peace between our clans. I can help your people see that Duffs are honorable, too."

It seemed strange to go back so soon, but all Maggie said was, "Have ye discussed it with Owen?"

"Not yet, but the hard one to convince will be my mother."

"She won't want ye to go?"

"She won't want to go *with* me, but go with me, she must." Cat gave her a very pointed stare. "I'm thinking you don't need her hovering around, protecting her boy."

Maggie was surprised and touched by Cat's intuitive reading of the situation. Their absence would have helped if Maggie planned to jump right into marriage. But perhaps it would be best if those who loved Owen the most weren't around when Maggie played the incompetent bride and forced Owen to publicly end the engagement.

# CHAPTER 6

After crossing the narrows and back, Owen came out of the water close enough to the front of the group to feel satisfied, to show he wasn't the most powerful, that he was one of them. Several women cheered, and he nodded to them. When they giggled and waved, he looked down at himself and thought it was time for his plaid to cover the soaked shirt before he gave the women ideas.

Fergus followed him up the rocky embankment, wringing water out of his shirt, flashing a lot of flank. "I'll fetch your garments, my lord."

"I know where they are. Go find your own, Fergus."

He'd lost the leather tie from his queue in the loch, and was brushing his hair out of his face when he saw Maggie talking with his sister. So Maggie had come to watch. He hadn't told her about the contest, but couldn't be surprised his sister had. Had Cat dragged Maggie along? He found his garments where he'd left them and, surprised by the good-natured taunts of the men he'd beaten, tried to respond in kind. Such banter didn't come easily to him. He was a serious man focused on serious research, including preparation for his first session in Parliament next year. But this was his clan; these were the men he'd lead into battle if it became necessary. He was determined to know them better.

But all the while he dressed and bantered, he kept glancing at Maggie. Once he caught her staring. She quickly turned away, and he felt the satisfaction of knowing he unsettled her. To his surprise, his sister turned away quickly, too, a sure sign of guilt. What was Cat doing to feel guilty about?

"Mistress Maggie," called a round-faced young woman near the fire. "Come have some oatcakes."

Maggie hurried away, and Owen was able to catch up to his sister—who still didn't meet his gaze.

"Cat, is something amiss?" he asked. "Who is that woman with Maggie?"

Not that he was looking at Cat as he spoke. He was watching Maggie, who wore a smile he hadn't seen in ten years, as she broke apart an oatcake, then blew on her fingers. Her hair was tight to her head, but he was remembering the wavy curls of her girlhood, the curls he'd once spread upon the ground and admired.

"That's Kathleen, the maid assigned to her," Cat said.

He'd almost forgotten his own question, so engrossed had he been with Maggie and his memories. "So that's Kathleen," he murmured. "She doesn't look much like her brother."

"She did when she first arrived," Cat mused, "but she's had a hard time adjusting to life here. Their deprivation in the colonies has made her . . . overly hungry here. Mrs. Robertson and I thought it would be good for both her and Maggie to be with someone else who's a newcomer."

"Speaking of Maggie, I should thank you for bringing her down today. I looked in on her before I left, and she was so engrossed in the library that she didn't hear me. I left her in peace."

"Perhaps you should have intruded," Cat said, eyeing Maggie with worry. "She seems . . . unsettled. You need to be alone with her, so I've decided to take our mother and go visit Hugh and Riona for several weeks."

Owen regarded his sister with surprise. "Have you told Maggie?"

"I have."

"And she didn't beg to accompany you?"

Cat winced. "It's as bad as all that?"

"Almost. She's not happy about the marriage."

"I suspected as much, even though she agreed to marry you."

"Agreement isn't quite the same thing as gladness and excitement."

"Well, I wouldn't be all that glad to marry a man

I hadn't seen in ten years. But Maggie seems a brave woman, and I admire her. I want her to be happy, and perhaps she can be, if you give her time. Woo her, Owen. Treat her like a woman who has a choice instead of making her feel trapped."

He frowned. "I do not make her feel trapped."

They were *both* trapped.

"Not deliberately. But I think once Mother and I are gone, you'll be free to make her feel wanted." She cocked her head. "Maggie mentioned that the two of you spent time together one autumn long ago. Maybe you need to make *her* remember it. Now go be with her."

She gave him a push, as if he were a young man at his first dance. When he frowned at her, she rolled her eyes. He sensed she was barely holding back from sticking out her tongue. The edge of his mouth quirked up, and by her laughing eyes, he knew she'd seen it. She always could bring out the humor in every situation, a trait he didn't have.

He saw Maggie walking toward the loch, solemnly eating another oatcake, and he approached her. Her gaze roamed down his damp shirt, and the haste with which she looked back at his face made him feel satisfied. She might be resistant to marriage, but there was no doubt that she wasn't immune to him. And he wasn't immune to her.

"You look good here, among my people," he said, reaching up to slip a lock of her hair back behind her ear.

She gave a start, her eyes wary. "You think flattery will help ye get your way?"

"It's worth a try. Didn't some man try to work his wiles on you before now?"

She narrowed her eyes, but didn't answer.

"Why did you not marry?"

She didn't say anything for a long moment, just stared out across the water at the bare hills to the north, the direction of her home.

"I felt I'd know the right man when I met him," she said at last, then arched a brow at him. "It never happened."

"Perhaps because you'd already met the one man meant to be your husband—me."

She gave a snort that was anything but amusement. "Even *you* don't believe that. If ye did, ye'd have come to court me long before now."

"Do you wish I would have?"

"Nay, I'm saying that we aren't destined to be together." She lowered her voice. "My dream is apparently trying to prove the truth of that in the worst way possible."

He ignored her reference to the dream, refusing to play along with her game by offering another rational argument every time she brought it up. "Were you angry that after Emily died, I didn't come to court you?"

"Not at all."

"I was eighteen, Maggie. I was sad about Emily's death, but relieved not to have to marry a woman I didn't choose. My education was my focus in those years, as it should have been."

"Ye don't have to convince me of that. I knew how little a marriage mattered to ye, and how little faith or trust ye had in me."

He was not going to defend himself or his behavior again, especially since she was only trying to punish him. "It matters to me now. Only twenty-seven more days."

She turned back to the water, revealing nothing in her unusual eyes. Looking at her slim back made him want to put his hands on her, feel the narrowness at her waist give rise to the curve of her hips. Time to distract himself.

"Did you enjoy the library this morn?" he asked.

She faced him again, then reluctantly said, "Not as much as I'd hoped. The room proves that my education was sorely lacking. I find little I can understand. But I'm not giving up," she added sharply. "There's a book on contracts I mean to decipher."

"Go ahead. I won't rescind your access to the library."

She thought him a monster, forcing her to marry, handing out rules on a whim. Did she not care that *he* was being forced to marry, too, losing the right to name his own wife? But she wouldn't take such a reminder kindly, he knew. He was irritated that she wasn't settling into her role, accepting her new reality. Surely she understood the duty of a laird's daughter.

But perhaps Cat was right, that he had much work to do if he wanted a comfortable marriage.

"A library was the one way I felt that my father did right by me," Owen said. "I would never deny you such a privilege. I look forward to introducing you to more when we travel to London early next year."

Those dark brows, so expressive, lowered again. "Travel to London?"

"I am a member of the House of Lords with my father's death, and I must take my seat there. I think you'll enjoy the city. Have you ever been there before?"

She shook her head. "Edinburgh is all I've known—all I need to know. I won't be traveling to England."

He ignored that, speaking patiently. "The sheer size of London will astound you, and it spreads outward every year. More than half a million people live there, and it continues to grow so much it might outpace the entire population of Scotland."

"That is not possible," she insisted.

"When we marry, you can come with me to find out. There are pleasure gardens to wander through, where globes light up the trees at night and people from all levels of society walk about masked. Every day men and women have great discussions in the coffeehouses about politics and philosophy and science. Is that what you'd like?"

"Ye cannot lure me into marriage with talk of foreign cities, Owen. Talk is an easy thing to use against a person, and not very successful."

"You think I'm 'using' talk, as if I spout lies?" he demanded.

"I think ye talk to try to get what ye want. Regardless, I won't be traveling to London. I'll never leave Scotland for the land of the enemy."

"It will be your duty as my countess."

"Then ye'd better find another countess," she said sweetly.

She moved to turn away and he took her upper arm, holding her close and leaning down. Their faces weren't far apart.

"I never took you for someone so suspicious," he said. "What happened to you, Maggie?"

"Life happens to all of us, Owen. *You* happened to me, too. Please release me so I don't embarrass us both by pulling away."

He was watching her mouth, and knew what she said, but once again he was caught up in the nearness of her, the lavender in her hair, the moistness of her lips. "Don't distance yourself, lass," he murmured. "Give this a chance."

But he let her go.

MAGGIE was grateful for the group of horses that slowly wound their way back down the glen toward Castle Kinlochard. It helped her hide her dejection at having to refuse a trip to London. She'd spent her life longing to explore and learn about the world, but going along with Owen's plans would only make him think she would marry him.

All around her, men bragged or teased, women laughed, and Owen remained at the center of it, and yet apart, their laird. He did not seem the sort to have an easy way with his people, which still surprised her. The boy she'd known for those few weeks ten years ago would have been far more at ease. What had happened to him? It couldn't simply be maturity and responsibility.

Over the next few days as Cat and her mother made preparations to leave, Maggie reluctantly spent time with them. If she wasn't poring over the law book— confusing Cat but making Owen frown at her—she was sewing pieces of tattered lace and ugly trim to her plainest gowns. Once his family left, she'd be ready for the next part of her plan, making Owen lose his desire for him. Then at last he might try to help her find another way to satisfy the contract.

She spent her nights trying to have another dream. She used several methods: she stayed awake late, hoping exhaustion would trigger something; she made herself think about the dream constantly during the day; she even tried writing it down just before going to bed. Nothing worked. Each morning saw her more and more exhausted with her failure, and Cat watched her with worry.

And then came news of another fire, this one in

an uninhabited cottage. No one had been hurt, but it seemed the arsonist was taking a daring step closer to such a risk. Owen increased patrols throughout the countryside, but continued to publicly insist someone was only taunting him. She didn't know what he privately thought, because she hadn't asked him.

On the final night before his mother and sister were to leave, Owen followed Maggie to her room.

She put a hand on his chest, barring him from entering behind her. "Nay, go be with your family. Ye won't be seeing them for some time."

Fergus had followed, and now stood uncertainly at the end of the hall. He didn't seem to know where to look, and ended up staring at the ceiling. Maggie would have laughed under other circumstances. She appreciated Fergus's abilities as unaware chaperone.

Owen jerked his head at Fergus, who obediently stepped back down the corridor, out of sight. Owen leaned his forearm against the doorjamb above his head, which made almost a cozy tent for them to speak beneath.

With his thumb, he brushed her cheek. "You have circles beneath your eyes growing darker each day," he said quietly. "Do not concern yourself about another fire or Martin Hepburn. I've talked to his neighbors. Martin might not get along well with people, but he's never been accused of a crime. It's hard to believe he'd start a fire on clan property."

She nodded, holding the law book tightly to her

chest as a barrier against him. Her base thoughts lingered on the impressive width of his chest that gave evidence of his ability to fight anyone to protect his land and people.

"I will discover the truth, Maggie. I protect what's mine."

She felt suddenly trapped by the heat that smoldered in his dark eyes. Days of avoiding him only meant that his presence seemed to affect her even more. Exhaustion had sapped her ability to resist him. When he leaned down to kiss her, it took everything in her to let her mouth go slack. Her emotions rioted inside her, making parts of her ache in a way she hadn't felt since . . . he'd kissed her ten years before.

He slanted his head and parted her lips with dogged determination, deepening the kiss. He caught her against him, and she shuddered, all her resolve dissolving, forcing her into a last desperate rebellion: she bit him.

He jerked his head up with a mild curse, and she quickly stepped into her room and closed the door against him.

"Sorry!" she called. "I just don't ken how to do anything right."

Eyes closed, body humming with awareness and need, she rested her head against the door and listened. The wood seemed to vibrate with his touch, but he only grumbled something and walked away.

THE next morning, Owen knew the shadows beneath his own eyes might rival Maggie's. He'd barely been able to sleep. The kiss he'd meant to seduce her with had caused him more than the pain of frustrated desire. He'd been shocked she'd bitten him. Why had he thought spunk and determination a good thing in a bride? But he reluctantly admitted that he didn't want a weakling for a wife, and he certainly wasn't getting one.

"You haven't taken your eyes off the McCallum girl," Lady Aberfoyle said.

He glanced down at his mother. They stood just inside the great hall, near where Maggie was giving Cat a friendly hug good-bye. And then Maggie disappeared down a corridor. She'd already made a formal curtsy to his mother, who hadn't appreciated the gesture.

"Mother, we're to be married," he said, trying to keep his tone patient. "You'd have to be more worried if I was indifferent to her."

"I do wish you'd reconsider and find another way to fulfill the contract. Do you know that in times past, these McCallum women actually made and sold thread in Edinburgh?" She sounded as aghast as if they'd offered their bodies on the street.

"I appreciate that they're hardworking women trying to better their clan," he said, an edge to his voice. "You certainly have had friends who've done the same. Life in Scotland is not always as easy for some as it is for us."

"Easy? And do you think your father and I haven't worked hard for this life we've given you?"

"You worked hard making sure Cat did not have to live under the marriage contract."

Lady Aberfoyle flinched. "Your father kept things from me, you know that."

"And I know you guessed some of what was happening, how Father was lying to Hugh McCallum about his betrothed. You and Father set this in motion. There's no stopping it now."

"Even if you wished to?" she said in a hesitant voice.

"I don't wish to. I know my duty. Safe travels, Mother."

He should have kissed her cheek, but instead he opened the door and led her outside to the stairs down to the courtyard. A dozen mounted men would guide the Duff women for the long day's journey to Larig Castle.

A servant told him that Maggie was in the library, a place he knew she thought of as her refuge, outside of the room he'd given her. It was good that he had something to offer her that she cherished.

He stepped into the open door and saw Maggie seated at a table with two large books spread out before her. She looked up and regarded him soberly, saying nothing.

"Cat and my mother have left," he said, stating the obvious.

She nodded, then lowered her gaze to the books

again, as if in dismissal. But just as he was about to demand her attention, she shoved the books away from her, until one teetered on the far edge of the table.

"Your sister has a knowledge of this library I envy," she said tiredly. "I might not appreciate your mother, but I can be grateful on Cat's behalf that your mother granted her the education I was never allowed."

"Maggie—"

"Oh, they tried to give me a woman's education," she said with bitterness. "I can read and write. My mother tried to teach me to sew, to knit, but even playing the viol was difficult. I cannot hold a fan with any mastery."

She was trying to convince him that she was a failure at the womanly arts, but he didn't believe her. And then her expression turned sad, and her next words rang with truth.

"I cannot understand these books. I've never read literature before. I feel like the ignorant Highlander we're always accused of being."

"I don't need a wife who comes to me knowing every one of life's skills." He was still angry that she was fighting a situation they both simply had to accept. It seemed illogical and flighty, not some of the good womanly attributes her mother had tried to instill in her. Why did she have to be so abnormal from other women—going on about childish dreams, threatening to break the vow she'd made to him? If he had to be married to a woman out of obligation, thank God that at least she sometimes amused him.

And there was always the promise of their wedding night. He allowed his gaze to drop below her face, lingering on her full breasts and narrow waist. Her hips were hidden from him, but not for long, a little over three weeks. He was counting down the days.

Maggie let out a noisy sigh. "I thought we were having a conversation about education, something supposedly so important to you, but instead your mind seems on—on—" She waved her hand between them.

"I was telling you what I preferred in a wife. This"—he waved his hand as she had—"is one of the things I definitely prefer."

"I've already said I won't marry ye!"

Owen knew she loved her brother, and that saving Hugh's life and honor was why she'd agreed to the betrothal in the first place. Their marriage would save lives wasted in a needless feud—her clan would still have access to their prized land, where they'd been sharing the perfect ingredients for the whisky that had been making both clans coin ever since the marriage contract had been signed at Cat's birth.

And yet Maggie kept insisting that a dream of his death was making her reject the best solution to satisfy the contract. He'd be flattered that she cared about his well-being, if he wasn't so frustrated.

"Maggie, I'm not going to discuss our marriage again. It will happen and there's nothing you can do to stop it."

"I can refuse to say the vows."

"In front of both our families, whom we're protecting with this farce of a marriage?"

She flinched.

"Let's return to your education. I can work with you on your studies, answering questions, explaining things. It won't be long before you'll be learning from every book in this library—including that one on contracts."

She watched him with suspicion. "And . . . ?"

"And we'll have time to discover each other as adults instead the foolish youths we once were." *You'll learn to trust me.*

"Ye mean the foolish youth *you* once were."

He'd been sailing through the calm waters of his life, challenged by little, mastering everything he tried. But Maggie was a storm blowing in, one that a captain could stand on the deck and face with bold challenge.

After a heavy sigh, she said, "Very well, I cannot resist the lure of these books. They'll help me figure out a plan to salvage the contract between our families. But Owen, I'll not marry ye."

"There isn't another way to satisfy the marriage contract, Maggie. You're the only McCallum daughter, and I have no brothers. This courtship and marriage are the only logical decisions to make, whereas you seem to want to base this decision only on emotions and flights of fancy."

"Flights of fancy?" she echoed, those storm clouds rising up again in her sea-colored eyes.

He took another step closer. His words had been a challenge, for Maggie didn't move, only lifted her chin and glared at him.

He cupped her cheek with one hand. "You look tempting when your emotions blaze."

She tried to push his hand away, but he only used his other arm and pulled her closer.

"You cannot pretend you didn't enjoy our last kiss." He dipped his head.

"No pretense is necessary."

She kept space between their bodies, and he wasn't about to force himself on her. There was no need. He buried his face against her neck, nuzzling her hair, bringing out all the sweetness of lavender.

"The scent of you intoxicates me," he whispered against her ear.

He gently bit her earlobe, and she gave a start.

Then Owen went against every instinct and stepped away from her, hoping he left her wanting more. "We'll start your education tonight."

"Education?"

"Not your education in lovemaking." He enjoyed her blush. "Until this evening."

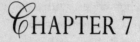

# CHAPTER 7

It wasn't until Maggie was outside that she felt she could breathe again. She'd felt desperate to be away from the oppressive opulence of the castle and everything it was supposed to mean for her future.

The courtyard was relatively empty after the departure of Lady Aberfoyle's traveling party, but still, she could see grooms raking hay in the stables, hear the carpenter's saw. She longed for a little garden where she could pace in peace, but everything was grown in the fields surrounding the moat. At least she thought so until she went past the corner of the towerhouse and found a little stone half wall near the well, surrounded by purple rhododendrons.

She stepped past the wall, and though part of the courtyard was still visible, she felt a little more at peace.

Until she remembered how easily Owen had set her pulse racing just by biting her earlobe.

Biting her earlobe!

It should have been revolting or at least annoying. She should remember her anger at how he'd treated her so long ago.

He'd been standing so close, she'd felt the heat of his body, smelled the scent of the outdoors. As he'd spoken, his breath on her cheek was shockingly erotic. And then he'd . . . smelled her, smelled her hair or her neck or . . . even now, it made her tremble. Why? The sensation of arousal was so frustrating and inexplicable. But arousal it had been, for she'd felt a clenching deep between her thighs and a heat that shimmered across her skin.

And then he'd bit her, and she'd actually lost strength in her knees. Only sheer stubbornness and pride had kept her from falling into his arms. It was both appalling and alluring. She'd agreed to his tutoring plans like a woman not in control of herself.

But what else could she have done?

Too often she felt like a coward for not sacrificing her future and her freedom for her clan, as her brother had tried to do. Hugh would have died for their clan, but she couldn't be the one to condemn Owen to death.

There was the dream, always there was the dream, the one that was still so vivid she could hear the slowing of Owen's heart beneath her ear after she'd thrown herself on his chest. She shuddered and hugged herself, trying to focus on the blooming loveliness of a rose climbing a trellis, but that was as red as Owen's dream blood.

What was she supposed to choose? Honor for her clan by trying to marry a man who would die if she did so?

She wasn't giving up her fight against Owen's fate. If she couldn't have the dream by thinking about it, there had to be another way to trigger it. She'd once heard of a woman who'd lived in Inverness a hundred years before who saw visions through a hole in a special rock. Could Maggie find some sort of talisman to bring on her dreams?

Feeling foolish, she examined the ground in the tiny garden, but it was well maintained, with no stray rocks. She hurried to the bridge that crossed the moat, and found narrow stone stairs that led down to the inner shore of the moat itself. Bent over, she searched for rocks, knowing how odd it would be to find one with a hole in it. There were mossy and wet, and the smell of swampy vegetation wrinkled her nose. She passed beneath the stone arch of the bridge, where shade blocked out the cloudy sky. When she spotted a rock with a hole in it, she felt utterly foolish as she held it up to her eye for a long moment. Of course nothing happened. She didn't see visions when she was awake.

Overhead she could hear the faint rumble of footsteps, but she ignored it, still squinting through the rock, until she heard a voice.

"She came this way," said a man gruffly.

Maggie straightened and lowered the rock as she recognized the voice. It was Kathleen's brother, Gregor. She stood still as more than one voice floated down from above.

But it was Gregor who spoke the loudest. "Don't ye see? The McCallum wench has driven away Lady Aberfoyle."

Driven away? Maggie thought with indignation. Who would believe that?

But she couldn't hear a response, only the murmur of voices. Was no one standing up for her, standing up for peace? Did they want an endless war where their children might die?

"Surely ye see the way she has Himself all twisted up," Gregor scoffed. "How is that good for anybody?"

She wanted to remind everyone that Gregor's family had fled rather than stay and support the clan. But that would only make Gregor hate her more.

And if he somehow found out about her ability to see the future . . .

Worried she wouldn't be able to control her temper, she remained beneath the bridge until she heard them all leave. She wouldn't run to Owen like a child complaining about bullies. But Gregor made her feel . . . nervous, ill-at-ease, and she wasn't used to it. She'd taken for granted being the daughter of a chief. Though her father hadn't shown any sort of love, at least she'd been accepted by everyone else in the clan, even when her mother had kept her away and safe in Edinburgh much of the time.

Now she was alone, looked upon with suspicion—by everyone including Owen, who refused to trust her.

OWEN stood beside his uncle near the charred shell of the abandoned cottage. It rose alone on a bleak hillside, surrounded by pastures for cattle. Once it would have been a welcoming sign of light and warmth for a clansman, but now its roof had caved, the stone was stained with soot, and black smoke continued to rise desultorily into the sky. In the distance, his gentlemen were walking the hills and woodlands, searching for anything that would give them clues as to what had happened.

Harold stood with his hands behind his broad back, his expression impassive.

"And no one saw anything," Owen said grimly.

Harold arched a brow. "I said that, aye."

"I know, but I'm frustrated. At least last time someone saw a man running from the burning byre. But I guess this remote cottage had been abandoned for a reason, being so far away from the village."

"No real reason. Old Abercromby and his missus never had bairns. The missus only died a few months ago, years after her husband, and it's been waiting ever since."

Owen snapped his fingers. "Now I remember. It

was on the list of cottages to be refurbished before a new couple moved in."

Harold nodded. "It'll take even more work now."

They were silent a long moment. Owen kept hoping one of his men would give a shout of discovery, but it didn't happen.

"I thought the first fire was a prank that got out of hand," Owen said.

Harold shrugged.

"But twice? This has to be deliberate. It's not as if a lightning storm had happened in the night. Could this brigand be angry that I'm the chief?"

"'Tis not as if ye were elected from a group of eligible men. The clan has always known ye'd inherit the title and the chiefdom."

"He could have been waiting until I inherited to vent his anger, but it seems unlikely. If it's because of the peace with the McCallums, that's been an ongoing process for over twenty years. Surely there would have been an outcry before now."

"But your sister was to leave us to marry. Bringing a McCallum here might have changed things."

And there was nothing to deny about that. Maggie had changed everything—including his plans to choose his own wife, someone perfect for him. What those "perfect" characteristics might have been, he'd never had the chance to narrow down. But he was a logical man, and having regrets wasn't logical. He'd made his choice, and the rest of the Duffs would just have to accept it.

"Have you made certain the patrols will pay particular attention to such out-of-the-way places in the future?" Owen asked.

Harold nodded. "I'll have another discussion. This will not happen again. But will we be able to find the culprit?" He spread his massive hands and shrugged.

Owen didn't like such uncertainty. He was the chief, his people's protector. Someone out there was determined to cause problems, and Owen had to be the one to stop it. He wouldn't have Maggie in danger. Just the thought made something cold and ugly settle deep in his chest, and he didn't bother to examine it too closely.

THAT evening before dinner, Maggie prepared herself carefully, choosing her plainest gown and watching as Kathleen wrinkled her nose but said nothing. The lace "decorating" the stomacher looked as if a five-year-old had sewn it on, and after the maid had gone, she'd carefully ripped the hem. She pulled a few strands of her hair out of its neat chignon, loosened the laces of the bodice, and strategically placed several folded petticoats inside as if she was gaining weight. She looked at herself in the standing mirror and had to grin.

In the great hall, she saw Owen glance at her, then glance again, but he displayed no emotion. To her dismay, he put on a show before his clan, kissing her hand and leading her in triumph to the dais. She was prominently on display, the subject of wide-eyed stares. She hoped Owen felt embarrassed, even if only secretly.

She also couldn't help wondering who in the crowd had been with Gregor, wanted her gone, perhaps was even setting fires to gain Owen's attention.

Maggie pointedly set her law book down on the table beside her plate and saw Owen look at it, then at her. After giving him a polite smile, she put her head down and began to read, painstaking though it sometimes was.

At one point, Harold came and said something quietly to Owen, then left the dais again.

Maggie frowned and tried to keep her nervousness hidden. "Is something the matter? Is it another fire?"

He arched a brow, then said with obvious reluctance, "It was about the last fire."

"I was told ye went to see it today."

"There are no secrets among the clan," he said dryly.

"You and I have several," she reminded him.

He ignored that. "There was nothing to see there, and Harold just informed me that although the men searched long and hard, they found nothing to implicate anyone."

"I wish ye would have told me you were going. I would have come with ye."

"Assuming I would have permitted it, and I would not have."

"And why not?" she asked, affronted.

He leaned toward her. "You're telling me you won't be my wife. Why would I give you a place at my side?"

"So ye're punishing me now for telling ye the truth?"

"This isn't a punishment. If anything, I'm granting you my protection. I won't risk you being hurt, Maggie."

"So ye really think the fires are happening because of me." She wilted a little inside.

"I believe the fires are happening because of *me* and my decision to change the contract. My people do not know me as perhaps they should. The patrols have been increased. It will not be so easy to find a solitary target to burn."

She regarded him solemnly. "I do believe ye're trying to make me feel better."

"I am not."

"Good, because 'tis unnecessary. I can handle anything that happens here. Since I'm involved, I wish to be told the truth and not kept in the dark."

"If I deem it safe."

She groaned and said heatedly, "You are not my father, Owen."

"No, I am even more important in your life—your future husband."

"I've already said—"

He held up a hand. "Don't bother saying it again. Now I suggest you finish your meal."

Darkness had fallen by the time dinner was done, and when she would have retreated to her room, Owen took her arm.

"Come with me to the library," he said.

Suspiciously, she clutched her law book to her chest, in case he tried to take it from her.

With a sigh, he said, "I have the telescope prepared for you to see the moons around the planet Jupiter."

Reluctantly, her imagination was captured. "There are moons around Jupiter? I remember ye telling me about the planet long ago." *When ye were trying to seduce me while lying to me about your betrothed.* "Have ye not changed your tactics to get a woman alone?"

He leaned in and gave her his most seductive smile. She caught her breath, even though she knew he was putting on a show.

"Do you wish to come or not?" he asked.

"I'll come. I don't want to make ye seem rejected before your clan."

"Your concern moves me," he said dryly.

When he would have straightened, she drew him closer and spoke with a sincerity she hadn't planned. "It *is* concern, Owen, whatever ye might think. I fear for ye."

They looked into each other's eyes for a long moment. And then he shook his head, and the rejection pierced her, though she should be used to it with him.

In the library, she knew he was trying to make

things simple as he talked about the telescope, showing her the eyepiece mounted on the side of the polished wooden tube. Never once did he make her feel inferior because she had so little knowledge of her own.

"This is a reflecting telescope, invented in the 1660s by Isaac Newton, who died earlier this year."

She nodded solemnly and let him talk on about the different mirrors used in the various telescopes, and how they reflected light. She didn't understand most of it, but for once, she didn't allow herself to become frustrated. He would teach her, she saw that now. He didn't think of her as a mere woman, too stupid to understand manly concepts. Being treated that way was . . . refreshing. He seemed like a different person, as if the weight of his responsibilities as chief and earl fell away, and the guarded way he held himself around her faded. He was just another scholar, full of enthusiasm for learning. His father had tried to crush that thirst for knowledge, but Owen hadn't allowed that to happen.

"Just six years ago," he continued, "John Hadley presented a revised version of Newton's telescope at the Royal Society. I was fortunate to be there and see its demonstration," he said, his eyes unfocused as he remembered what was obviously a momentous occasion for him.

"Ye spent most of your time in England," she observed. "I'm curious why ye didn't become a Hanoverian instead of a Jacobite. By all rights, ye should have been more loyal to the Crown than our King Over the Water."

"I won't forget that Scotland's king—England's true king—had his throne taken away from him, and we Scots had more and more taken away from us. We were promised our equal place in Parliament, and then it was denied us. Those rights still haven't been fully restored. There are new customs and excise taxes—"

He broke off when Maggie stared at him in disbelief.

"I did spend my entire life in Scotland," she pointed out.

"Then you know I could go on with our grievances," he answered smoothly. "It still infuriates me. Famine only made things worse. When the Jacobites tried to bring our king back to Scotland and his rightful rule, I supported it."

She frowned. "My brother Hugh was eighteen during the Fifteen rising. He fought in it. But you were only sixteen. Surely ye didn't participate."

He looked back through the eyepiece of his telescope.

"Owen?"

"No, I didn't fight," he said, meeting her gaze, "but not because I didn't want to. I was in Scotland when the call came to gather the clans. My own people went. I planned to go with them. And then I was hit from behind."

Maggie inhaled with surprise.

"When I woke up, trapped in a coach, we'd already

crossed into England. My father kept me a prisoner at one of our estates for that entire autumn and winter. Over ten thousand Highlanders gathered to defend our country and our king, and I wasn't there."

"Ye ken it didn't turn out well, Owen," she said quietly. "So many mistakes were made. The Earl of Mar delayed when he should have pressed forward. Men deserted while our leaders argued over what to do next. And then when we finally fought at Sheriffmuir, Mar refused to engage our entire army, and the Duke of Argyll and his much smaller force were allowed to withdraw." She sighed. "Even the Scottish contingent that marched into England surrendered. How ironic that both sides claimed victory."

Owen was watching her with interest. "You know the details well."

She shrugged and felt a warm embarrassment steal over her, then silently berated herself for it. It wasn't in her plan to win his admiration—she was supposed to be his idea of a terrible wife. Why couldn't she keep her mouth shut and play dumb? It was too late now. "My mother brought me back to Larig Castle as the clans were gathering, figuring I'd be most safe there. My brother eventually returned from the battle, wounded, and—and he told me everything." She'd almost said she helped nurse him back to health, but she didn't want Owen to know she had any healing skills.

"I didn't know Hugh had defended us," Owen said. "While he fought, I read books. Are you not impressed?" he asked bitterly. "Clan Duff was represented by my uncle Harold and many of our men, while I was safe in England."

She understood far more than he was actually saying. Was that guilt he was trying to hide? Could that have been part of the reason he rarely came home?

"But I learned from all of it," he continued. "I've made sure these last years that although the Disarming Act was supposed to deprive us of weapons, we've taken good care to hide ours away. Let the Campbells and the Hanoverians and Whigs do without; we'll be ready to defend what is ours."

He sounded like a warrior, like a Highlander, and it made something deep inside give a little quiver of need.

To distract herself, she asked quickly, "Does the watch bother ye here?"

"They don't dare. Those companies can police the Lowlands and the burghs. We take care of our own in the Highlands."

Maggie saw the determination in the coldness of his deep brown eyes as he stared out the window. She imagined he looked out across the breadth of his land, unseen in the dark, and like many men, he must wish the soldiers would try to come against him, so that he could fight. It was an uncivilized urge for a civilized man, and it made him far too attractive to her.

She deliberately turned back to his telescope and gestured.

The edge of his mouth lifted in a faint smile. "I lined up the telescope where Jupiter is, but let me prepare it for you. You'll be amazed that there are so many moons around one planet."

Trying to ignore his nearness, she bent over the telescope to look through the eyepiece. He didn't let her ignore him, of course. He guided her position at the telescope by placing his hands on her hips to move her, then touched her back as he bent over her to make sure she was looking through it correctly. There was only one eyepiece—how wrong could she get it?

She studied the white disk in the black sky, and when Owen told her how to see the moons' shadows against Jupiter, she finally started losing herself in the wonder of it all.

She straightened and looked up at Owen. "That is . . . magical," she breathed. "To think that there are other moons, other planets, that men have developed ways to see them through the vast reaches of the heavens . . ."

"Not just men. I read the works of a French astronomer, a woman named Jeanne Dumée."

"A woman?" Maggie breathed, stunned.

"She said she hoped to convince people there was no difference between the brains of men and women. I didn't need her to tell me that. I grew up alongside a formidable woman."

His relationship with his sister was as strong as hers

with Hugh. It made her think more kindly of Owen, when she couldn't afford to.

She said, "Cat was very lucky to be allowed to show her intelligence. Though your father was cruel to my brother, he seemed to allow Cat to grow up with dignity and a freedom many women lack."

Owen shrugged. "He deliberately chose when he would allow either of us that right."

She thought of Owen confined to his home, reading for endless hours when he wanted to be with his clan fighting for Scottish freedom. For a long moment, they seemed held near one another by invisible strings of tension that pulled her closer regardless of her rational wariness. Her skin felt too sensitive for her body, and somehow she knew touching him would make things both better and far more dangerous.

But he turned back to the telescope and started lecturing again, and she told herself to feel relieved. She put her hand on the law book to remember her priorities.

# CHAPTER 8

The next morning, when Owen informed her he was leading his men on a hunting party for a few days, Maggie was relieved. He knew it, she knew it, but he only shook his head and made his plans, giving her a resounding kiss in the great hall as he departed, where everyone could see him. He took obvious delight in telling her to talk with Mrs. Robertson about an upcoming festival the castle would be hosting. When she looked aghast, he settled her down by telling her that her family would be invited, too. Then Maggie retreated to her room to begin a sewing project that made her gleeful when she imagined Owen's reaction. Mrs. Robertson seemed relieved she had some form of womanly inclination, but Maggie made certain the housekeeper couldn't see exactly what she was sewing. Maggie noticed that Mrs. Robertson didn't bother to mention the festival, and Maggie didn't bother to bring it up, knowing she needed to pretend indifference. Mrs. Robertson was probably relieved to handle it herself.

In the afternoon, Maggie spent hours in the library, struggling through books on marriage law and making little headway. By evening, she was exhausted and suffering a headache, so she made her excuses to miss supper in the great hall and ate quietly from a tray in her room. With plans to find her bed early, she called for Kathleen's help undressing, then dismissed her for the night. Maggie practically sighed her pleasure as she pulled down the counterpane on her bed.

She jerked in surprise at what was nestled in her clean sheets—a stick, bare of bark, with the letters of her name carved backward in it. There was nothing else, though she tossed back all the bedding just in case.

The stick seemed ugly and foreign against the white sheets, a representation that someone had invaded her room and left this to . . . what?

It was a talisman, she suddenly realized, and shivered. A talisman or charm, and she knew enough of superstition—had educated herself because of her fears of what others would think of her—to know that it was the mark of witchcraft, specifically a mark of evil intent.

Was it supposed to make her fear a curse, which she didn't believe in, or implicate *her* as a witch? No one knew the secret of her dreams except Owen—or did they? She suddenly felt very vulnerable and frightened. Without thinking, she picked up the ugly thing and tossed it onto the fire, where flames licked greedily before consuming it.

She hugged herself and watched, even as she wondered if the same person behind this had started the fires on clan lands. Had this person grown bolder when no one connected those fires to accuse the McCallums? Was she now to be the focus of someone's hatred? She needed to tell Owen and—

Then she groaned aloud. She'd burned it, had only been thinking that she didn't want the evidence of hatred anywhere near her—hadn't wanted a servant to find it in her possession.

But now she had no proof to show Owen that this villain had penetrated into the castle itself with his threats.

Cursing her impulsiveness, Maggie straightened the bedclothes and reluctantly climbed in. Someone hateful had invaded her room, touched her bed, threatened her. It was a long time before sleep claimed her, and even then, she awoke several times in the night, fearing that someone was trying to enter her room. She slept better only when she pushed a chest in front of the door.

Two days later, Owen rode home through the gates of Castle Kinlochard with the hunting party and searched the crowd for Maggie's lovely face. He'd been unnaturally concerned about her in his absence, even though he knew his uncle had the castle's safety well under control. She wasn't with the servants crowded around to deal with the carcasses of partridges, duck, and deer being unloaded from packhorses. And then he spotted her at the top of the stairs, at the double doors leading into the great hall. She wore a dark gown that had been altered to downplay her figure, just as she'd done to her other gowns. The skirt was parted, showing off an underskirt made of different colors that clashed garishly, and the neckline was sewn with uneven edges. He could only imagine how appalled her lady's maid must be.

The new attempt to make herself unpresentable reluctantly amused him. He'd countered by trying to show her that there was nothing she could do to make him break their betrothal, that he wanted her regardless. Could this all be part of a plan with her brother? The man he'd sent to investigate the McCallums had yet to return.

Owen was far too preoccupied with Maggie, he thought with resignation. On the nights he'd lain across the hillside heather, wrapped in his plaid, he imagined what her hair would look like when he removed all the pins and let it fall about her shoulders. He wanted her eyes hot with wanting him, like he'd only glimpsed once or twice until she shuttered her thoughts from him, hid behind her stubbornness.

Now in the courtyard, he lifted his arm in a salute to her where she stood on the landing high above, and she nodded. He saw people looking from him to her, and that was good. Those who were against peace between the clans had to see that this marriage was a foregone conclusion.

He dismounted into the muddy courtyard, and a groom came to lead his horse away. Taking the stairs two at a time, he saw Maggie's eyes widen, even as he reached to take both of her hands in his, a deliberately romantic gesture. He pressed her warm hands to his cool lips, then looked up at her.

She eyed him speculatively. "Who are ye trying to impress? 'Tis certainly not me. Ye've only been gone two nights."

He studied her closely. "You are well and safe?"

"And why wouldn't I be?"

But she didn't quite meet his gaze, and he frowned his concern.

"Your uncle was practically my bodyguard," she rushed on, "and I could swear there were several other 'shadows' near me, too. Remind me next time, so I don't think a villain has me in his sights."

"I will remember."

Her words were lighthearted, but he sensed a . . . falseness about her, as if there was more she could be saying.

Taking her arm, he led her into the great hall, where servants were feeding the hunting party.

"I assume the hunt was successful?" she asked.

"In more ways than one."

"And what does that mean?"

He lowered his voice. "My uncle organized the hunt, but assumed I wouldn't go."

Her brows knit with puzzlement. "But ye're the chief."

"Harold believes I consider myself an earl before a chief. He only knows my father's example, of course."

She seated herself in the chair he pulled out for her. "So . . . this was a test?"

"Perhaps. He subtly implied the rough trip across mountain might be too much for me." He took a deep sip of his wine.

"And ye're not offended."

"It was a challenge I appreciated, one that was necessary to my men."

"And ye think challenges are simply for men?"

He eyed her. "I didn't say that."

"Nay, but ye've implied it, especially by the way ye had your uncle traipsing around like my nursemaid."

"I wouldn't let him hear you say that," he said dryly.

"I am able to take care of myself," she said. "Next time tell him that I once went toe-to-toe with a British soldier."

"Of course you did."

She narrowed her eyes at him and said in a low voice, "Are ye accusing me of lying—again?"

He cocked his head, aware that he was approaching

a line that she'd drawn between them. "Perhaps exaggerating for the enjoyment of your audience."

"Those are pretty words for lying. I tell the truth—*all* the time."

And maybe there was some part of her that thought she did, but it didn't change how he felt about her ridiculous claims to be some sort of seer. Perhaps her parents had been so busy ignoring her that she'd fallen into the hands of a superstitious group of women. Or she'd found a way to manipulate people by claiming powers. One coincidence that ended up coming true couldn't change his mind.

But he wasn't about to say all of that. "Then go ahead and tell me how you and a redcoat faced off."

"Aye, I will. He boldly stared at me one day as I walked through town, followed me home, came right into the parlor, and told my mother he intended to court me. She rebuffed him politely—we weren't *that* stupid—and we hoped that that would be the end of it."

Owen suddenly realized that sounded very real, very dangerous. "How old were you?"

"Twenty."

She was like a little rooster, so much bluster and crowing, but very helpless against a bigger opponent. He felt a stirring of dread as he imagined her at the mercy of a man.

"What happened next?" he demanded. He heard himself sound cold, icy, but it was the only way to keep down the heat of rage that was building up inside him. What was happening to him—what was she doing to him?

"He started following me, day after day, not bothering to hide, his red uniform blindingly obvious, his ugly smirk promising perseverance. My mother suggested I find a husband, but I would not be forced to marry."

Maggie gave Owen a look that plainly said she still felt the same.

"He was not invited to private parties, of course," she continued, "but at public dancing assemblies, British officers did as they wished. Finally, he found me in a corridor after I'd needed a moment's privacy, and pulled me outside into the garden."

The defensive righteousness in her voice was slowly fading away as her gaze unfocused. She was obviously seeing into the past, leaving her body so tense that Owen felt if he touched her, she might shatter. He felt an unfamiliar urge to comfort her, and it made him uneasy. This woman who was upsetting all his plans was part of a bargain, not a love match. He couldn't imagine ever trusting her enough for that. But she was suffering now, and he didn't like how her suffering seemed to hurt him as well.

"He tried to take liberties with me," she said, her chin up with bravery. "I fought him, which surprised him."

"You are fierce. I like that in a woman."

As he'd hoped, it seemed to distract her from the terror of her memories, and she rolled her eyes at him.

"Aye, weel, I would have felt better with a pistol or at least a dirk. But luckily, he was tippled, and I ended up breaking a vase over his head before giving him a bloody nose."

It was hard not to look at her with open admiration, but he managed to conceal his emotions. She was a spitfire, which he'd known from the beginning. Brave and clearheaded, even when under attack. "Did he leave you alone after that?"

"Aye, he did, but he turned his sights on another girl less able to defend herself."

Now her changeable expression became haunted, and he found himself even more tense.

"Her father took matters into his own hands when it seemed the worst had happened, calling out the redcoat. They fought, and the redcoat was killed. Although many stood up in defense of the Scot's actions, they hung him regardless, and the girl was ruined." Her voice was soft by the end, but she showed little reaction.

"I'm sorry," he said, knowing it was another in a long line of tragedies that a Sassenach had caused.

She took several deep breaths, and when she met his gaze again, her eyes were cool. "'Tis in the past," she said at last. "And that story is the proof that I can handle any challenge."

He studied her for a long moment, at the way her

unusual eyes sparkled with determination and pride. Without intending to, he found himself taking her hand and bringing it to his lips again, but not in the flamboyant way he'd done so in the courtyard. He heard her breathing quicken, and his own matched it.

Until she pulled away and said brightly, "Did ye kill many poor animals on your hunt?"

She didn't want his sympathy, and he felt uncomfortable having tried to give it. "Many. I have excellent aim."

"Then the castle will feast." She hesitated, then turned that challenging gaze on him again. "Do ye remember the first dinner we shared?"

"Ten years ago in Edinburgh?"

She waved a hand. "Nay, not that. I knew ye wouldn't remember."

She went back to her bannock.

Curiosity got the better of him. "You're going to leave it like that," he said dryly.

"Very well. We were young when our parents forced us together for a meal. Ye were fourteen to my twelve. Ye didn't even look me in the face, so angry at being kept from whatever ye'd meant to be doing that night." She lifted her chin. "I thought ye a spoiled child."

"I do not remember that dinner, but if you were twelve"—he glanced down at her chest—"you might have changed a bit since then."

She gave him a faintly sarcastic glance. "So have you."

"For the better." He leaned toward her, inhaling the lavender scent that was a part of her.

"Aye, ye continue to delude yourself that way." Shaking her head, she turned back to help herself from the serving bowl full of boiled broccoli and onions. He allowed her her silence as she ate, but eventually he engaged her once again, remembering her evasiveness when he'd first arrived at the castle.

"What did you do to occupy your time while I was gone?" he asked.

"I did not pine away for ye, if that's what's got in your head."

"You can be a cold woman, Maggie McCallum."

"Ye don't need me to make ye think good of yourself. Ye've always had that in hand."

Owen heard a chuckle behind him, and turned to see Harold, whose eyes still twinkled, though his lips barely curved upward. Fergus stared straight over their heads at the other dinner guests, but his mouth twitched.

"I'll repeat my query so that we can have a civilized conversation," Owen said. "What did you do to occupy your time?"

Maggie sighed. "I spent most of it in the library, if ye must know. Your books are varied and fascinating. I tried to find the most basic and easiest to read. I feel . . . quite ignorant."

"When I read a new book, sometimes it takes me

days or even weeks to understand the complexities of the theory proposed."

Though she nodded, her frown didn't recede. She only wanted what he wanted, he told himself, knowledge of the world. It was rare to find that in anyone. Most were simply concerned with their own lives and struggles and never thought beyond their own villages.

"You'll be happy to know," Maggie added, "that I also spent much time sewing, a very proper womanly occupation."

He couldn't help looking down warily at her ridiculous gown.

She just blinked her big, innocent eyes at him before saying, "Mrs. Robertson told me that you were very particular about your shirts, and I insisted that I could handle the directions well."

"You made me shirts?" he said, barely withholding a grimace. He had them sewn professionally in London and Edinburgh.

"I did. I'll show you this evening so that ye can wear one in the morning. I felt so very much like a wife," she said sweetly.

That didn't bode well . . .

LATE that afternoon, Maggie stood at the balustrade outside the open doors of the great hall. Below her, the men prepared to compete with their swords, part of Owen's attempt to acquaint himself with his men. They were as jolly as if on an outing in the countryside, rather than about to risk serious harm or even death by simply practicing. She'd been around the bravado of men her entire life, but sometimes it still surprised her.

She found herself watching Owen wherever he went. He wore an air of confidence, of command, that came from a lifetime of knowing he was heir to a chiefdom and an earldom. Men watched him or made way for him, showing respect for the position, and perhaps beginning to show the same to the man himself.

While the two dozen men discussed the rules of their competition, Maggie thought about the meal she'd shared with Owen. She regretted becoming so defensive that she'd confided such a personal story about her past. She'd never told anyone other than her family, had spent weeks and months, even years, wishing she'd done more to stop the soldier before men died. Such regrets seemed to be a refrain in her life, she thought bitterly.

Owen had simply listened, hadn't passed judgment, hadn't downplayed the event. She didn't want to know about a thoughtful side to him, one that made him even more attractive to her.

She'd almost told him about the evil talisman, but hadn't wanted to discuss it in such a public place. Whoever had done such a thing wanted her to be frightened, wanted to see her reaction, and she wasn't going to give that person the satisfaction.

While Owen was hunting, Maggie had overheard Mrs. Robertson mentioning a healing woman in the village, and Maggie had made it a point to try the occasional subtle query to discover just how far this woman's gifts extended. Kathleen, practically as newly arrived to the castle as she was, didn't have any knowledge herself, but she'd proven useful in finding others who did. Maggie had become quite heartened to realize people associated the mystical with this woman, as well. Perhaps the healer would be the perfect person to help her experience the dream—if Maggie could find a way to discuss it without revealing too much.

Maggie had walked into the village, an ever-present gentleman following behind. In an unsettling turn of events, the old man, Martin Hepburn, had taken to following her about when he saw her. He never approached her or said anything, but wherever she went, on the green, or down a wynd between cottages, she could look behind and see him spying on her. Could he have been the one to place the talisman in her bed? He didn't live in the castle—wouldn't he have seemed out of place wandering the corridor of the family bedrooms? Or he could have had someone do it for him.

And then Maggie was distracted from her reverie when Owen swung a sword at his first opponent, the blade reflecting the sunlight like lightning. With powerful strokes, he drove the man backward again and again, parrying ripostes with the targe on his left arm. He lured his opponent into a deep lunge, and in the blink of an eye, disarmed him by catching hold of his wrist.

Maggie's mouth went dry at the display of power and technique. Other combatants were still battling each other, but those around Owen cheered, and the defeated man hung his head good-naturedly. Had her relationship with Owen been different, she would have cheered, too, enjoying the muscles of his bare legs as his plaid swayed about his thighs. After disarming his second opponent by using the man's lunge to throw him to the ground, Owen paused to discuss a technique with his foe, demonstrating for the man's benefit. More than one man listened intently. He was tutoring his gentlemen with patience, enthusiasm, and obvious knowledge of his subject. It wouldn't be long before every man here followed him without even a hesitation.

In the final battle to decide the winner of the entire challenge, Owen faced his uncle Harold. Every combatant watched, as well as the servants from the household and even some of the villagers who had come in from their fields. So many people gathered around the training yard that if Maggie had gone down the steps to be with them, she wouldn't have been able to see the fight. On one side of her was Kathleen, eyes glistening with eager excitement, and on the other, Mrs. Robertson, who was waving and cheering for Harold Duff.

Just before commencing, Owen looked up at Maggie and saluted with his sword. Heads lifted to glance up at her, some even with interest, but fires had been set, witchcraft threatened, and more than one man had protested her marriage to Owen. Would one of his own clansmen try to kill him on his wedding day if he married her?

Then Owen and Harold started to battle, and the crowd had to surge back to avoid the combatants, who ran at each other, slashing swords, thrusting, parrying with their targes. First Harold was the aggressor, then Owen, and it went back and forth for some time. The cheering was so loud Maggie felt like her head was ringing. Kathleen jumped up and down; Mrs. Robertson whistled with a piercingly loud trill.

After a particularly athletic encounter, Owen and Harold circled each other. Both of their swords hung from tired arms, but their footsteps were alert. Owen was wearing a grin, and Harold's eyes shone even as his face streamed with sweat.

And then suddenly Owen launched an attack, his sword weaving with an intricate maneuver—only to be captured beneath Harold's strong arm, while the war chief's own sword stopped a foot from Owen's chest. A wild cheer surged upward and the two men fell back. Owen breathed as heavily as his uncle, both smiling at each other.

Shaking her head, Maggie said, "They'll all be drinking their whisky in celebration tonight."

The housekeeper gave her a disapproving stare. "They'll be hungry. I'll see to their feast."

"Thank ye, Mrs. Robertson," Maggie said, striving to sound polite when she was irritated. Maggie was a competent woman—she hated appearing negligent to anyone, as if she didn't know that exhausted men needed to eat. But it was necessary to keep up the appearance of making Owen a terrible wife.

The old woman nodded and went back inside. Maggie looked at the open doors for a long minute as other servants, talking by twos and threes, meandered inside.

"I think she'll like ye eventually," Kathleen said with encouragement.

Maggie's stomach was tight with the knowledge that it would be better if Mrs. Robertson never liked her. Perhaps the shirts Maggie had made for Owen would help ensure that.

# CHAPTER 9

$O$wen stood in the center of his clan, his gentlemen, and felt tired but satisfied. Men who'd seemed leery of him a sennight ago now stood around him dissecting the matches that had been held, analyzing the techniques and who could improve. Though he'd lost, Owen felt the results well worth losing to a man twenty years his elder. His uncle's skill and knowledge had been legendary, and it was good to see he still deserved the title of war chief.

Much as he told himself he'd been competing with his men to better reacquaint himself to them, it had the further bonus of invigorating him in a way he hadn't imagined. He'd thought of himself as a man of science, elegant and urbane. But displaying his physical prowess had made him feel like a warrior, like a man who could defend his own—defend his woman.

And to improve his mood even more, he'd received word from the man he'd sent to investigate the McCallum finances. They were not a wealthy clan, but they were not in debt either. Though the late chief might have been a drunkard, he had had competent lawyers and factors representing him. Merchants and bankers alike respected the clan and did business with them. Hugh did not need to conspire against Owen for financial reasons, it seemed. But Hugh's behavior as the new chief was still relatively untested. What if their finances were good because they'd found other uses for Maggie's dowry, and she and her brother were too proud to admit it?

He glanced up at the entry to the great hall, at the landing at the top of the stairs. Maggie still stood there, and for a moment, it was as if they were but steps apart, so much did he feel compelled by her gaze. But was he simply showing off for her? Could a display of muscle truly win over a woman who invented stories when things didn't go her way?

But he couldn't keep being angry with her, not and see her wedded and bedded. She'd gone beyond being just his duty to being a challenge. Perhaps his physicality could be used as a potent weapon against her. He wanted to touch her all the time—why hold back? Surely it would be a better weapon in his battle to save their clans by marrying.

So that evening at supper, he kept his chair close to hers, let his knee rest against hers, brushed her hand when they reached for their silverware. Maggie gave him irritated glances, but she was a little too flushed and bright-eyed to make him believe she was unresponsive. She leaned farther and farther over that ridiculous law book she was reading, as if she could bury herself in the words. He kept this up throughout the meal, until she tried her own distraction.

"Remember that I have the shirts I sewed for ye."

"Then I'll come to your bedroom right now and try them on."

"What?"

Her eyes widened with panic, and it was a fine sight.

"But I didn't finish my supper," she insisted.

He pushed back his chair, and took her hand.

"But—"

He didn't let her take up the law book she made a lunge for, only pulled her from the room, leaving behind the amused chuckles of his clan.

In her room, she faced him with her hands on her hips. "That was uncomfortable for me. Your people are probably appalled at your behavior."

"They think I'm smitten."

"A lie if I ever heard one," she scoffed.

"Is it?" He took a step toward her and she didn't back down, only lifted her chin as if to dare him.

And he was tempted. But he wanted her off balance, kept wondering about his methods.

"Did you enjoy the sword fighting?" he asked.

She blinked in confusion, but rallied.

"You gave a tolerable response to your uncle's obvious superiority."

He felt the rare urge to laugh, but didn't give in to it.

"I train often, even in London," he told her. He moved smoothly by her and went to the dressing table, where her brush and hand mirror awaited. There were tiny bottles of women's things, and he touched them one at a time, noticing over his shoulder that she'd fisted her hands. "There are many men who'll train in the sport, even if they have to fight a Scot. I see that the Sassenach weren't as good for my training as facing a Highlander would have been."

He lowered his voice and faced her again. "Nights sleeping in the heather and among rocks were a reminder of a more primitive part of myself: being with the men of the clan, putting meat on the table for my people, defending a man against a wild stag. At heart I am such a man, Maggie, and such a man thinks about bedding his wife and making her revel in the glory of physical sensation. I thought constantly about what you look like beneath those garments."

Maggie felt heat flush beneath her bodice, up her neck and across her face. She was far too aware that they were alone in her room, with no one nearby to serve as a distraction. It was just the two of them, and he wielded his wicked flattery like a sword against her. And she was far too susceptible. He was touching her things, intruding on her life—and bringing about his own ruin, she reminded herself, taking a deep, calming breath.

He came another step closer. "I never would have imagined being so distracted by a woman."

Something in her traitorously wanted to believe him, wanted to be distracting to a man, had never imagined what a heady, powerful feeling it might be.

But it wasn't true. It was all a ruse to assure her cooperation.

She licked her lips and tried to summon a cool tone. "I think ye're talking yourself into an obsession for something ye can't have."

He passed by her, circling her. She held her breath, then gasped when he kissed her neck, his warm, damp lips making her shudder. Why could she not remain cold to him, when she wished for it so desperately?

"Such an innocent reaction," he murmured, then blew across her damp skin.

"Then ye misunderstand my reluctance to be touched by ye."

He chuckled.

Where was his anger? It was easier to do battle with an angry man. Humor was a new tactic that reminded her too much of those autumn weeks they'd spent together.

And then she remembered her plan for tonight. "I ken ye're waiting anxiously to see the shirts I sewed for ye. Let me get them."

Heading for a chest against the wall was a face-saving retreat, she thought wryly. She held out both hands, offering the shirts, perfectly pressed and folded.

He barely gave them a glance, was watching her

as if he meant to pounce. She dropped the pile on her bed, then shook out the first one. Her stitches at the neckline were even—deceptive, she knew. She peeked over the top of the shirt to find him frowning at it.

He immediately wiped the frown away and said, "Thank you for taking the time to perform such a wifely deed."

She gritted her teeth, then spoke with dismay. "Oh, dear."

"What is it?"

He couldn't hide the wariness, which delighted her.

"I do believe I made a mistake. I am so thoughtless! My mother always told me to pay more attention to my sewing, but nay, I only wished to be outside, looking for frogs." She winced. The little boy he'd been had loved frogs, too.

"I don't see a mistake," he said pleasantly.

She shook the shirt out even farther, and a third sleeve materialized on the right side. "I'll never be able to look Mrs. Robertson in the face again! Already she thinks I'm hopeless in the womanly arts."

"Nonsense," he said smoothly. "When I wear it, I'll have an extra handy cloth with which to clean off my sword."

She gaped at him. Why wasn't he irritated? Why wasn't he growing tired of her? It was so frustrating. Then he put his hand into his coat and removed an unfamiliar object, a several-inch long piece of triangular glass.

"Your mention of frogs reminded me that I had thought to continue your lessons this night with a prism. But the experiment won't work here, since the setting sun is in the wrong window."

And then he took her hand and led her toward the door. She couldn't pull from his strong grip, and damn him, she was intrigued by what kind of experiment could be done with a strangely shaped piece of glass.

But she made certain to grab the shirts on her way out.

At the end of the hall, when he pushed open a set of double doors, she saw a massive, curtained four-poster bed, with a satin burgundy counterpane.

"This is your bedroom," she said warily, and let go of his hand to remain near the door.

"So it is." He arched a devilish brow.

He began to open the chests that lined one wall and searched through. Curious in spite of herself, she studied the paneled walls with their intricate carved decoration, the bare wig stand that had probably been his father's, for Owen showed no inclination to wear a wig as so many men did. The furniture was heavy and masculine, finely made for an earl.

"I can't find any sheets," he muttered.

"Sheets?" She glanced wide-eyed at the bed.

As if he read her mind, he began to toss bed pillows to the floor and pulled down the counterpane.

"Owen, I absolutely will not—"

He yanked a white sheet right off the bed, then

grinned at her aghast expression, as her insides quaked.

He draped the sheet over a chair and placed it across from the window. As he pulled shut the curtains on the setting sun, moving from one window to the next, he said, "The light is almost gone. We must hurry."

The room was suddenly full of shadows, his body almost a blur of movement, as lacking in shape as a ghost. She had a pang of foreboding about her dream, but let it go.

He gathered a section of the curtain up, then glanced around with a frown. "Need something to—ah."

To her surprise, he unpinned the brooch from his shoulder, and the loose ends of his plaid fell to dangle along the outside of his belt. Next he flung off his coat and waistcoat until he was only wearing his shirt and plaid, tucking the excess plaid into the belt at his waist. In his shirtsleeves, the width of his shoulders made her catch her breath. Oh, she shouldn't be here.

Using his brooch, Owen pinned up a section of the curtain until it let in a narrow beam of light, then lined up the sheet-covered chair across the room.

He motioned Maggie forward. "Come closer and watch. This is how Newton proved that white light is a mix of colors."

She hesitantly approached, not wanting to be too near the bed. It wasn't just that she didn't trust him— she didn't trust herself around him.

Owen put the triangular piece of glass into the

light—and she gasped as the light appeared a rainbow of colors on the white sheet.

"You've seen something like this before, with rainbows or puddles of water," he said. "Scientists used to think that a prism or other things somehow dyed the sunbeam into different colors. But Newton took another prism and held it into the multicolored light, and it reformed back into a white light, proving that white light contains all the colors mixed together. Fascinating how it all works, isn't it?"

She stared at him. His enthusiasm and wonder matched her own, and she felt rather overwhelmed. The world was a strange and miraculous place, and knowing men in some far-off city had explained parts of it didn't make it any less magical. But men hadn't explained dreams, didn't deem them worthy to be studied, to be believed.

He lowered the prism, and the rainbow disappeared. His smile faded, his brown eyes became almost black as he regarded her with that awareness to which she was so susceptible. They were alone, the setting sun almost gone. The air fairly shimmered with the tension between them, almost as much as the white of his shirt against his dark, sun-touched skin. She was closer to the bed than she'd meant to stand, and suddenly, it loomed like something alluring and exotic and foreign, no longer a simple bed for rest.

"Maggie."

He said her name in a deep, rough voice that set

her to trembling. She should leave. But he crossed the fading beam of light and took her into his arms. His kiss was as deep and rough as his voice, taking from her, drinking from her, making her think of the darkness of passion as an ocean current at night, sweeping her away. She forgot all about resisting him or playing ignorant about how to kiss.

His big hands on her back slid lower, cupping her backside and pulling her against him. Through her skirts she could feel the hard length of him. Knowing he wanted her was thrilling and intoxicating, making her forget the danger of desire between them. The future was suddenly something she couldn't control, shouldn't know.

And then he was kissing her brow and her cheek, and down her neck. He slid his hand up her body and cupped her breast above the stays. She moaned. She felt trapped within her garments, wanting to shed them and any resistance she thought she could sustain against him.

She suddenly realized that the padding she'd donned at her waist interfered with his touch, and snapped her back to the reality of her plight.

She couldn't lose herself. She'd been granted a gift she couldn't ignore.

She turned her head aside, and he straightened.

"Maggie, your knowledge of kissing has come a long way."

She ignored his teasing. "Don't ye see, Owen? Dreams can be just as baffling as science before it's explained," she cried. "Ye've no problem accepting the word of a scientist ye've never met, but ye cannot believe in me."

She pushed away from him, breathing hard.

"Maggie—"

"Nay, 'tis your turn to listen to me. Maybe ye won't believe in this either, but ye deserve to know. Something happened while ye were gone."

"And what was that?" He folded his arms over his chest and regarded her impassively.

"Someone entered my room and left an item in my bed to frighten me."

She sensed the tension in him as if it were a snake coiled within his skin.

"What was it?" he demanded.

"A talisman, a sort of evil charm. It was a stick carved with backward lettering, a clear symbol of witchcraft. I do not know if they meant to frighten me or implicate me, but ye're the only one who knows about my . . . talent."

"And you think I told someone."

"Of course not," she said with conviction. "Ye wouldn't embarrass yourself that way."

"Embarrass myself? What has that to do with anything? I will always protect what you tell me in confidence. We are betrothed."

"And someone doesn't want us to be."

"Show me the talisman."

She winced. "And there is the problem. I was so appalled that someone was trying to implicate me as a witch that I tossed it into the fire. I have no proof to show ye, only my word."

"And I believe you."

She blinked at him. "Ye do?"

"Why would you invent such a story?"

"I—I wouldn't," she agreed, not bothering to hide her surprise. "Do ye think it's the same person who set the fires?"

"I don't know. The fires could have been against me and my ascension to the chiefdom."

"Or because ye betrothed yourself to a McCallum," she pointed out.

"But this is aimed directly at you."

She hugged herself. "Aye, but again, it could have been meant to reflect badly on ye."

He said nothing for a long moment, his head down in thought. "I will ask Mrs. Robertson if anyone was seen lingering outside your door."

"Don't tell her about the talisman. The charge of witchcraft—I've always feared it."

She waited for him to tease her, but he only studied her solemnly.

"I never want you to be afraid here," he said in a husky voice, "and now someone has made you so."

She shrugged, feeling uncomfortable. "Someone is

trying to drive me away. Such a coward seldom acts openly."

"But you won't be driven away?" he asked, an eyebrow raised.

"Nay. I'll leave when the contract is settled between our families and not a moment before."

He lowered his voice and spoke. "And I say you'll never want to leave."

She rolled her eyes.

"But for now, I will increase the men guarding the towerhouse."

She stiffened.

"The fires are enough of a reason. There's someone trying to ruin the peace between the McCallums and Duffs. Between you and me, Maggie, we won't let that happen."

For two days, Maggie resisted every effort to help prepare for the festival, even though her family would be attending. Mrs. Robertson's coolness grew into icy disdain, but she doggedly kept Maggie informed, as if the woman could will Maggie to prove herself capable of being a Duff bride. Kathleen chattered nonstop about it, trying to remake Maggie with just her kind flow of words. All Kathleen had were the stories people told her about the coming together of the whole clan for a several-day event of food and games and fun.

"My brother is being a curmudgeon about it," Kathleen confided one morning.

"How can he not be interested in meeting more of the Duffs?" Maggie asked, hiding her suspicions about Gregor.

Mrs. Robertson lifted her head from her lists and frowned at Maggie as if to say, *Ye're interested in talk of Gregor but not making your husband proud?*

Maggie felt a little sick inside. She'd always been an obedient young woman, and had never realized how important the respect of the staff truly was. But all she needed to do was remind herself that Mrs. Robertson would thank her if she knew Maggie was trying to save Owen's life.

But not if she thought Maggie was a witch.

"Gregor claims that the festival is frivolous," Kathleen said, as she tied the laces crossing Maggie's ugly stomacher. "That takin' days away from work is somethin' that—" She broke off, and her face flushed scarlet.

"That McCallums would do?" Maggie finished quietly.

"Ye know I don't think that!" Kathleen said in a rush. "I've come to know ye as a good mistress and a kind woman."

"I appreciate that. When my family arrives for the festival, Gregor will see that they can work just as hard as a Duff, and can be just as fair."

"I'll tell him, mistress, I promise." Kathleen swallowed several times and forced a smile as she returned to the laces.

Maggie pitied the maid her hard life in the colonies, and imagined it must be difficult to deal with Gregor, a man who would turn against Maggie simply because of her last name. Would he try to frighten her with the talisman? Sadly, he wasn't the only clansmen in the Highlands to hate simply because it had been taught to him.

For a moment, Maggie imagined being the one to bring healing to both clans, to stand at Owen's side as his wife and end the bloodshed forever. Oh, she was becoming more and more drawn into that world that could never happen. It made her remember being in his arms in the near darkness, his bed—their marriage bed—so close. But she was not a woman who could blithely forget the harm that could happen to Owen if he married her. She wouldn't give up on discovering the truth of her dream.

She took a deep breath. "Mrs. Robertson, ye've mentioned a healing woman in the village."

Kathleen didn't lift her head, but Mrs. Robertson straightened and eyed her warily.

"Aye, Euphemia. Are ye feeling ill, mistress?"

"Nay, I've simply heard that the old woman is a seer. My mother has interest in such things." Oh, the lie came far too easily to her, and she hoped God could forgive her. "She'll want to visit, I know, so I thought I'd be certain if Euphemia is an honest woman."

"Och, honest as our King Over the Water," said Mrs. Robertson. "She's a wise woman, too, with potions and charms to help ease sickness or fight the evil eye. But aye, though she's hesitant about it, she's a seer," the housekeeper added with some reluctance.

"But has she warned people to their advantage?" Maggie asked.

Kathleen looked at her, baffled.

"Fate deals its hand to us all," Mrs. Robertson said in a stilted voice. "Little can be changed. Does your mother understand that?"

Maggie cleared her throat. "Of course. Aye, my mother can be a bit obsessed at times."

Kathleen's eyes seemed to shine with pity, before she said brightly, "Will ye be attendin' the spectacle the men are puttin' on today, mistress? They're havin' another competition. Wrestlin' done the Scottish way," Kathleen said with pride. "Gregor used to show his friends in the colonies."

"Then I hope he has success," Maggie said, her mind beginning to race.

Everyone would be distracted by the spectacle. She should be able to slip away to the village and speak to Euphemia about her dreams. Perhaps the woman could help her relive it again, or maybe Euphemia even had success trying to change what her visions had shown her.

# CHAPTER 10

Maggie had never imagined that the entire village might crowd into the castle courtyard to see a wrestling event. Sword fighting always seemed so much more dashing and dangerous to her. Or perhaps it was simply the spectacle of seeing who could defeat their new chief. Maggie didn't stand above the crowd on the first floor balcony as before, but mingled among them, looking for Euphemia, but she never saw the elderly woman. The clan was growing used to her now; some gave deferential nods, but others didn't meet her gaze, and some turned away altogether. She told herself all this would help prove to Owen that she wasn't fit to be his bride, but she still felt terrible—and so very lonely.

Scottish backhold wrestling was always a feat of brute strength. The men paired up, and she easily found Owen, who leaned forward to "hug" his opponent, hands clasped together at his back, right arm beneath the man's left, Owen's left arm over the man's shoulder. Maggie had watched many times in her youth, and knew the loser was the man who touched the ground with anything other than his feet. It was simply two men, using every muscle in their bodies to remain standing, while knocking over the challenger.

Owen easily slid his foot behind his opponent's, then pushed him over it, forcing the man to the ground. It was best two out of three, but Owen won the second match as well, and would face another challenger. There were plenty of brawny bare legs and flying kilts as the men upended each other, making the women squeal with delight. Maggie unabashedly enjoyed the sight.

Watching Owen move, the display of his muscles, gave her an unwelcome shiver of awareness. He'd been far too solicitous with his caresses, his touches, many of them seemingly innocent—though she had her doubts. No one needed to touch someone as much as Owen touched her. She was beginning to anticipate it each time he was so close, to gird herself to resist any enjoyment. She constantly flinched and frowned at him, trying to prove herself irritated. She wasn't certain it was working, for he looked too satisfied with himself.

But she couldn't think about that now. She had plans for the day.

It was easy enough to slip into the dark tunnel beneath the gatehouse and then across the moat bridge. The village was just down the lane, and she'd had the cottages and their owners pointed out on her last visit. It was strange how deserted the place seemed. An occasional chicken pecked at the grain near a cottage door, but no people weeded their small gardens or remained on watch over cattle on a nearby hill. The sky had been threatening rain all day, and a wet mist settled over everything. Maggie shivered and moved through the center of the village and beyond, to the last solitary cottage, alone before a thick copse of trees. There was a well nearby, and a little bench as if its owner liked the peaceful view. She turned and took a deep breath, never tiring of the beautiful mountains surrounding the loch that threaded its way through the glen.

Maggie knocked. It was a long time before the door opened, but she was patient, knowing Euphemia's age. The door slowly creaked open, and two bright eyes peered out at her from the gloom.

Then those eyes went wide. "Mistress Maggie?"

Euphemia drew the door all the way open, and Maggie saw the little wizened woman with her hunched back, white wispy hair gathered into a long braid, and her face as crinkled as a dried apple.

"Good day, Mistress Euphemia," Maggie said. "I wasn't certain ye'd know me."

"Of course I know ye, lass," Euphemia said, her voice high-pitched and rough with long use. "Everyone does. Ye're to marry our chief. And ye wear those silly gowns."

Well, at least some people were noticing, she

thought, since Owen was ignoring her lack of style completely.

Euphemia narrowed her eyes and stared hard at Maggie, who wondered what gifts the old woman truly had.

"Come in, my wee bairn, I was just having a cup of buttermilk. Would ye like some?"

Maggie followed the elderly lady inside, and had to duck beneath all the herbs hanging to dry from the ceiling beams. It was a single room, with a peat fire on the floor in the center, smoke escaping through a hole in the roof directly above. Euphemia gestured to a wooden table with two chairs, and Maggie took a seat. The cup of buttermilk was warm and nourishing, and reminded her of the summers of her youth in Edinburgh, when she'd looked forward to going back to the Highlands for the treat.

Euphemia sat down very, very slowly, and Maggie could hear the creaking of her joints.

"Ahhh," Euphemia said after her first sip. "Now tell me why I've been lucky enough to be visited by the chief's future wife."

Maggie hesitated, staring into old, old eyes that had seen the joys and sorrows of everyone in this village. They were intelligent eyes, a deep, deep blue, full of sympathy as well as curiosity.

"May I trust that what I share with ye will go no further?" Maggie asked quietly.

Euphemia crossed her arms over her chest, and

chewed her bare gums together briefly before saying, "A woman like me knows how to keep secrets, mistress."

Maggie took a deep breath—and told her everything, about the dreams of her youth, the dream that ended any chance of a marriage with Owen, her attempts to discover what happened next. Through it all, Euphemia remained silent.

Suddenly thirsty, Maggie took a deep draught of buttermilk, sat back, and gave a long, weary sigh. For a small moment, it had felt good to share the worst with someone else. But then . . . the fear suddenly overwhelmed her. What had she done? Why had she trusted a stranger with something that could ruin her life should it be discovered?

"Och, my wee bairn," Euphemia said gently, "ye need have no fear of me. I have met others like ye, and they yet lead uncomplicated lives."

Her expression was sly and merry, and Maggie gave a shaky smile. "Are . . . *you* like me?" she asked.

Euphemia's smile faded a bit, but not her humor. "Nay, I do not have dreams in the night, but visions, mostly at dusk. I hear things, too, but perhaps someone already told ye that, for ye to seek me out." She chuckled, a dry old rasp. "Ye do not need to tell me who, lass. I don't hide my true nature."

"How do you bear it?" Maggie asked. "I've seen how people with our gifts are treated. I've been able to keep the truth to my family and a few others, but here . . ." She looked out the window and swallowed against the lump that arose in her throat. "I'm a Mc-Callum, Euphemia, the enemy."

"Ye don't seem so threatening to me."

The gentle kindness of her voice was almost Maggie's undoing, but she willed the stinging in her eyes to recede. "Perhaps not to ye, but I've heard cruel whispers. A byre and a cottage were set to burning; I've been followed about. And recently, someone left a talisman of witchcraft in my bed, a stick with letters carved backwards."

Euphemia sat back in her chair and narrowed her eyes. "'Tis terrible to do such things to a girl only trying to mend a feud men started centuries ago."

"How can I marry Owen if it will mean his death?" Maggie asked bitterly. "He doesn't believe that he'll die; he thinks I'm only trying to deceive him. And maybe it *is* all a deception in my mind—I don't even know the true ending of the dream. Can ye help me, Euphemia? I don't want my actions to renew this terrible feud, but . . ."

"Aye, his lairdship cannot be allowed to die," the old woman said. "He's a good man, a good chief."

"So ye think my dream means that he *will* die?" Maggie demanded.

"That I cannot know, lass."

"Can *I* know? Can ye think of any way I could have the dream again? I've tried everything I know and nothing works. I keep seeing him lying on the floor, pale and blood-spattered." She shuddered.

Euphemia put her hands to her thighs and rose to her feet. "I ken of only one thing that might help. Come with me."

The old woman took down a cloak from a peg near the door, and without asking questions, Maggie helped her don it. A walking stick came next, and then the two of them went outside.

Maggie froze upon seeing Martin Hepburn standing in the middle of the lane, surprise and guilt mingling on his face. She tried to step in front of Euphemia, in case he meant them harm, but using her walking stick, Euphemia pushed her aside.

"Martin, off with ye," Euphemia ordered.

His face flushing, he turned in a dignified manner and walked back toward the center of the village.

"Why is he following me?" Maggie asked with frustration.

"Pay him no mind, lass."

Maggie fell into step as the old woman took a dirt path that led past her house and began to slope upward. Maggie didn't know how long she could ignore Martin and his unsettling behavior toward her. But for now, she would concentrate on Euphemia.

To her surprise, the old woman was as steady on the hillside as a goat. For half an hour they climbed a rocky path, passing the occasional curious cow that lifted its head from chewing grass and blinked at them. The mist burned off. The glen fell away below them, and by glancing over her shoulder, she could see the towers of Castle Kinlochard looking more like a child's toy. The wind picked up, and Maggie felt tendrils of hair escape her chignon. Euphemia moved slowly but steadily. Gradually the path curved along the mountain, and soon any sign of civilization disappeared.

The path flattened at last, where their small mountain crested. Beyond loomed more mountains, but on the windswept summit was a sight that took Maggie's breath away. Rising up from the short scrub grass were standing stones, like jagged teeth against the cloudy sky. There were only three of them, and one was squat as if broken. They stood side by side, sentinels left by distant ancestors. With the mountains as a backdrop, they reminded her of the columns of a wild cathedral.

Maggie let out a soft "oh" of appreciation, yet barely spoke above a whisper. "Euphemia, how incredible."

Narrow-eyed against the wind, the old woman said, "No one can say why they're here, why they're scattered throughout Scotland and beyond. Some say they were men turned by enchantment into stone. Others say they are but monuments to men killed in battle. Perchance they were used in rituals long since lost to time."

"Ye don't use them yourself?"

"I have found my gift inside me alone. Believe me,

I have tried to use them, but they are not for me. Yet they bring me solace when I need to think."

"May I . . . walk among them?"

Euphemia said nothing for a long moment, just studying her with old, shrewd eyes. "Aye," she said slowly. "And touch them. Perhaps they can give you the strength to find your answers."

Gooseflesh swept across Maggie's skin as she walked toward the stones. Two more were lying on the ground, half sunk like stones in mud. The tall grass clung to her skirt as if pulling on her. The stones were taller than she, and as she moved among them, whenever their shadows fell upon her, she shivered. At last she touched one, putting both palms on it and closing her eyes.

But nothing happened to her, no vision, no sudden realization. Not that she'd expected it, since she'd only experienced her gift in dreams. But still, she was disappointed. The stone was as cold as she imagined, rough where it had been chipped away, smooth in other places.

"The stones have not given ye inspiration," Euphemia said, coming to stand beside one and placing her hand on it with deliberate intent.

Maggie shook her head. "I cannot expect something to magically happen. I spent many years denying my dreams, forcing them away. Perhaps I made enemies of whoever gave me such a gift."

"Why did ye deny yourself?"

"There was a woman I dreamed would drown. I did not stop it from happening, and the guilt is sometimes still a terrible burden—one I well deserve."

"Och, ye don't even ken if ye could have stopped it, lass," she said kindly.

"Have ye ever changed a vision foretold to ye?"

"Nay, and I stopped trying long ago."

Maggie felt her shoulders slump with disappointment.

Euphemia continued, "I've accepted my glimpse through the curtains of time, and come to peace with it."

Maggie thought about Owen—had he come to peace with the knowledge he'd had of his betrothed's death? Or had he simply forgotten it all? "The dreams shaped me in a way I've not often acknowledged. I was afraid to become close to people outside my family, for fear I'd see something I could not change."

"And Himself?"

"I keep my distance, aye," she whispered, then leaned her forehead against a cold stone and sighed. The wind whirled around her.

"Ye cannot be second-guessing your life."

"Can't I? Do your visions make ye hold back? Ye don't live in the center of the village, do ye?"

Euphemia's smile was secretive. "Perhaps my customers prefer privacy; perhaps I prefer privacy. Or perhaps I've a lover no one needs to know about."

Maggie's head came around to gape at the old

woman—and then they both laughed. "Glad I am to hear that."

They walked a while longer on the mountaintop, taking in the beautiful view of the glen so far below, the loch a narrow, glistening line through it like a finger.

"Do ye think I'll be able to discover the end of the dream?" Maggie asked, just before they were going to leave.

"I think ye cannot count on that, mistress. Ye can only hope. Make plans accordingly."

Maggie went first going back down the steep path, turning to offer her hand where Euphemia might need it.

"Have you given thought to being honest with everyone about your gift, mistress?" the old woman asked. "Perhaps ye're a wise woman like me. The village could use another. I won't live much longer."

Maggie gasped. "Ye've seen your own death?"

Euphemia gave another raspy chuckle. "Nay, I just feel it in these old bones. I cannot live forever."

Though Maggie hadn't received the help she wished, she found herself smiling all the way back to Euphemia's cottage.

OWEN felt that his frown was a like a thundercloud preceding him as he entered the village. Most were still back at the castle, enjoying the refreshments he'd ordered, but a woman carrying a bucket scurried out of his way, eyes wide.

After the wrestling competition was over and he couldn't find Maggie, he'd been angry that she'd left the safety of the castle, and that his men had been too distracted to pay attention to her departure. When Mrs. Robertson had admitted Maggie's interest in Euphemia, it had given him a measure of relief. On the quick walk, his anger had mostly turned to exasperation. But now that he saw how empty the village was, how anything could have happened to Maggie with no one to see even a clue, his exasperation merged into worry. She made rash decisions without thinking through the consequences. He wanted her safe within the castle walls, not wandering alone, an easy target.

And now he couldn't stop thinking of a person who'd set Duff property on fire, risking lives, or would frighten a young woman by leaving superstitious nonsense in her bed. It was a threat, even if Owen didn't believe in the ancient ways it stood for. He'd dealt often with crime in the cities, but it didn't seem right, here at home.

But Maggie was exactly where Mrs. Robertson had suggested, at Euphemia's cottage. He saw the two of them sitting on a little bench, Euphemia drooping as if tired. She was so much tinier than he remembered. He'd been frightened of her as a little boy, because everyone seemed so in awe of her. When he was a little older, he and some other boys had dared each other to touch her front door, and she'd opened it wide even as he'd been an inch from touching it. He'd run away, convinced she was giving him the evil eye. Now she watched him approach with lively interest, and then looked from Maggie to him with expectation.

He stopped before the bench and nodded his head. "Euphemia, it's been many years since we've last spoken. You have not changed much in all that time."

"Neither have ye, my lord, though ye've gotten tall and brawny."

"Have you convinced my betrothed to marry me?" he asked.

Maggie's eyes went wide.

"Surely you had to know everyone is compelled to tell their troubles to Euphemia," he continued. "Of course, most wouldn't have come here alone with the village practically deserted."

Euphemia gave a hoarse rasp that must have been a laugh. "She's a stubborn girl who knows her own mind. There's no hurrying her."

Maggie made a point of looking behind him. "Where's Fergus? Ye may not like me walking about alone, but he feels the same about ye."

"I left him basking in the glory of second place."

"Second to ye?" she inquired, tilting her head.

"Nay, second to Gregor."

To his surprise, Maggie's face paled.

She asked, "Did ye wrestle him yourself?"

He shook his head. "I lost just before the finals. Why do you look so relieved?"

"Gregor is an angry man."

"And how do you know that?" he asked. "Has Kathleen been confiding in you?'

She smoothed her skirt over her knees, before taking a deep breath. "I heard him tell others I drove away your mother and sister."

He stiffened. Euphemia's wrinkled eyes narrowed even further.

"Say nothing to him," Maggie continued. "'Twill crush Kathleen, who's having a difficult enough time settling in here after what they've been through."

"I'll remain silent—for now," he warned. "I know he's angry at the failures of his life. Did you think he'd take that out on me in a wrestling competition?"

Owen couldn't keep the disbelief from his voice. He was also surprised that once again Maggie showed that she cared about him. He'd thought her dream of his death was just a way out of the marriage, whether instigated by herself or her brother. But here she was, worried about a clansman hurting him. It made him feel confused about her true motives.

Maggie looked away, chin raised mutinously. "Gregor makes me uneasy."

"And you wandering about, without telling me, makes *me* uneasy."

It was hard to imagine that the competent blacksmith would use a fear of witchcraft against a helpless woman.

Owen glanced speculatively at Euphemia, but spoke again to Maggie. "Why did you come here?"

Euphemia was the one who answered. "And could she not have been explorin' the village and come upon me? Perhaps we agree that wrestling is a foolish pursuit for young men."

"You don't think that," he said. "I remember you cheering along with the rest when I was younger."

Euphemia actually giggled. "A man's bare chest glistenin' in the sun—nothing wrong with that."

Maggie glanced at her friend, her unusual eyes full of amusement.

Euphemia let out a sigh. "Ah, weel, 'tis not easy for me to walk to the castle anymore."

Maggie bit her lip and looked away, her disbelief obvious. Owen didn't believe the old woman either. But at least she'd been there for Maggie. Could Maggie's capitulation be aided by a wise woman's counsel? No, he knew he would be the one to accomplish that. And he'd been looking forward to it more and more.

He looked past the cottage and up to the top of the nearest mountain. "Have you been to the standing stones?"

Maggie glanced at Euphemia, and he knew the truth before she spoke it. He could be his own seer where Maggie's expressive face was concerned. So much for the old woman having trouble walking.

"Then come up with me," he said. "I haven't been there in years."

He put out a hand, and though Maggie ignored it, she rose.

"Euphemia, are ye certain ye don't need my help?" Maggie asked.

Euphemia practically giggled. "Young lovers need time alone. Go on with ye." And without waiting for them to depart, she stood slowly and went back inside.

Owen gestured for Maggie to precede him past the trees and up the sloping path. He watched her hips under the ugly gown, thought of sliding his hands beneath and finding the tiny waist she was trying to disguise. She was becoming like the gift he longed to explore, a present far superior to the wrapping.

When they reached the summit, Maggie hugged herself, rubbing her hands up and down her arms, before going to touch the stones without the fear some might have shown.

He could see a low line of clouds heading east, the ones that had left his clothing damp with light rain during the competition. The wind picked up, bringing with it the scent of vegetation and earth—his earth.

"Takes one's breath away, does it not?" he asked. "The view reminds me of all I'm now responsible for."

"It cannot be a surprise to ye," she said dryly.

"It's not. I've been raised to assume this position my entire life. But it's different than I imagined."

She glanced at him, those unusual eyes inquisitive.

"The knowledge that ye're responsible for the welfare of hundreds of people is surely daunting."

"If I make a poor decision, people will suffer. Were we not to marry, many others would suffer in both our clans."

She stiffened the moment he mentioned their marriage, but instead of changing the subject, she said, "I'd like to read our marriage contract. I've been studying your law books and—"

"There's no need."

"I *demand* to see it!"

"There is nothing there to give you hope nor to trap you. Your brother surely read it—he would have told you if there was something vague. I know you intend to invite him to the festival, but that might not be possible if things are still unsettled between us."

She stiffened. "Owen, no more threats. My brother has to come. I need to see my family."

Coldly, he said, "Or you need to beg him to take you away from here."

"I wouldn't do that, and ye know it," she insisted, her voice rising. "I will not give up on peace between our clans. I promise to find a way to settle things without the risk of marrying ye."

"Risk?"

She quickly glanced away from him as if taking in the view. The wind briefly buffeted them both, just as life was doing to them.

He turned his frown on the stones. "Is that why Euphemia brought you here, to see if old stones had some mystic connection to you or these supposed dreams?"

He saw a tick in her jaw from clenching her teeth so hard, but she didn't answer.

"You should not have brought up our private struggles with her, Maggie."

"What choice did I have?" she demanded. "Ye won't listen—ye'd rather risk your death in an attempt to prove I'm a fool."

"You think I take pleasure in proving you wrong?"

"Victory, triumph, whatever ye want to call it. Ye're used to being right and won't accept that there are things ye don't understand."

He said nothing—he'd already said it all. He didn't like being suspicious of her plans for her brother, but it reminded him that much as he was trying to seduce her, he could never trust her.

But there was her concern for his safety . . .

Maggie let out an exaggerated sigh. "Surely there's another woman you can marry, far more sophisticated than I, who would make the perfect wife for an earl. Ye had to negotiate with your father for the right to choose your bride. That meant much to ye. Surely ye had plans, lists of suitable women, perhaps. There must be a distant McCallum relative ye can marry in there somewhere."

He caught her by the upper arms so he could look into her face.

"I am amused by your image of me with dozens of

women on some sort of marriage list." And then the truth came to him, and he said it without considering the consequences. "You know why none of those women interested me? They're sheltered by their fathers; they care only about themselves or Society. And yes, some of them might do the occasional charity, but they don't know what it really means. *You've* lived among your people, *you've* experienced harsh winters and bad crops and fevers. *You* were born to be the wife of a chief. And in eighteen days, you'll be one."

She flinched.

"You're simply afraid of your destiny," he continued, "afraid that you're not in control."

"I don't care about control!" she cried. "And destiny—such a vague word. Can ye believe in destiny, Owen?" She advanced on him. "It sounds the same as believing in dreams."

"Not the way I'm using it."

She groaned. "And how was I any good for my people? My mother took me away, hid me from my father, kept me removed from my friends and others when they needed me the most."

"Don't make yourself guilty for another's sins. Those London women didn't make me think about marriage. Only when I saw you again did I know what I had to do."

Her resistance was a wall she built higher and higher between them. He put his fists on his hips and stared hard into her eyes, willing her to trust him. The wind picked up; his plaid flapped at his knees, her gown seemed to skim over the grass, and still their gazes did battle.

He wanted her trust, but he didn't intend to grant his own. For the first time he truly considered this assumption. Was he just as guilty as any Duff clansmen of assuming that a McCallum trying to get out of a sworn marriage contract could never have a valid reason simply because of who she was? But how could he trust her when she wouldn't let go of this notion of dreams that came true? It only served to remind him of the foolish mistakes of his youth, where he let his emotions for Maggie overrule his duty to Emily and his clan.

"So ye weren't thinking of marriage in London," she said, "but surely there were women."

"Women?"

"Women ye spent time with."

"You mean mistresses?"

"Ye had them. All men do."

"Do they? I didn't know it was a rule."

"Ye're avoiding the question." She took a deep breath, and the wind whipped dark curls of hair about her head. "I don't love ye, Owen, but it doesn't mean I want ye to die. Maybe ye should find another woman who'd be more suitable, less deadly."

She started back down the hillside, going too fast. And then she stumbled and fell, dropping out of sight. Owen raced after her.

# CHAPTER 11

The gravel gave way before Maggie, and directly in her path were two small boulders that hadn't been there before. Trying to avoid them, her feet slipped from beneath her. She cried out, desperately flinging both arms wide, but could find nothing to hold on to. She slid sideways down a rocky slope, rather than following the path that hugged the hilltop. She came to a halt hard against a boulder, and she felt her ankle twist with a sharp pain. But she didn't let go.

As she panted and tried to see how far away the path was, she felt rocks and dirt raining down on her.

"Maggie!"

Owen's voice from above her was urgent, but she wasn't fool enough to think he cared about her except as a pawn between their clans. Then his arm smacked her hard on the back as he tried to catch himself on the same boulder. He came to a stop beside her, while gravel continued to fall all around them. With his arms he shielded her from the worst of it. Her ankle throbbed dully, but that faded compared to the worry that someone might have placed those rocks where she and Owen wouldn't see them until it was too late.

But they were rocks on an incline, she scolded herself silently. They could have shifted because of their earlier passing. She was letting this unknown villain make her paranoid.

She remembered Martin had lingered at Euphemia's cottage, and she shivered. But the man was old—surely they would have heard him attempting to climb the steep path?

When the last pebble had fallen and the silence was unbroken, she lifted her head to face Owen. His face was streaked with dirt, brow furrowed with what could be anger or concern.

"Are ye all right, lass?" he demanded.

She heard the brogue in his voice for the first time, and she didn't like how it warmed her. She felt a cacophony of emotions, from unease to need to desperation to confusion.

"Maggie, answer me."

The brogue was gone, but she knew she'd heard it. "I'm fine. I turned my ankle, but nothing serious."

"You should not have rushed down the mountain like that," he said sternly.

"Nay, I shouldn't have."

He opened his mouth as if to continue lecturing her,

but she'd already given him the answer he wanted to hear. "Then come, let us see how your ankle is."

He rose to his feet, and she allowed him to lift her by the hands. Gingerly, she set weight on her ankle, then tried to hide her wince. He started to put his arms around her, and she put a hand on his chest.

"Nay, ye won't be carrying me or we'll take a tumble. I've hurt myself worse. Just let me hold your arm."

She could see his jaw clench, but he had no choice except to go along with her. They moved slowly through the gorse and bramble back to the main path, then she tried to keep as little weight on her foot as possible. The soreness eased a bit, and soon she was only limping by the time the path began to level out behind Euphemia's cottage. The old woman was not in sight, which frustrated Maggie. Now Euphemia couldn't say if she'd seen Martin go by.

They spoke little as they made their slow way back through the village. People were returning from the castle now, standing in their doorways, chatting with neighbors or feeding chickens. More than once, Owen had to explain that she was fine, a mere ankle twist, and she felt more and more like a clumsy fool.

But she never saw Martin.

As they left the village behind and the castle walls rose up above them, Owen asked, "Did Mrs. Robertson tell ye about the clan assembly being held tomorrow?"

She hid a wince, knowing Mrs. Robertson had done no such thing—quite deliberately, Maggie was certain. Maggie had asked for such treatment, after all.

"We did not discuss it," she said. "'Tis not my place to become involved—I am not her mistress."

She waited for him to insist she was wrong. She wanted an argument over this, another reason to prove herself an unsuitable wife.

But he only spoke mildly. "You're right, of course. You don't have the experience yet to host such an event."

"But I—" and then she stopped herself. She'd been about to say that of course she had the experience; she'd been in the Larig Castle for several assemblies, helping the housekeeper and the staff. But she couldn't allow pride to get in the way of proving herself incompetent to Owen.

She waited for him to display that little smirk that irritated her beyond measure, one that said he knew what she was up to. But he only looked concerned.

"The housekeeper will have everything in hand," he said, "so no need to bother with the details. And you'll need to rest your ankle, of course."

*Of course.*

But she was too curious. "Will ye be passing judgment for your people," she asked as the castle seemed to rise ever higher above the trees, "or will this all be about the business of the clan?"

He narrowed his eyes. "Considering my father was

seldom here to handle the justice himself, and passed the duty off to lesser chieftains, I imagine many personal concerns have built up within the clan."

"Have ye ever done this for the clan before?"

His pause was so slight she almost missed it.

"Of course not. I was not the chief. But I have been there when my father handled it. Much of it is common sense and only takes a laird to enforce."

She'd heard many a conflict brought before her own father that were not so easy to settle hard feelings. But she didn't point that out. Owen was overly confident; perhaps she could use that to her advantage.

They passed beneath the gatehouse and the secret rooms above, where once warriors would use their advantage over invaders below. Out in the misty, muddy courtyard again, she glanced at Owen, whose expression was set. She didn't say anything more. Let him believe he'd won. She'd be like their ancestors and descend on him when he least expected it.

O<small>WEN</small> saw that his uncle Harold was waiting for him in the great hall, but he wouldn't allow Maggie to hobble upstairs alone. He raised a hand to Harold, silently asking him to wait, and the grizzled old man nodded and eyed Maggie's limping gait.

Owen studied her face, saw the pallor of her attempts to show that she wasn't in pain. Many women of his past acquaintance would have been using their distress to garner sympathy, and instead, she was trying to pretend she was fine. Her pride might damage her ankle even further.

He picked her up, one arm behind her back and the other beneath her knees. She gasped and reared her head back, as if she didn't want to be too close. Other men might have taken offense, but he thought of her behavior as part of the challenge—he seduced, she resisted. He intended to win.

The whalebone hoops sewn into her petticoat caused it to lift her skirts high, and she quickly pressed it down.

He spotted a passing servant and called, "Send Kathleen with ice from the ice pit. The lady has an injured ankle."

Maggie gasped. "Do not waste precious ice on my ankle."

"Nonsense. If we were at our estate in York, we'd have a large supply of ice from the icehouse."

"A house—devoted to ice?"

She sounded reluctant to be so curious.

"Yes, many of the larger estates are building them with double thickness of walls, sometimes half buried in the ground."

As he went up the circular stone stairs, he was careful to keep her head and feet from knocking the walls, a tricky feat with the hoops fighting to expand her skirt, and in a narrow space meant to defend from warriors trying to battle their way to the upper floors.

But Maggie had put her arms about his shoulders as

if to make herself smaller, a satisfactory result. At her bedchamber, he shouldered open the door to find the room deserted.

"Kathleen will be along soon," he said, gently placing her in a comfortable chair near the hearth.

And then he pushed her skirts up to her knees and lifted her foot in his hands. "Hold all your skirts back."

"Owen! 'Tis indecent! I will not be touched so familiarly by a man—*ever.*"

He eyed her with hidden amusement. That was a claim he could quickly prove false, but it dawned on him how . . . amusing he found her. He actually admired the way she held to her plan to prove herself the most improper wife, against whatever he tried. It was sure to be a losing effort, of course, but she wasn't ready to concede.

"You're being very brave," he said, giving her his most sincere and understanding tone. "What a perfect quality in a wife."

She started to push the skirts down, and he counteracted her by placing his other hand on her knee.

"Maggie, stop."

She did, but her tension vibrated down her leg. She wanted to win, just like he did.

He could feel the slight swelling of her ankle, and that reminded him of how he'd felt when he'd seen her disappear down the mountainside: the shock, the urgency, the fear. It had been surprisingly potent, had driven away his self-possession, his belief that he was always successful holding himself to proper dispassion. He would not care for her like that, as if she was more important than anything else. She would play a part in his life, his lady wife, but only one part.

Was that, too, because she was a McCallum? But she'd lied to him when they'd first been together, and she was lying again.

But he'd lied to her about Emily, hadn't he? He certainly wasn't perfect.

He didn't like questioning himself. When he came to a conclusion, it was because he'd given it great thought and made a rational decision he never regretted. But Maggie was making him rethink all his assumptions about her—his assumptions about himself.

The tension between them rose swiftly, with his hands on both her ankle and knee. Whatever he thought of her character, it didn't alter his desire for her. Her flesh was warm through her stockings, and he felt a keen desire to slide his hands higher, until he reached bare skin above her garters.

"Unless you'd like me to draw little circles on your skin with my fingers," he said in a husky voice, "I suggest you remove your garter and stocking from your injured foot."

Her eyes went wide, and he was treated to the sight of their unusual hues, one blue, one green. He'd seen more than one old woman make the sign against the evil eye when Maggie passed, and he hoped she did not notice such things. Or had it always been that way for her? Again, a softening toward her moved through him, and he reminded himself of their relationship by unbuckling her leather shoe, removing it, and letting his palm gently cup her foot before moving slowly, lingeringly up to her ankle. He trailed his fingers up her calf and gently caressed behind her knee. The hoop bulged her skirt too high. All he had to do was spread her knees to see—

"That's enough!" she cried in a breathy voice. "Please turn your back while I remove the garters."

He didn't want to turn his back; he wanted to watch her reach beneath her skirt and touch her own thigh. But she was cooperating, so without rising, he faced the other way, resting his folded arms on one bent knee and struggling to master his control.

"My ankle is barely swelling," Maggie pronounced.

He turned around to see her smoothing down her skirts.

He arched a brow. "Do you want me to force the issue?"

Letting out an exasperated sigh, she lifted until her skirts just reached mid-calf. Allowing her to win the moment, Owen took her bare foot into his hands and felt her tremble.

Swelling had distorted her ankle, but not by much, and some bruising shadowed her skin. He moved her foot gently about, his fingers tracing the delicate bones within.

"I do not feel a break," he said at last.

"I told ye that, Owen. Didn't I walk all the way back on it?"

"When I saw your expression downstairs, I knew I'd made a mistake allowing it. Your pride overrules your good sense."

"Pride?" she echoed defensively. "'Tis simply common sense. I felt no stabbing pain. Everyone has twisted an ankle a time or two. This supposed concern of yours is simply an excuse for touching me."

He gave her his best roguish smile. "Touching ye? Aye, that is a secondary benefit I appreciate."

"Aha, did ye hear your voice? There's a trace of the burr there, just like when ye followed me down the mountain. Why do ye hide it?"

"I do not hide it. I spent much of my life in England, and my speech evolved."

"Evolved, did it?" she scoffed. "Your parents made ye hide it like they were ashamed. I've heard your cousin Riona, remember. She, too, has lost the musical sound of Scotland."

He knew how to quiet her. He lifted her foot and placed a gentle kiss on her ankle, his gaze never leaving hers. He saw her lips softly part in shock, her tongue slide out to moisten them. He continued to press gentle kisses up her calf, until he could no longer see her face because of the rise of her skirts. She quivered under his touch, but didn't stop him, and he grew more and more bold. His vow to touch her as much as possible was working. He put both hands on her knees and began to separate them—

And then a knock sounded on the door.

He stiffened and lifted his head to meet Maggie's gaze again. She strove to look relieved and triumphant, but he thought he detected a hint of disappointment.

She lowered her skirts and called, "Come in!"

The plump maid Kathleen entered, talking even as she juggled a basin filled with jagged ice. "I'm so sorry for the delay, mistress, but I didn't know where the ice pit was, and I had to send a boy to—" She broke off and almost dumped the basin as she spied him kneeling before Maggie. "Laird Duff—I mean, Lord Aberfoyle—I didn't know . . . I didn't think . . ."

"No apology necessary," he said, rising to his feet. "I ascertained that no bones are broken."

Puzzlement flitted across her expression, and he realized she might not have understood all the words he'd used. But she understood the important part, and gave a shy smile to Maggie.

"There, mistress, ye see? Let me help make ye feel better."

"I'll leave Mistress Maggie in your capable hands," Owen said.

He paused, remembering what Maggie had said about Kathleen's brother, Gregor. As if Maggie could read his mind, she beseeched him with wide eyes to keep silent, and he gave her a brief nod before departing.

He had much to organize before the assembly tomorrow, and he was glad to have that to focus on, ere his thoughts dwell too long on Maggie's soft skin.

THE next morning, Maggie came down the stairs holding herself to just the faintest limp. She'd remained in her bedroom for supper the night before, glad of the excuse to avoid Owen's arrogant gaze. Oh, he knew what he was doing every time he touched her. It had only been her ankle, for heaven's sake, and he'd caressed it as if it were her—her—

She barely stopped herself from putting a hand to her chest, as if she could still feel his bold touch there.

Memories of his advances at least kept her from dwelling on her frustration at how little Euphemia had been able to help her where her dream was concerned. And to think that Euphemia had stopped trying to change the outcome of her visions—oh, she refused to let that dishearten her. Maggie didn't *know* the outcome of her dream, that was the problem. Euphemia seemed to think Maggie should just make her decision without knowing the rest, but how could she?

So Maggie had lounged around during the evening, sending for servant after servant, claiming the trays of food either hurt her delicate stomach, or were too much for her sensitive nerves. Every moment of such playacting was agony for her, especially when Mrs. Robertson came herself with the last tray, and watched Maggie taste the chicken as if daring her to reject it. Maggie hadn't, but then she'd already proven her point to Owen, who surely heard how she'd unsettled his staff.

She saw Owen standing on the dais at his uncle's side, both of them leaning over a great account book spread before them. She didn't want to feel this . . . this flood of emotion that warmed her insides whenever she looked upon him. She felt lost and helpless that he could affect her so much. What if she couldn't hold her ground against him? What if the shameful feelings of lust weakened her, made her capitulate to the wedding, and then he died?

Nay. She wasn't going to let that happen. She was going to see that contract and discover if there was another way out that would satisfy both their clans. The fact that he withheld it from her gave her hope.

Owen looked up, and when he saw her, he frowned and left the dais to take her arm. "How is your ankle? Should you be up and about?"

"I am fine."

"Have your stomach issues resolved this morning?" he asked, his deep voice full of innocence. "I don't like to think of you distressed in any way."

She forced a smile, and secretly grumbled that he once again was twisting about everything she did to annoy him. Someday he would grow tired of that. "I feel much better today, and had a good breakfast." She eyed his garments, and noticed the tautness of the fabric. "Is that another shirt I sewed?"

"It is." Though he wasn't smiling, his brown eyes seemed to glow with hidden amusement.

"Oh, dear. I do believe it looks quite tight on ye."

He shrugged. "I'm happy to wear something you made just for me."

She gave an exaggerated wince. "I wasn't certain how wide to make it, especially in the hip area."

A corner of his mouth lifted. "I did have to tug it down quite firmly. It won't ride up."

"I didn't think ye needed much room there," she said, wide-eyed, while secretly knowing how men were about their male attributes. She had a brother, after all. "Or perhaps your girth is expanding. A paunch is something many men acquire over time." She eyed his stomach reprovingly. "Not something I'd wish for in a husband."

He leaned down and spoke in her ear, and his breath made her shiver.

"Then you'll have to keep me well exercised in bed."

Like a fool, she blushed. When his uncle Harold called his name, Owen smiled and left her.

As the morning progressed, more and more people gathered in hall, where the tables had been dismantled to make way for the crowds. Clan pipers and harpists took turns entertaining. Maggie wandered among the people, holding her head high at the sly stares, the whispered conversations behind her back, the shock many revealed upon seeing her different colored eyes. This was not unusual among strangers, of course, but always she feared a murmur of "witch." Such superstition still had a hold on many people, who could not explain the world with science, as Owen did, and instead held fast to the stories handed down through generations.

When Harold brought the crowd to order by banging his fist, everyone settled immediately as if they'd merely been waiting. A line began to form before the dais, leading back toward the crowd, and Maggie judged it as the hours passed, waiting until it shortened to put her plan in motion. She listened to interesting discussion about the extent of the land tacks in the area, the tenants, how the summer growing season was progressing due to storms or drought, an account of the size of their herds. She also heard that Owen held several assemblies across all the lands owned by their clan, for they stretched west to the sea.

One by one, the clansmen presented their problems to Owen, who consulted with his young gentlemen acting as his counselors. She'd seen this in her youth, and she thought he was fair and more interested in his people's lives than her father ever had been. He listened to a grazing rights dispute between two villages; discovered the health of a herd of cattle, each one taken after the death of a villager, to be bestowed on a newly married couple; found a husband and father for a widow and her children after a lively discussion among the gentlemen about which man would suit her.

The most serious case heard was that of a young woman accused of theft. Maggie had heard whispered stories about chiefs who handled the matter coldly, tying a woman by her hair to seaweed on rocks and waiting for the tide to come in and kill her. When Maggie was a child, her brother had once told her that their father had branded a man's hand for theft, and she had had nightmares for days.

Owen contemplated the woman in question, listened as witnesses described what she'd done, and how they'd caught her in time to be able to recover the property she'd stolen. Maggie held her breath, praying Owen wouldn't have her whipped or banished or killed. To her relief, he ordered the woman to be a servant on the land of those she'd wronged, working in their oat fields from dawn to dusk for a month.

The afternoon waned, and all could smell the delicious odors of the food that would soon be served, and grew restless and talkative. More than once, Owen had to raise his voice to ask for quiet. There were only two people left to explain their grievances when Maggie casually got into line behind them. Many people were milling about, their conversations gone to whispers before Himself, but they still were ready to be finished for the day and didn't pay attention to her.

But Owen did. He frowned briefly at her, and then turned his attention back to the person with the complaint. She stayed where she was, hands linked casually behind her back, and waited. If he was going to continue to deny her plea to read the marriage contract between their families, then she was going to demand the right in public. Many men might laugh at her behavior, for the laird had the last say. He was the supreme ruler, almost a god in these people's lives. They might go to church on Sunday, but every other day they had to follow Owen's wishes rather than God's. Of course, a fair chief's rules would follow God's . . .

Owen frowned at her again as he finished up with the person two people before her. Once the man stepped aside, and the next man moved up, she would do the same. It would be obvious to Owen that she was bringing a grievance.

As if he understood exactly what she wanted, Owen narrowed his eyes at her and gestured with his hand toward the corridor. So he thought she'd allow a discussion in private about the contract, when he'd already refused her once? She wasn't taking that chance. She cocked her head as if she did not understand. Letting out a breath, he gave a curt nod, and Maggie knew she'd won. He would let her see the contract to keep her from embarrassing him in public. Satisfied, she turned away and began to walk toward the nearest wall, where she could watch the crowd. She'd become good at that over the years, seeming to be a part of things, but not really. As she watched the women talking, the way they touched arms, the fondness in their eyes for each other—she knew she didn't have that, hadn't had it for many, many years. She was hiding or suppressing so much of herself, it was difficult to offer deep friendship to any woman. She'd always managed to convince herself it was better this way. She had a deep connection to her brother, and even to her mother, although it was difficult to reconcile some of the things the woman had done in her marriage to a drunkard. Maggie knew the friendship of other women was far too dangerous when one had secrets.

There was a sudden commotion near the main double doors at the far end of the hall. A wave of disgruntled sound moved across the room, and Maggie heard a boy's voice crying above it. "My lord, my lord!"

Owen raised a hand, and immediately the crowd calmed to murmurs.

"Thievery, my lord!" the boy cried, so out of breath he had to bend at the waist, support his hands on his knees and pant.

The voices swelled with concern and outrage, and again, Owen raised a hand. "Boy, what is your name?"

"Arthur, m-my lord," he gasped. "My da sent me to tell ye he'd been overcome by strangers and two dozen cattle taken."

Maggie stared at Owen, hiding a wince at the realization that with so many men occupied at the assembly, an enemy had taken advantage.

"We know who did this!" rang out a man's voice.

Maggie took a quick breath as she saw Gregor elbow his way through the crowd and stand in front of the dais, hands on his hips. With rising dread, she guessed what he would say before he said it.

"'Twas the McCallums!" Gregor continued, catching the eyes of many men and nodding at them all.

Maggie clasped her hands together tightly and looked toward Owen. She tried to concentrate on his stern face to avoid the suspicious gazes of so many people.

"Nonsense," Owen said firmly. "Calling an old enemy guilty because of history makes no sense."

Gregor's face reddened, and more than one man eyed Owen with wariness. Maggie swallowed heavily, knowing she was part of the reason it would be difficult for him to earn the trust of all of his people.

"The McCallum and I have a contract joining our families," Owen continued, his voice calm and reasonable. "His sister lives among us, my intended bride. It would be harming his own family to harm us. Let us not jump to conclusions, but form a party and investigate. The war chief will decide our number."

Maggie took a deep breath, realizing she was letting herself grow light-headed.

Owen came around the dais and went to the boy, putting his hands on his shoulders and talking to him. Maggie couldn't hear them, but she knew many others were listening. Owen wasn't making a secret of the interrogation, just trying to get any detail from Arthur without making the boy even more nervous by putting him on display.

Ten minutes later, Owen moved past Maggie, leaving the great hall, and she hurried after him. Without hesitating, she followed him into his bedchamber, and then closed the door in Fergus's startled face.

As Owen unpinned the brooch holding the plaid over his shoulder, he eyed her. "Did you need something from me?"

The length of plaid fell to hang from his belt, and he began to unbuckle that, too.

Raising her eyes to his face reluctantly, she said, "I wanted to say I regret that Gregor could try to use my family against ye."

"The feud between our clans lasted centuries. The acceptance of peace and the fostering of goodwill will take at least our lifetimes." A corner of his mouth lifted. "You and I will be the beginning of it."

She briefly closed her eyes in frustration. "Owen, I've said I won't marry ye. And just now, in the great hall, ye promised to let me see the contract so that I wouldn't embarrass ye."

"I was not worried about being embarrassed," he said.

And his plaid fell to the floor, leaving him wearing the shirt she'd sewn. It was ridiculously tight across his hips, and she almost felt strangely touched that he wore it at all. She reminded herself that he was doing it to annoy her, not to please her.

Then he turned toward the window, and she could

see the perfect outline of his—she hastily lifted her gaze and called upon every skill she'd developed to keep her emotions hidden away. She was an expert, after the parenting she'd had.

"Then why did ye agree to let me see the contract?" she demanded.

He said nothing at first, just stood where she could see him—practically every part of him. And she only arched a brow and waited, willing herself not to perspire. He was tall, and leaner than some she knew, but oh, every muscle was put together perfectly. When he bent to unbuckle his leather shoes and remove his good stockings, she swallowed heavily, then got herself back under control.

"I didn't want *you* to be embarrassed, Maggie," he said. "When you're my wife, you won't want others to remember your reluctance to trust me."

She frowned, not knowing if he was being overly confident or simply considerate. And then he began to pull up his shirt—with difficulty at first—and at the sight of his bare thighs, she almost whirled to give him her back.

But she didn't. It was exactly what he wanted, to intimidate her, to fluster her, to show some kind of superiority. It wasn't the first time she'd seen a man naked, after all.

But it was the first time she'd seen *him* naked, and that made all the difference. Every part of him was perfectly made, from the width of his muscled shoulders to the narrowness of his hips. And his manhood . . . it looked very large.

He asked in husky voice, "So you want to see what you'll be marrying?"

"And now I've seen it," she said in a bored voice, and walked past him. She could almost breathe again when she reached the door.

She heard quiet footsteps approach behind her.

Over her shoulder, she said, "Tonight when ye return, ye'll show me the contract."

He didn't answer, and she made herself hesitate with her hand on the door handle.

"Owen?" Though she managed to use a warning tone, her voice had an uneven edge that made her wince.

"Yes?"

His breath actually touched her hair, and gooseflesh rippled across her skin. She could swear she felt the heat of his flesh even through all of her garments. Trembling, she realized if she opened the door, she'd back right into him.

"I wish you'd wear your hair down," he murmured.

She shivered as his fingers touched her hair behind her ears, then slid along her neck beneath the bun of her heavy hair, leaving a fiery path. Why was she tolerating this? Oh, because she wanted his goodwill about the contract.

She was lying to herself.

He kissed the slope of her neck, right where it met her shoulder. With a sigh, she let her head fall forward, giving him more access. He nipped her and she shuddered. His hands spanned her waist and then moved up her torso to cup her breasts and pull her back against him. She could not feel his skin but the knowledge of it against her burned.

"Blasted stays," he murmured against her ear.

She, too, was wishing them to perdition, but then lost her breath as his fingers trailed along the top, where her breasts rose above. When he dipped a finger down between them, she cried out. With his other hand, he turned her face so that they kissed across her shoulder. She arched to reach his hungry mouth with her own, and didn't notice that he'd begun to pull up her skirts, until a draft of air from the open window blew across her thighs.

She broke the kiss. "Owen! I said no touching!" But her voice sounded unconvincing.

But then his rough palms were sliding up along her hips, and it felt wicked and sensual and so necessary to her very existence. Her skirts got in the way, but he pushed them up and forward relentlessly.

And then he pressed himself against her bare backside. She felt the heat of his erection, the length cradled between her cheeks. She groaned, knowing she should fight this but unable to. She was trembling and weak and overcome with a passion that seemed to burn in her blood. He held her hips hard against him and rubbed himself slowly.

His breath was hot and fast against her ear. "Maggie, lass."

Her name was only a guttural whisper, but just the sound alone increased her need for him. She didn't know what to do with her hands, and for a frustrating moment, actually wanted to touch herself.

As if she'd summoned him, she felt Owen slide one hand across her belly and then lower. She forgot to breathe again, anticipating yet fearing his touch. When he cupped between her thighs, the sensation was so exquisite that she moaned, dropping her head back against his shoulder. His hand began to move then, spreading his fingers, dipping between her folds, moving deeper. He stroked her, and the sensation flamed inside her, higher and higher. His other hand caressed the tops of her breasts, then he tucked his finger beneath her stays to slide roughly across her nipple, as if he strummed the strings of a harp.

When he gently bit her shoulder, she felt the eruption of pleasure overwhelm her, shuddering through her, sensitizing her even more to the movements of his hand. And then he became still, his erection still pressed against her backside, his breathing harsh. In that moment, she didn't know what she was going to do if he wanted his own pleasure satisfied.

Instead, he removed his hands and stepped back. Her skirts fell all around her, hiding what should burn like her shame, but instead felt glorious.

"Go now, Maggie, before I make ye my bride in the ways of our ancestors."

She stiffened, glared at him over her shoulder, then marched out of the room on shaky legs.

Only as she reached the door to her room did she remember what he was off to do, confront enemies of the Clan Duff. Could he die, and this moment of her own pleasure be all she ever shared with him?

Or did her dream ensure that he could not die this way? She felt a bubble of hysterical laughter rise in her throat as she pushed open her door. Her smile died when she saw Kathleen's look of welcome fade into confusion at Maggie's expression.

Maggie held up a hand. "Forgive me. I'm trying to find a way not to cry, but it seems I cannot force any other emotion, though I try."

"Oh, mistress," Kathleen murmured consolingly, reaching as if to pat her shoulder with a familiarity that gave the maid pause. "His lordship will be fine. I've heard of cattle reivin'. A bunch of grown men racin' around the countryside chasin' each other like a child's game." Kathleen hesitated. "And I don't want ye to be thinkin' about those ladies who stared down their haughty noses at ye. Ye have beautiful eyes, and I told 'em there's nothin' hauntin' about ye at all."

Maggie withheld a grimace and simply nodded to encourage the maid's rambling speech, needing to talk about something, anything, except the ways Owen had touched her, the pleasure he'd given her without demanding his own.

Or was he saving that for later?

# CHAPTER 12

Supper in the great hall was a subdued affair. Many of the families had already returned home, and those that stayed anxiously awaited word from their men who'd gone with Owen and Harold. At last people found beds, even if some rolled up with blankets near the hearth. Maggie went up to her bedroom, leaving orders that Owen must come to see her regardless of what time he returned.

She told herself she wasn't going to let him out of showing her the contract, but honestly, she was worried about his safety, too.

She was wearing only her nightshift, combing out her hair, when the door suddenly opened and Owen stood there, bringing with him the odors of dampness and horse and sweat.

"You sent for me, mistress?" he asked dryly.

And then he looked down her body and froze, and the memories of the kisses they'd shared, how he'd pleasured her, were as sharp as if they'd just happened.

Owen slowly closed the door behind him, and Maggie used the moment to don her dressing gown as if it were armor. She cocked her head and eyed him with faint confusion.

"Owen, what are ye doing here?"

"You sent for me," he repeated, enunciating the words.

"I did not. Clearly ye misunderstood." But she hadn't thought this through, and didn't want a servant to suffer his anger because Maggie was trying to provoke him. She distracted him by saying, "What happened? Was anyone hurt?"

Shaking his head, he went to the wine decanter and poured himself a goblet, then took a long drink before answering. "No one was hurt, on either side."

She let out her breath.

"It seems several Campbell youth thought they could impress their elders and reive some cattle."

Maggie's breath left her in a rush, and she realized that there'd been a part of her that feared some stray McCallums had decided they were tired of the peace.

"They were easy to follow," Owen continued, "and just coming down from their whisky-fueled bravery when we found them."

"What did ye do to them?" She knew it was within Owen's rights to have them killed.

"Used our swords to paddle their backsides and sent them home to their mothers."

His grin was a white flash in the near darkness, stoking her desire for him as if the coals only slumbered, always ready.

To distract her wayward thoughts, she said, "Then the day was a success all around."

"It was," he mused, staring down into his goblet. "I'd anticipated that the tedious aspects of ruling the clan would take away from my enjoyment of my scholarly pursuits, but I find it's almost just as rewarding to change people's lives for the better."

"Almost?" she echoed wryly. "It seems ye prefer your dusty books to people."

"Sometimes. I mostly prefer discussing them with you."

Then he was studying her again, his shadowed expression intent. And she was remembering him naked . . .

Quickly, she said, "Don't be thinking your heroics or your flattery will make me forget the promises ye made today. Ye're going to show me the contract."

His half-lidded gaze slid slowly down her body, reminding her of the physical promises he'd made, too. She felt flushed, her skin overly sensitive to the soft linen of her nightshift against her unbound breasts.

"You have a quick mind, Maggie, not one to forget. I had my secretary find the document for you. Wait a moment."

When he was gone, she let out her breath in a rush and wiped perspiration from her forehead. It was not hot in the drafty stone castle, but she was feeling that way. After the pleasure he'd given her that afternoon, she would never feel comfortable being alone with him again.

Or had he hoped that the physical experience would make her forget wanting to read the contract?

He returned with a sheaf of papers and handed them to her. "How is your ankle tonight?"

Before she could escape his nearness, he caressed her arm, from shoulder to elbow, and she stepped away before he could go any further.

"Better," she said distractedly. "I barely limp."

And then she lowered her head and began to read the contract, trying to ignore him but, as usual, finding it difficult. While drinking his wine, he watched her closely, and it was awkward enough reading such formal language without his unnerving stare. She was relieved that her work deciphering the law book helped her understand most of it.

But neither her name nor his was written there, and she pointed that out.

"The amended contract is with your brother," Owen said.

"Ye don't have our betrothal in writing?" she demanded. "Our actual names? Ye ken what that means."

He frowned. "And what does that mean?"

"Ye don't have to marry *me*," she said. "You and Hugh can amend the contract any time ye like, apparently."

"You have other sisters you want me to consider?" he asked with sarcasm.

"Nay, but I have several cousins who would be perfect for ye. I'll send for them." She should feel relieved, glad that at last she'd found a way to escape the marriage contract and Owen's risk of death, while still keeping the peace between their clans. But the thought of watching him flirt with other women made her relief strangely hollow.

He studied her as if she was a specimen he was examining. "Maggie, is there something you need to tell me about your dowry?"

Puzzled, she said, "I don't understand."

"Is there a simpler reason you need to avoid marriage? Did you discover that your father didn't leave you the promised dowry? Or did your people need it more than you felt you did?"

"This has nothing to do with my dowry!" she snapped. "I've been honest with ye, Owen, and I don't appreciate ye trying to find different reasons to explain my resistance to marriage."

"Let me be honest with *you*. I don't care about your dowry, whatever it is. *You* are enough for me to have in this marriage."

She opened her mouth, but for a moment, could find nothing to say. It would be the dream of every young woman for her husband to want her just for herself. But he didn't. "Let's not forget our whisky land, Owen. Your clan has already begun to make a name for itself with our precious resources."

He leaned closer. "And let's not forget that your brother's forfeiture of marriage to my sister would have taken that land away from the McCallums permanently. I didn't need to marry you at all."

"And now I'm supposed to be grateful for your pity?"

"It wasn't pity!" he said with obvious frustration.

"Good. I prefer a practical decision taking into consideration the future of both our clans. Which is why Dorothy or Helen will do just as well for your wife."

He set down his wine goblet with deliberation. "Go on *dreaming*, Maggie. I'll see you in the morning."

She flinched at his choice of words. "That's ugly of ye, Owen. After all, I'm trying to save your life, regardless of how ungrateful ye are."

Without a word, he closed the door behind him, and she was left fuming at his need to find another reason she was resistant to the marriage. Because of course, it couldn't be the simple truth that she'd been telling him from the beginning, she thought sarcastically. She sat down at her writing desk and began a letter to her brother, pushing aside her anger to cheerfully praise the upcoming festival, and asking him to bring two of her cousins to enjoy the event, though she didn't explain why . . .

FOR the next few days, Maggie had a bit of reprieve from Owen's attentions as he concentrated on the paperwork generated by his decisions at the assembly. Although once she was in the library struggling through a book on natural philosophy, and Owen took time from his schedule to discuss the many branches of the science. During their discussion, she occasionally found herself studying his face, the sober, intent way he explained everything to her, yet with an element of excited wonder he tried to hide, as if "wonder" was a childish emotion. He would never be the kind of man to think his life had to be the same routine, day in and day out, not when simply studying the world gave him such pleasure. He saw endless possibilities stretched out before him, the promise of new discoveries. Quantitative discoveries, of course, she reminded herself angrily, not discoveries as vague as dreams or visions. Nothing to do with deeper emotions. Maybe she was focusing on educating herself for some of the same reasons. Because she didn't have to look at the woman she'd become, one who held back from life, who couldn't take the risk of anyone knowing her truest self. She'd offered that to Owen not once, but twice, and felt humiliated and disregarded when he'd branded her a liar.

But she could not change Owen, and she had to focus on the fact that he expected the discoveries of science to help mankind, to help his people. He would never be a man who kept himself apart. He wanted to be familiar to them, to know them in return. To that end, they had another manly competition, target shooting. The men of the nearby villages and the castle barracks met up in the field on the far side of the moat and took turns impressing each other with their marksmanship.

More than once she'd caught Gregor glaring at her, as if he was thinking of the McCallums he'd like to be shooting. It made her uncomfortable, casting a dark cloud over the event of the day.

This was the first competition that Owen won outright, and afterward, she saw Gregor monopolize him for several long minutes, and she could only wonder what the smithy was saying.

She told herself it wasn't important if she herself was accepted by the Duff clan—her replacement would be arriving soon. Maggie hoped that in some small way, her presence here had already begun the healing, easing the way for Owen's McCallum wife. She had beautiful cousins, and she knew Owen would be just as attracted to them as to her. He'd done nothing to show her he had any deeper regard for her than as a woman to warm his bed and stop a feud. They had the occasional discussions, but he could have those with anyone. And if it made her feel a deep sorrow, it was the price she'd have to pay for keeping him safe.

Suddenly, she heard a child cry out from the midst of a pack of children gathered to watch the competition. Owen strode within their midst, and soon he emerged leading a young boy, whose dirty face was streaked with tears—and blood was dripping from his hand.

Maggie rushed toward them. "What happened?" she demanded, taking a handkerchief from within her sleeve and wrapping it about the boy's bleeding palm.

"It seems James here thought a dirk-throwing competition should be next, and decided to show his friends what he could do."

The boy, who could not be more than ten, sniffed back his tears and said nothing.

"Could you help him, Maggie?" Owen asked.

"Take him to the great hall and send for hot water. I'll fetch my sewing."

When they met again, she was surprised that Owen was still with James, and in fact, was bathing the boy's hand over a basin of now pink water. Mrs. Robertson stood back and watched fondly, and Maggie couldn't help thinking that such a display of compassion did Owen well before his people. But that was cynical of her.

She set to work, cleaning the wound with soap, even as the boy cried silent tears without resisting her. After warning James to remain as still as possible, Maggie carefully sewed the wound closed with a few stitches. His face paled and he twitched, but he was a good patient. At last she covered the wound with a salve Mrs. Robertson supplied, bandaged it, then let the boy go, with the admonishment to keep it clean and have his mother apply fresh bandages each day. James ran from the hall as if she'd tortured him. Maggie watched ruefully.

"What a fine seamstress you are," Owen murmured in a teasing voice.

Startled, Maggie turned to him, only to find him leaning far too close. She shivered when he continued to whisper in her ear.

"What a good wife and household mistress you'll make. Such compassion."

She frowned at him—had he steered the boy to her deliberately to prove a point, that she was very capable of being a competent wife? Saying nothing, she packed up her sewing and left him, her nose in the air when she heard him chuckle behind her.

At midday on the eve of the festival, a rider came to alert the castle that the McCallum party had been spotted and would arrive before supper. Maggie flew into a flurry of activity, including a last examination of all the guest bedrooms, knowing and accepting that she was behaving as if she didn't trust Mrs. Robertson.

Maggie was surprised by how much the nearly three weeks of being away from her family had affected her. It wasn't as if she'd never been apart from her brother for months on end, but then she'd had her mother. Now . . . she had no one to confide in, no one to feel safe with, no one who believed in her.

In her mind, she saw the image of Owen, felt again

the way his hands had touched her days ago, but not once since. Feeling desired was not the same thing as feeling cherished.

The thought of safety made her pray that Gregor could control his animosity while her family was visiting. The McCallums had been respectful to Owen when he'd been at Hugh and Riona's wedding celebration; surely the Duffs could do the same.

Kathleen arrived to help her change for supper. Maggie usually didn't do such a thing, but she'd spent hours in the gardens choosing flowers to grace the tables, and felt dirty and sweaty enough to take a bath.

She looked at the lovely gown Kathleen had laid out—not one of the ones Maggie had altered to make her unattractive. It was best if she appeared normal for her family; she didn't want them to become suspicious. But she was still going to pad her waistline when Kathleen had gone.

As Kathleen was helping her tie the laces of her open bodice over the flat stomacher, Kathleen appeared flustered and red-faced.

"What is it, Kathleen?" Maggie asked. "Ye don't have to be nervous about my family."

"Nay, mistress, I promise I won't be, but I have somethin' to say, and I don't mean to make ye feel badly."

"Go on."

The maid raised a pleading gaze to Maggie's. "I want to apologize for my brother. I couldn't decide how to say it, and maybe I waited too long, but . . . He had no business tryin' to talk his lordship out of marryin' ye that day at the target shootin'."

Maggie stiffened, unable to be surprised. She'd seen the way Gregor had been looking at her when he had Owen's ear. But Owen hadn't said a thing.

"I'm embarrassed by his terrible behavior in a place I want to call home . . ." Kathleen's voice trailed off as she stared at Maggie. "Ye didn't know, did ye?" the maid whispered. "Och, his lordship was sparin' yer feelin's and I made a mess of things."

Maggie put a hand on Kathleen's shoulder. "I already knew your brother was not fond of a McCallum marrying a Duff. Think nothing of it." She almost wished Owen had heeded Gregor's words. Then it would be over, and she wouldn't have to see Owen's dead face in her dreams.

She thought of the fires that had been set, the talisman in her bed, the rocks in the way of her descent. Could Gregor have been the one who raced up the slopes to hurt her? He was younger and fitter than Martin.

She changed the subject to chatter about her family, finding herself describing Hugh, Brendan, and her mother to the interested maid.

Before supper, she found Owen standing on the landing outside the great hall, looking across the battlements and into the distant hills. Below them, the courtyard was a hum of activities, with booths being set up for the peddlers to sell their wares. Owen glanced down at her with a faint smile, and put an arm around her waist.

"Ye look lovely today," he said dryly, glancing pointedly at her gown.

She answered primly. "Thank you."

His look became sober as he returned to the view.

"Are ye worried about the reception of my family during the festival?" she asked. "Kathleen told me her brother tried to talk ye out of marrying me. Ye should have listened."

He shrugged. "His words meant little to me. There will always be people unable to accept change. They have to learn that McCallums and Duffs aren't so very different."

For a strange moment, she almost thought he was telling himself that.

His mouth tilted up. "And besides, I believe Gregor was only hoping to make me miss my next shot."

And then he put his arm around her waist, right there in public, and she had no choice but to allow it, short of embarrassing him.

To her surprise, he squeezed her padded waist a little tighter and leaned down to whisper into her ear, "I like that you're rounded in all the right places."

She stiffened.

"It makes me think of the pleasures of exploring your womanly softness in my bed."

Frowning with annoyance, she elbowed him, and he chuckled but didn't let her go. He was pointing out that he knew the truth of her deception and teasing her about it at the same time.

But his familiarity reminded her of other places his hands had been, and once she'd remembered such intimacy, she couldn't forget it. She wanted to . . . squirm as if she couldn't get comfortable; she wanted to press closer to him; she wanted—

She wanted to find a replacement wife and leave, before her treacherous thoughts made her even more miserable.

"I believe I see your family in the distance," Owen said.

She gasped and stood on tiptoe, as if that would help.

"I see a glint of light off metal," he added.

"They have to be armed for the journey," she hastened to assure him.

Amusement crinkled his eyes. "I have traveled roads before and understand the necessities. I know they don't mean to invade."

She felt a blush stealing over her but kept her gaze focused in the distance. Several clansmen came up the stairs, nodding respectfully as they moved past through the open doors to the great hall.

"Everyone we care about will be here," he said quietly. "We could marry. The banns have been read once so far, and I could pay a stipend to speed up the process."

Surprise gave way to tiredness. "I will not marry

ye, Owen. But I won't embarrass ye by talking about it with my brother—at least not in public."

Owen gritted his teeth. "He's the one man who'll understand the stubbornness I have to put up with."

"He's used to stubbornness, because he's full of it himself. I'll be curious to see if his relationship with our mother is improving. Unlike him, I ken what it's like to feel powerless against a chief, against a father, against a strong, violent man. My mother suffered for many years. Hugh can't truly understand that. My prayers were answered when my mother and Hugh reconciled, but there's still a wariness there. Speaking of mothers," she added, changing the topic, "*yours* was not happy about our marriage. Such a shame ye'll still have to marry a McCallum, though it won't be me."

"These last weeks with your family will surely change her mind about *you*," he said pointedly.

"We'll see," she said. "Oh, look, they're much closer!"

And she broke away from Owen and headed down the stairs. She knew he followed her to the courtyard, but she didn't wait for him, just hurried across the mud, holding her skirts to her ankles. Someone had spread straw across the courtyard, covering the worst of the mud, and she appreciated that. She passed beneath the dark of the gatehouse and crossed the stone bridge over the moat, just as the McCallum party reached the far side. Maggie waved excitedly and walked between the horses ridden by her brother Hugh and his new wife, Riona. Riona bent to briefly clasp her hand, and the sun touched her golden hair like a halo. She looked . . . radiant. The tender way Maggie's warrior brother regarded his wife had Maggie blinking back tears. Their happiness was all that she'd hoped for Hugh, considering he'd been pledged to a different bride since childhood.

But then he'd kidnapped the wrong bride, and had fallen deeply in love. That love had started Maggie on this journey to save her clan. She'd accepted Owen's expedient offer of marriage, and before she'd experienced the newest dream, had even told herself she'd find a way to be happy without love. She'd always assumed she couldn't truly let herself love a man, because she'd need to keep secret her dreams and that would be a betrayal of trust.

Yet . . . Owen knew her every secret, and though he didn't believe in her gifts, he didn't treat her as a pariah. He even wanted to marry her regardless. Oh, it was for their clans, she knew, but . . . he was making her rethink all her assumptions about marriage. She felt a pang of loss, knowing she'd never be able to explore that relationship with him—not if she wanted him to live.

She was relieved to pull herself out of such thoughts by looking at the excited expression on her ten-year-old brother's face. Brendan's mother had died birthing him, and he'd never known the identity of his true father until recently. Having been raised by his grandmother, he'd never left the vicinity of Larig Castle. Now he looked in wonder upon the Duff stronghold.

"Maggie!" he called. "There's a moat!"

She laughed. "And there are fish and frogs and lots of things ye'd like."

"Those are little boy games. I'm going to see the training yard."

"Oh, of course. I'm sure ye'll enjoy that, too." But she hid a smile as she watched him look down over the bridge at the water with eagerness.

Next came her cousins, Dorothy and Helen, waving to her from the center of the traveling party. They looked upon Castle Kinlochard with wonder and excitement. They were sisters, Dorothy a redhead and Helen a reddish blond, and it was the amusement of the clan at how different they were from each other. Dorothy was forthright and passionate about her opinion, whereas Helen was demure and ladylike in her pursuits. Surely one of them would appeal to Owen.

Her own mother wore a tremulous, worried smile, as if she had lived in fear for Maggie. Maggie gave her a reassuring smile in return, but she wasn't so sure she'd convinced her mother. Theirs was an unusual relationship. The two women loved and understood each other, for both good and bad. Her mother was there to comfort and listen, had never disregarded her dreams, even when Maggie was a child. She'd kept Maggie's secrets, and in return, Maggie had tried to comfort her over the mistakes that had

driven Hugh away. Lady McCallum had known that
her husband abused young women and been powerless against him, except to remove her children from
his influence. It had taken years for Hugh to learn
to forgive her for not confirming to the world that a
serving girl's bastard child was her husband's and
not Hugh's. Lady McCallum had been terrified of
her husband, damaged, unable to stand against him.
Maggie had sympathized and found herself hovering between Hugh and Lady McCallum for much
of her life, soothing both sides, trying to encourage a healing of their bond. Hugh's wife, Riona, had
helped bring that about, and Maggie would always
be grateful.

And then she saw Owen's sister, Cat, and their
mother, Lady Aberfoyle. Cat searched Maggie's face as
if she was desperate to know that all had gone well
with their betrothal. Cat would be disappointed when
Maggie and Owen separated. Maggie smiled at her,
and Cat smiled in return. Apparently Maggie wasn't
all that successful in her reassurance, because Cat's
smile faded and she seemed to search the castle as if
looking for her brother.

"Need a ride?" Hugh asked, and reached down for
Maggie.

Smiling, she clasped his hand, and as he lifted, she
found the stirrup with her foot and used it to turn and
sit across his thighs.

As they approached the gatehouse, she saw Owen

standing on the far side, arms folded over his chest, his expression impassive. She had the urge to beg her brother to gallop away from here, before her heartache grew even worse.

"Are ye well?" Hugh asked with quiet concern.

Did he sense something? She didn't want to worry him, so she gave him a bright smile. "I am. Everyone here has been kind. I've simply missed my family."

He searched her gaze much as Cat had done, but then glanced up and saw Owen, so he said nothing. Maggie let her breath out quietly in relief. She would have to tell Hugh something soon, for he'd understand exactly what was going on when she threw Dorothy and Helen in Owen's path. Or maybe Hugh already suspected her motives.

"So everyone will welcome McCallums to their Duff festival with no qualms?" Hugh asked dryly.

"I didn't say that . . ." she admitted, thinking of Gregor.

"But you have felt safe here?" he demanded.

"Owen makes certain I am safe." And that wasn't a lie.

They left the darkness of the gatehouse and emerged into the gloomy overcast sky that hung over the castle, as if anticipating what was to come. Owen reached both hands up to her, and she leaned forward and let him take her waist and lower her to the ground. Again, he put his arm around her, reminding Hugh of his claim.

Her brother dismounted and reached to clasp Owen's hand. "Aberfoyle."

"McCallum," Owen answered.

She wanted to roll her eyes. The two men had been on first-name basis before, but apparently the defensiveness hadn't gone away.

Grooms came forward to take the horses as one by one the guests dismounted. Four clansmen had ridden along to guard the party on the journey, and Owen had ordered rooms in the barracks prepared for them. He and Maggie led the rest of the group up the stairs to the first floor great hall. At last Owen released her to go to his sister, whom he hugged fervently.

Cat smiled up at him, cupping his cheek. "You look good, Owen, bronzed by the sun. You've been out with your men, I see?"

"The competitions have continued," Maggie said. "Your brother finally won one of them."

Cat laughed. "Let me guess—target shooting."

Owen gave nod. "You know me too well."

Lady Aberfoyle came forward next, and Owen dutifully leaned down to kiss her cheek. As he did so, the countess studied Maggie. The disdain she'd originally offered Maggie seemed gone, so at least the visit to the McCallums had done some good. That would be a relief for Owen, whichever McCallum he married.

"Margaret!" her mother cried, throwing her arms about her daughter.

Maggie hugged her tightly back, and to her surprise, felt a sting of tears. It felt like ages since she'd had someone to confide in—Euphemia had briefly stood in for her mother, but since she'd been able to help so little, she hadn't eased Maggie's concerns. Her mother wouldn't be able to either, but still . . .

As they parted, Maggie saw Brendan bow his head to Owen.

"Lord Aberfoyle, I like your castle," Brendan said.

"Thank you," Owen replied, smiling. "I hope you explore it as if it's your own."

"I may?" He shot a look at Maggie. "Oh, that's right, my sister'll be mistress here. I'll be back." And he ran outside.

Maggie gave Owen a grateful look.

"And who are our other guests?" Owen asked.

Maggie recognized the faintly sardonic tone of his voice as he regarded the lovely sisters. The two young women squealed as Maggie rushed forward to embrace them both at the same time.

"Oh, Maggie, ye were so kind to invite us," Helen murmured, gazing around at the great hall with awe in her eyes. "Who would have thought we'd ever be dining in the Duff castle?"

Dorothy shook her head. "There's been peace between our families for years, ye silly lass. 'Twas bound to happen." And then she smiled at Maggie. "But truly, ye were gracious to think of us."

*I hope ye still believe that after the festival,* Maggie

thought. She turned, linked both her arms with her cousins, and presented them to Owen. "Lord Aberfoyle, may I present Dorothy and Helen McCallum, sisters to each other and cousins to me." She cocked her head toward Dorothy. "'Tis our grandfathers who were first cousins, were they not?"

Dorothy nodded, and then said as an aside to Owen, "We might be distant cousins to the chief, but when Maggie was home, she made us feel close."

Maggie felt a twinge of regret for being away so much and losing the close bond she'd once shared with her cousins. But with her father there, there was little else her mother could have done to keep her safe.

Owen bowed like the gentleman he was, and Helen's face turned a becoming shade of pink as she blushed, though she said nothing. The sisters curtsied as if forgetting Maggie still held their arms, and she stumbled forward as they sank.

Hugh laughed aloud, and she shot him a sisterly frown, even as Riona elbowed him. Maggie had known the moment she met Riona that the woman was perfect for her brother. It had just taken some sacrifice on all their parts to make it happen.

A sacrifice Maggie couldn't continue with, and her guilt threatened to swamp her. She reminded herself that she had other options, then gently pushed her cousins forward a step. "Owen, would ye show Dorothy and Helen to their room? I'll guide the rest of my family." She grinned at Cat and Lady Aberfoyle. "You ladies already know your own way."

To her surprise, Lady Aberfoyle went to Lady Mc-Callum. "I promised to show you our home, Sheila. Come see what we've done."

"I've been looking forward to it, Edith," said Lady McCallum.

Maggie gaped as the two older women set off together, disappearing down a corridor. While Dorothy and Helen began discussing the tapestry as the two knowledgeable weavers they were, Maggie turned wide eyes on her brother, and Owen regarded his sister curiously.

Hugh spread his hands. "We don't know how it happened, but they've become friends in but a sennight. When first they met, they eyed each other like rival cats about to hiss and claw."

"Hugh," Riona scolded mildly. "The women aren't animals."

"But Hugh's right," Cat conceded as if with regret. She glanced at her brother. "Owen, I spent the entire journey there reminding Mother that your happiness was more important than the hatred her parents had taught her, that a new day of peace was upon us. When we arrived, she was polite and distant with everyone until she met up with Lady McCallum. I don't know what they sensed about each other—"

"A kindred spirit?" Riona interrupted with a smile.

Cat chuckled. "Perhaps that's as good an explanation as any. They apparently hadn't expected it and insisted on resisting for many days of sarcasm and biting comments."

Hugh exhaled a deep sigh. "'Twas exhausting. I wanted to enjoy my new bride, not judge every dispute between two old—"

"Hugh!" Maggie said, glancing apologetically at Owen and Cat. "So how did they realize they could be friends?"

"You mean besides the reminder that their children would be marrying each other?" Cat said.

Cat smiled from Owen to Maggie with such hope that it was painful when it faltered as she stared deep into Maggie's eyes.

"It was as simple as discovering they were both fond of embroidery," Riona said. "Lady Aberfoyle saw what Lady McCallum was working on, and they stiffly began to discuss it."

"For two entire days we had to listen to that at every meal," Hugh said, shaking his head.

"It was better than their arguments," Cat pointed out.

Maggie was relieved to see that Cat was comfortable with Hugh now. Cat had been worried about her cousin Riona's captivity turning into a good marriage. Apparently her fears had gone.

"Let us allow our guests to refresh themselves before the meal," Owen said.

"Dorothy, Helen!" Maggie called, ready to foist them off on Owen.

Owen lifted a hand and Mrs. Robertson smoothly glided forward as if a signal had been arranged. "Aye, my lord?"

"Please show Maggie's cousins, the Mistresses McCallum, to their bedroom." To the women, he said, "We hope you do not mind sharing one room. Many guests are expected for the festival, and every room will be full."

"We don't mind," Dorothy said forthrightly. "After all, we assume Maggie brought us here to consider men for our husbands. The more guests there are, the luckier we might be."

Maggie looked everywhere but into Owen's knowing eyes. Hugh was regarding her suspiciously, too.

Helen blushed again. "Dorothy, ye're far too free with your words. Lord Aberfoyle doesn't care about such things."

"We aren't offending him," Dorothy insisted. "'Tis not as if we're here expecting a trial marriage to begin."

The sisters brushed shoulders as they laughed, and Maggie saw Riona and Hugh regard each other with their own special smile. Their marriage had begun that way.

Maggie was startled when Owen slid his arm into hers. "Come, let us show our guests to their rooms together. While they're resting, we can make sure the evening's entertainment is ready."

"Oh, but Mrs. Robertson—"

"—can use our help."

He turned to Hugh, and Maggie watched that careful shield come up between them again, as if they were so concerned to be civil to each other that they could not be themselves. But Owen said nothing, just gestured to the corridor down which their mothers had disappeared, then led the way.

But he didn't let go of Maggie's arm.

# CHAPTER 13

$O$wen wasn't surprised that Maggie soon found a way to avoid him after they saw her family settled. She escaped to go find her mother, leaving him to stare after her, and Hugh to give him a narrow-eyed glare. Could the McCallum chief be regretting the contract, regretting handing over his sister to a stranger? But Cat was the stranger Hugh would have taken to wife, had Owen's father not deceived them all. It was difficult to believe Hugh would want the contract broken, after all that had been done to save it.

Owen had taken no chances, doubling the guards patrolling the battlements and stationed in the great hall. He wasn't just preparing in case Hugh tried something—he wanted to keep Maggie's family safe from whoever had decided that the marriage shouldn't happen.

If Hugh was planning treachery, he was doing a good job disguising it. Anyone could see the love he had for Owen's cousin Riona. Riona wouldn't countenance a betrayal—if she knew about it.

With a bow, Owen took his leave and returned to his room to change, even as he wondered what Maggie had in store for him this evening. When she'd first mentioned having cousins he might favor, he'd put it off to her desperation to delay their wedding.

Each night as he lay alone in bed, he remembered the touch of her bare flesh, how she'd trembled but not stopped his exploration. She'd been as aroused as he, so moist in her depths that he'd done more than he meant to, unable to resist showing her what their nights together would bring.

And her reaction to her own surrender?

Threatening to find him McCallum cousins he was supposed to consider as his wife. She'd even told him exactly what she intended, and he'd dismissed her words as mere bravado. And then he'd taunted her about her dreams, and felt guilty about it ever since—and angry with himself for feeling the guilt at all. In a moment of frustration, he'd struck out at what she considered her biggest vulnerability. She'd called him cruel, and sworn she was trying to save his life. Was she honestly telling the truth about this dream—a truth only she might believe in? It just seemed beyond belief to him.

The logical thing for Owen to do was to watch Maggie and Hugh together and try to find out the truth. That made a lot more sense to him than believing that her dreams came true.

*She'd been right about Emily,* a voice whispered inside him. He ignored the doubt like always, but it was getting more and more difficult.

He still had to deal with her newest plan to get out of the marriage: foisting her cousins onto him. He should have known never to underestimate her. It shouldn't be this difficult for a woman to marry an earl, he thought, pacing from one end of his bedroom to the other. Many women in London would have married him for the title alone, though it was Scottish.

And then he stopped pacing as an idea began to form.

OWEN was eminently satisfied with the meal that evening, the choicest chicken, partridge, and heathcocks, mixed with salmon and haddock, courses that went on for hours. Through it all, his clan musicians played, harpist and piper, and the bard recited deeds from Duff history.

In the spirit of the evening, he'd seated Dorothy and Helen on either side of him on the dais, moving Maggie down a seat. She seemed delighted with the seating arrangement, engrossed in conversations with her brother to her right.

And Owen was stuck with her two cousins. They weren't unappealing, just very . . . young, newly in their twenties. They hadn't seen anything of the world beyond their village, had experienced little except the farming seasons. Dorothy was bold with her questions, and often encouraged her shy sister to tell of her feminine pursuits, but beyond polite conversation, Owen experienced no pull of interest, nothing compared to what he felt every time he saw Maggie laughing at something her brother said.

And it made him realize he hadn't seen her laugh at all in these last few weeks, not once, though she'd been a laughing girl when first they met. Those different-colored eyes sparkled with mirth, and there was a relaxation about her that made her seem even warmer and more appealing. With her family she seemed genuine and open, which she'd never granted him.

Because she didn't want to marry him.

He felt a stab of loss that surprised and unsettled him.

After the feast, the tables were cleared from the floor so that the dancing could commence. Owen took the opportunity Maggie wanted him to have, dancing with each of her cousins first, a country dance, and then a minuet. But he kept an eye on Maggie as he did so. She began with sedate clapping, keeping time easily to the music. He hadn't failed to notice that before her family had arrived, she hadn't enthusiastically joined in whenever there were guests being entertained. He'd assumed that she felt herself a McCallum amid Duffs, or that she wouldn't let herself be his hostess. But these last few days, he'd begun to accept that she'd told him the truth, that she couldn't relax among people, that she never let herself have close friends because of the dreams she kept secret.

That wasn't true with her brother, of course. But when Hugh tried to pull her into a dance, she'd demurred and he'd acquiesced as if he was used to it.

And then Owen stepped on Dorothy's foot. She was polite about it, but he realized he was more interested in watching Maggie than in dancing.

Yet he kept dancing, switching to partner Helen. Every time he smiled down upon the girl, he thought he glimpsed Maggie's own smile briefly dim. And for the first time, he considered that if not for her dream, maybe Maggie would have eventually welcomed the marriage. He imagined her excited for wedding plans, open to long discussions, eager for his kisses, looking forward to the wedding night as much as he did. What would it have been like not to feel that he was forcing her against her will, like a tyrant.

He should be angry that a vague dream was more important than the reality of their marriage. But anger had gotten him nowhere. He was far too enthralled with his betrothed, feeling like a boy at his first dancing assembly trying to secure the attention of the loveliest girl there.

And Maggie was very lovely, he thought, as he brought Helen back to where the McCallums gathered. Then he noticed how isolated the McCallums were, that none of his clan was making any attempt to make them feel comfortable by mingling with them. He couldn't force such a thing, he knew, but perhaps his dancing with the McCallum girls would do more than just make Maggie jealous, but encourage his own people.

Standing near Maggie, his arms crossed over his chest, he regarded the merriment in his hall, the abundance of food he'd been able to offer his guests, and felt satisfied. Not that it was a competition with Hugh, he reminded himself.

He noticed Gregor and his sister Kathleen standing against the wall right behind the McCallums, Gregor's dark eyes hot with anger. For a man who'd spent most of his life in the colonies, Gregor burned with a hatred that seemed irrational. Kathleen was beseeching him about something, her expression one of worry and even fear.

Fear?

Owen thought again of the fires which he'd never been able to solve. When nothing else had happened, he'd let it go, believing it was a prank that the culprit regretted. Then Maggie's bed had been violated with a symbol of witchcraft, but connecting that to anyone had proved elusive, since Owen couldn't actually tell anyone about the talisman. But watching Gregor, knowing how the man felt about the McCallums . . . Owen decided to remind his men to be aware of what was going on around them, rather than imbibing too freely.

He bowed in front of Maggie and offered her his

hand. He saw her hesitation, the way she glanced at her brother as if he could save her. Owen ground his teeth together.

Then she slid her cool hand into his and followed him into the center of the dancers. The dancing took all their fortitude, all their breath, and he saw that though she might stand apart from a crowd, she'd found time to absorb the basics of dance. But she was making a concerted effort to be a step behind him.

"I'm sorry," she said breathlessly. "I'm a poor dancer."

Another exaggeration, he knew.

"Perhaps my cousins—"

"No. I'm dancing with *you*, Maggie McCallum, my betrothed."

He overpowered her, guided her into the steps as if she truly didn't know them. She kept up with him because she had to, and soon her natural grace surfaced. He enjoyed swinging her about, feeling her hand in his, moving between couples only to meet up with each other again. Her waist was lean and lithely muscled beneath that extra padding, and he had to think about account books to keep from becoming obviously aroused.

As they circled each other, Owen was able to pitch his voice so that only she could hear.

"I wondered if you were going to insult me by refusing to dance."

She tipped her fine nose in the air. "I almost did. I'm

not fond of dancing. But ye're our host and 'twas my duty to—"

He stopped her with a laugh, and she eyed him, affronted.

"You did not dance with me out of duty," he said into her ear. The lavender scent of her hair was exotic and overwhelming. "You remember what I did to you with just my hands."

Biting her lip, she spun away from him, but the dance brought them back together.

"How dare ye refer to our private business in public," she practically hissed.

He liked her on fire. "Your brother can see that angry expression of yours. Is that what you want him to think, that you're unhappy?" The moment he said those words, he realized he was still concerned about her brother's intentions.

But Maggie was swept away before she could answer.

A minute later, the dance brought her back. "He'll ken the truth when I don't marry ye, after all."

"But you would restart a feud tonight?"

She exhaled loudly, then pasted a false smile on her face. "Nay, not tonight, not ever. I've told ye that."

"Find a better expression, because that looks positively gloomy."

"Gloomy!" she said, her new expression affronted.

"That's better."

Taking her by the waist, he whirled her around. He didn't bother saying anything more—he'd made his point. When the dance had finished, he didn't return her to her brother, but took her with him back to the dais, where he offered her wine. She took the goblet and sipped.

"Shall we discuss Dorothy and Helen?" he said.

"Are they not lovely lasses?" she asked sweetly.

"Quite lovely. You warned me you'd bring them and I'll tell you right now that you wasted your time. I'm uninterested."

"You aren't very interested in me but for warming your bed," she shot back.

"You know that's not true. I have the kind of discussions with you that I could never have with your much younger, innocent cousins."

"Are ye saying I'm old?" she demanded.

He cocked his head. "You chose to have them sent for. Do you believe you're too old?"

"Ye know I don't." She took a deliberate sip of wine. "But are ye saying I'm not innocent?"

He cupped her face and looked into her eyes. "Oh, you're an innocent. I think I gave you the first pleasure of your life. And I'll give you even more, even better, every night of our lives. And don't go all stiff on me. Your brother is watching." He pressed a gentle kiss to her mouth and released her. "Go on, be with him. You've missed your family, I know."

MAGGIE wanted to run to her room. Her emotions were roiling inside her, confusion, anger, despair—desire. Owen did all that to her, and more. He was too devilishly appealing to her poor, *innocent* cousins. Watching him with other women had been a startling pain in the center of her chest, and that had made her afraid. She couldn't grow to depend on him, to want him—to love him. Every deeper emotion she felt for him would only be worse if this terrible dream came true—but she wasn't going to allow that to happen. If she had tender feelings, then very well, she would use them as even more motivation to save his wretched life.

But there was her brother, his heavy brow low and dark. He was alone, for his wife was standing with their mother and Lady Aberfoyle some distance away. Taking a fortifying breath, Maggie went to him.

One eyebrow lifted as he regarded her. "What is going on with ye, Maggie McCallum?"

He only used their surname when he was upset.

"I—what do ye mean?" she asked lightly.

"Och, ye're terrible liar, always have been."

"That's not true. Trust me, I'm far too good at it now."

He rolled his eyes. "Why do ye think I got between ye and Father so often? Your expressive face revealed everything ye were thinking, and got us into even more trouble."

She put a gentle hand on his arm. "Ye mean I got *you* into more trouble," she said quietly.

He shrugged that off.

"Don't be like that, Hugh McCallum." She tossed the surname back at him. "Ye may be chief now, all bluster and command, but I'm dealing with another man like that, and believe me, it's helped me see through ye. Ye rescued me, protected me, comforted me when I was a frightened little girl. I'll never forget it, and I'll love ye until I die."

Apprehension rose in his eyes. "Ye're saying this *now*? Are ye frightened, lass? Is that what ye're telling me though ye're talking in circles?"

"Nay, Owen would never frighten me," she said, answering it in a way that wasn't a lie.

"But . . . things aren't right between ye. I can see that. I hurt for ye." The final words were a rumble deep in his chest.

She barely kept herself from flinging her arms around him, wishing he could make everything all right, as he'd done in their childhood.

But she couldn't tell him the truth—she knew that now. He believed in her dreams, had seen the outcome firsthand. If he thought she'd suffer tragedy on her wedding day, he'd stop it outright, regardless of what it did to the peace between their clans. And how would Gregor and his ilk take such an insult? She shivered.

"Hugh, I'm simply getting used to him. Less than three weeks ago, I agreed to marry him, a man who might as well be a stranger."

"I don't believe that—I saw how ye were with him.

Something happened long ago, something ye didn't tell me. And ye wouldn't tell me after ye were betrothed to him."

"Hugh, we were celebrating your wedding," she said with exasperation. "The past—it didn't matter. It *doesn't* matter."

"I didn't like hearing there was something between ye and a man."

"But I knew it made ye feel better about accepting the betrothal," she pointed out.

He didn't say anything, just put his hands on his hips and waited her out.

"He was barely a man then," she said reflectively, "just eighteen to my sixteen."

He frowned so deeply she thought his eyebrows would hit his nose.

"And?" he urged.

"Mother was trying to make peace with the Duffs, since ye were engaged to Lady Catriona—Cat. I met Owen once at a dinner when we were children, and I made no impression on him," said dryly. "But years later, Mother deliberately chose to live in the same tenement, and we became friends for a few weeks."

"Friends," he echoed, his voice full of doubt.

"That's all we were." *To Owen.*

"Did he lead ye on?"

"We flirted, Hugh, that was all." Did Hugh not remember that Owen's first betrothed had died? That made this even easier. She'd never told Hugh about the dream she'd had in connection to Owen, humiliated that Owen had believed her a liar—and worried that Hugh would challenge him over her honor. She couldn't let Hugh know she'd had another dream, the first in many years. "He had a telescope even then, and I was fascinated to look at the stars."

"It only took a telescope to lure ye to him?" Hugh said.

She gave his arm a push, a smile easing its way onto her face. "He didn't lure me. We were friends. And then I discovered he was betrothed, and I knew our friendship was inappropriate, so I ended it."

He searched her eyes as if he was trying to read her soul. She met his gaze with her best attempt at earnestness. It was all true. Sort of. Oh, this balancing on the edge of truth and falsehood was far more difficult with her brother than with Owen.

Hugh sighed. "But things are still awkward between ye—at least on your side. He just kissed ye."

"Ye sound accusatory, like I shouldn't be kissing my betrothed, when before ye were married, you and Riona—"

He put a finger to her lips, and she grinned at him.

"At that time, I considered her my wife in the ways of Scotsmen for centuries," he said quietly.

Her smile faltered. Owen had said he would do almost that same thing. Men.

Hugh lowered his voice. "Does he know about ye, lass? *Truly* know ye?"

She knew that he was referring to her dreams. She shivered. "He knows. I've tried not to dream for many a long year, Hugh. I'm hoping it never happens again."

"How did he take it?"

She shrugged. "As well as can be expected for a man of science."

"I'm sorry, lass," he said gently. "But it's best to start a marriage with truth. I can tell ye that from painful experience."

"We will make things work, have no doubt, Hugh."

"Truly? Then why did ye specifically send for Dorothy and Helen?"

Hugh was being far too logical and protective. "I wanted them to be exposed to a wider world."

That was true, too. When Hugh found out what she was doing, he'd be furious. She could only hope that by that time, he would understand the reason why.

OWEN was standing with his uncle when Hugh approached them. Owen offered the *cuach* of whisky, and Hugh held the handles and took a long swig before wiping his mouth with the back of his hand.

"Aye, I can tell where that was made," Hugh said.

"You cannot," Owen chided. "You know we share the land, so you're simply assuming." But Maggie had known, too. He pictured her that first day, full of bravado in the castle of her ancient enemy, beautiful and brave. He imagined what it must be like to spend the rest of his life away from his family and people. It wouldn't be easy, and yet she'd agreed to give up her freedom for peace.

And he'd felt sorry for himself for being unable to choose his own bride, he thought with disgust. At least he could choose where to live, how to spend his money and time.

"Are your tastes not as refined as mine, Aberfoyle?" Hugh said lightly. "From just a sip I can tell what was first in the casks that aged the whisky, whether it be bourbon or sherry or another spirit."

"Aye, I've been told that the best have such rare gifts," Harold mused. "Ye're a lucky man. As is your sister—a lucky woman, that is. She claimed the same sensitivity." After another swig, he handed the *cuach* back to Owen before he left them.

An awkward silence stretched between the two men.

"We do have something in common besides Maggie," Owen said at last.

Hugh eyed him. "And what would that be?"

"We've both newly been elected chiefs of our clans."

"An election, ye say? In my case, aye, but in yours—ye would inherit the earldom regardless. I imagine the chiefdom is a given."

Owen shrugged. "There is truth to that. But what surprises me is that the chiefdom is different than I thought it would be."

"Different? Did ye not watch your father all those years?"

"Your father was here in the Highlands, ruling his clan. Mine did so from a distance, more through intermediaries."

"'Twas not as if I wanted to model myself after my father's idea of being chief," Hugh said with sarcasm.

"Aye, I know. Maggie told me about him." He gave Hugh a sober look. "She told me what he did to the serving girls."

Hugh's eyes went flat, and he took another draught of the whisky.

"I'm not sure she gave me the full truth," Owen continued. "Did he hurt her as he hurt them?"

Hugh spoke forcefully. "He did not. I made sure of that."

"As did your mother, by taking you both away."

Hugh nodded.

Owen leaned back against the table, relief relaxing the tension in his shoulders. "I hadn't realized how much I feared that there was an uglier truth until just now. Not that it would have mattered to me in terms of wedding her," he added.

"'Tis good to know." Hugh perched beside him on the table. "Does that mean ye've grown to love my sister already?"

"Love?" Owen barely kept from scoffing, not wishing to offend a happy newlywed. "It would be impractical to need such emotion when dealing with a negotiated marriage."

"Impractical? Ye're a little cold-blooded, aren't ye?" Hugh shook his head and took another drink.

Owen snatched the cup away and took his own. "I'm hardly cold-blooded." *Ask your sister.* "I'm being practical. Unrealistic expectations set a bad precedent."

"Ye're a walking university, aren't ye? No wonder my sister isn't happy."

Owen didn't take offense. "Then you see it, too."

Hugh released his breath and gave a nod.

"Any idea what I can do about it? I'm already showing her I'm not cold-blooded," he added wryly.

Hugh grimaced. "I don't want to hear about that. Maggie . . . she's always been a little withdrawn, a little different. Maybe it does come from having a father like ours. Maybe it comes from the dreams she used to have. If ye're patient, and show her ye can be trusted, things might change."

Owen glanced at Hugh, who was watching the dancers, but in an unfocused, sober way. Did Hugh actually believe in those dreams? Hugh had been an MP in London, had seen more of the world than the ghillies who lived in their timeworn cottages. Yet did he cling to the old ways and believe in seers and dreams? If the McCallums took such things seriously and raised their children that way, no wonder Maggie believed.

Owen looked down at the whisky that no longer appealed to him. "She told me once that she helped save a little boy everyone believed had drowned."

Hugh nodded. "I wasn't there, but I heard what happened."

Owen released a frustrated breath. So Hugh only had secondhand stories to back up Maggie's claims.

"They gave up searching the loch for him after a long day," Hugh said. "That night, Maggie dreamed he was alive, and she led his parents right to him, where he huddled beneath a rocky ledge beside the loch. They were still talking about how she'd saved the boy days later when I arrived."

Owen frowned, but said nothing.

Hugh arched a brow. "She says ye're a man of science, and I guess that means ye've had a hard time believing her."

Owen nodded.

Quietly, Hugh said, "She was only fourteen when she dreamed about a girl in her death clothes. She didn't understand what she was seeing—she was so young—and the girl was a stranger. They found her hanged the next morning. Maggie blamed herself, as if she'd put the rope around the girl's neck. Instead, it was our father abusing her that caused her death."

Owen had thought his father cruel, but compared to the torment inflicted by Maggie's father . . .

Hugh's words had cast a melancholy spell, and the two of them remained silent for a long moment.

Hugh gave a great sigh. "I can't tell ye what to believe, but my sister has always been trustworthy."

*If only I could trust that* you *were telling me the truth,* Owen thought.

Owen looked out to his people and saw that the musicians and dancers were beginning to tire. The torches had slowly begun to fade, making the mood of the great hall grow more somber and reflective. It was time. He found the healer Euphemia by the hearth. Her eyes twinkled as if she'd been waiting for him. He led her forth by the hand, and everyone hushed on cue.

And then Euphemia began to speak. He remembered this part of the Lughnasadh festival well, because as a young child, he'd been a little bit afraid of her. She'd seemed ancient even then, but didn't seem all that different twenty years later.

In a mesmerizing voice that all quieted to hear, Euphemia spoke of the festival that celebrated the beginning of harvest, where the grains were almost ripe enough, and the first fruits of the season, bilberries and wild strawberries, were ready to be picked on the morrow. It was a time of joy, but also a time of tension, because winter was ever nearer, and the harvest had not yet been reaped. They would cut the first oats and make a bread from them as a ritual offering for a successful harvest. She even referred to the days before Christianity, where Lugh was a sky god worshipped by the people. He was the patron of both scholars and warriors—and Euphemia smiled at Owen as she said this.

He, too, was under her spell, as she began to speak in a singsong voice a poem about their ancestors and their worship of Lugh. Owen was glad Father Sinclair wasn't in attendance.

At last her voice melted away. Euphemia took one of the last torches and led the villagers out through the courtyard. Those that were staying in the castle either rolled into their plaids or followed servants up to their assigned quarters.

Owen looked for Maggie and saw her with their mothers, and her eyes shone with wonder as she watched Euphemia and her followers leave. Then she realized Owen was studying her, and for the briefest moment, he felt a connection she'd been taking obvious pains to deny. Lughnasadh was a time to begin anew, begin new employment, anticipate the harvest—start trial marriages. He let his eyes show her all the passion she inspired in him.

She turned away.

# CHAPTER 14

Maggie was still buried beneath her pillows when she heard the knock on her door. Groaning, she lifted her head and blearily looked around. Through the diamond windowpanes she could see the first gray light of dawn. Even Kathleen never tried to awaken her this early. And Owen wouldn't dare.

Someone knocked again.

There was a whole castle full of people who could be lost, looking for their own rooms . . . With a sigh, she crawled out of bed, managed to slip into her dressing gown and simply hold it closed in front of her as she approached the door.

And then she remembered the threats against her. There were far more guards stationed in the corridors, but still she asked, "Who is it?"

"Your mother."

Maggie opened the door.

Freshly dressed for the day, her mother stood there, smiling expectantly. "Good morning, Margaret."

Maggie leaned her head against the door and blinked slowly. "Is it? 'Tis too early to know."

"May I come in?"

Maggie sighed. They'd always been close, and her mother had had an evening to study her. Maggie had known this discussion would be happening sooner rather than later. Without even lifting her head from the door, she backed up a step.

Lady McCallum chuckled. "Ye cannot be *that* tired."

"I am. But I'm glad ye're here." She leaned to kiss her mother's cheek.

Lady McCallum surprised her with a hearty hug. "Oh, my lass, I've missed ye. We've never been so long parted, ye know."

"I know." Maggie smiled as she closed the door.

Her mother regarded the room with a critical eye. "These fine Duffs like to show off their wealth."

"Ye mean they like to make their guests comfortable."

"Mmph," was the woman's answer to that.

"Come sit with me, Mathair."

She sat on a cushioned chair before the fire, and Lady McCallum took the other one and drew it close.

"I could hold your hand all day if ye'd let me," the woman said.

Maggie smiled. "I'm not a little girl."

"But I feel the need to reassure ye like ye still are." Her mother searched her eyes, her own filling with worry. "I didn't like sending ye off with a man ye'd barely ever met."

"I know. But I'm well."

"Pshaw, don't try to lie to me. I see ye swaying those young men—even your brother—but I ken ye to your bones. Has it been so terrible here?"

"Nay, it has not, I promise, Mathair. Owen is respectful and kind. He has this incredible library, and he's teaching me all about the wonders of natural philosophy and astronomy and—"

"Ye aren't telling me what's in his heart, lass."

"I don't know what's in his heart," she answered wistfully. "And it doesn't matter, not truly. His kindness and generosity are more important." She had to pretend they were more important than his trust.

Lady McCallum bit her lip and looked away, blinking rapidly, before she said, "Aye, and it's growing up with such a man as your father that made ye think this, that love is unimportant. Take it from a woman who never had it from her husband—the love of a good man is everything."

Maggie's chest tightened almost painfully, as if her heart could shatter. "I can't marry him," she whispered.

She waited apprehensively, as if her mother would talk about duty to the clan and ending the feud.

Instead Lady McCallum's eyes went wide and she squeezed her hand. "Tell me everything, my wee lass. Let me help."

Maggie took a deep breath, aware of the magnitude of such a decision. And then she said, "I think I've been having dreams about Owen my whole life."

She thought her mother would gasp or perhaps even brush that aside, but all she said was "Go on."

So Maggie told her about the dreams of the little boy who'd practically grown up beside her almost as a comforting companion, the stolen weeks with Owen when she'd been sixteen, her confession of her dream about his betrothed, Emily, and his reaction.

Lady McCallum clapped her hands on top of her thighs and shook her head. "'Tis a sad thing to like a boy and be so disappointed in his foolishness. But he was young, then, Margaret. Don't ye think he's wiser to the mysteries of the world?"

"Aye, the mysteries of the planets or electricism. Those things can make no sense but he'll still believe in them! But not in me." The vehemence in her voice took her aback. She told herself to calm down.

"Ye know that for certain, do ye? Ye've discussed your gift?"

"My curse," Maggie said dully, a rejoinder she'd always given her mother, though they'd usually been bantering. "And aye, we've discussed it again. It didn't go well. He just can't believe in the old *superstitions*." She emphasized the word sarcastically.

"But ye haven't even experienced it in years. Maybe—"

"But I had another dream about him!"

The despair in her own voice shocked her and must have shocked her mother, too, because she regarded Maggie with wide eyes. The silence between them stretched taut.

"He's going to die," Maggie whispered, trembling. "If he marries me, on our wedding day, he'll die."

She could actually see her mother visibly pale.

"Oh, Maggie, ye saw such a thing in your dreams?"

Maggie nodded, feeling the tears well up and spill over. She dropped to her knees in front of her mother and wrapped her arms about her waist.

"Oh, my wee lass."

There were tears in Lady McCallum's voice, too, and they just hugged each other and rocked for what seemed like a long time. At last, Maggie lifted her head, and her mother handed her a handkerchief so she could wipe her face and blow her nose. She sank back into her own chair.

"Tell me the dream," Lady McCallum said, her voice laced with both firmness and concern.

"There isn't much to tell," Maggie said bitterly, "and that's much of the problem. Owen woke me up before I could see the complete dream."

Her mother arched a brow. "He woke ye up?"

Maggie waved both hands. "'Twasn't like that. He heard me scream and came to wake me up the first night I was here. All I saw was me in my wedding clothes, and Owen lying on the floor, blood everywhere, his face white as death." She hugged herself, her entire body trembling.

"But was he dead?"

Maggie shook her head. "Not yet, but I screamed and clutched him, and my clothes became spattered with his blood. And then—he woke me up."

"So ye don't really know he'll die."

"Do ye think I don't realize that? I've spent my entire time here trying to have the dream again, to discover the ending, but nothing works. I've even discussed it with the healer, Euphemia—"

"The one who seemed to enchant the entire hall with just her voice?"

Maggie nodded. "She took me up to the standing stones, as if there was magic somewhere, anywhere, that might help me. But there's nothing. So I resolved not to marry him, and have looked for another way to satisfy the contract and keep the peace between our clans."

Lady McCallum eyed her skeptically. "He still wants to marry ye."

"He thinks I'm being ridiculous, risking the marriage contract this way. He looked at me with such disdain. He doesn't believe he could die. He doesn't like losing, and thinks he's always right, and he wants me in his—" She broke off, blushing.

"In his bed, aye, such is the way of men. And ye

want to be with him, too. I can see the passion between ye two as if it were a color shimmering around ye both."

"Passion isn't love," Maggie said defensively, "'tis just lust." But she was so worried that it was too late for her, that she was falling in love with him even though he couldn't respect an intrinsic part of her. She liked their long discussions, she respected the loyalty and care he showed his people, he was so considerate of her cousins, even though he knew exactly why they were here. And most of all, she loved the way he made her feel like the only woman who mattered.

But could there ever be a love without trust? And why was love suddenly so important when she'd agreed to this marriage thinking they'd tolerate each other and save their clans?

"Ye had dreams about him as a child. Ye think fate didn't plan for ye to be together?"

"Then why did fate give me this dream?" Maggie cried with anguish.

Lady McCallum took her hand and squeezed.

Maggie choked back her tears. "I'm not going to cry anymore. I have a plan to solve everything between our clans. He can marry another McCallum girl."

Her mother tsked. "Dorothy or Helen. I knew something was afoot, but couldn't place it. Ye can see they don't appeal to him, not with the way he looks at ye, Margaret."

A hot blush stole over her. "He's barely spoken with

them. They're very different from each other, yet lovely in their own right—one of them is bound to appeal to him."

"Margaret—"

"What else can I do? I can't marry him! And I can't disappoint Hugh. He is so honorable, and it practically broke him to know his love of Riona jeopardized the clan. Ye weren't there, Mathair—those two foolish men would have fought to the death if I hadn't insisted we find another way. And Owen proposed. Obviously, that was a poor plan, as the fates have decided to show me. So I *will* find another way, and Hugh will never have to feel any regret or guilt."

Maggie was vastly relieved when, after a quick knock, Kathleen stepped into the room, and Maggie no longer had to keep convincing her mother— convincing herself.

On the first day of Lughnasadh, there was always a berry-picking excursion, celebrating the ripening of the first fruits of the season, followed by a horse race. Owen knew which one he usually attended, and the one he ignored. But not today. Today he had a woman to woo.

To his frustration, Maggie had invited two other women to accompany them on what could have been a romantic walk across the mountain. Instead, as he politely carried baskets and let the ladies pick bilberries and wild strawberries, he had to listen to Maggie coax details of their lives from both Dorothy and Helen.

They were sweet girls, and they were overjoyed to be away from home for the first time, but neither of them was the woman he would marry.

The only woman he wanted—to be truthful, the only woman he'd ever truly wanted to marry—was eating bilberries and staining her mouth a luscious purple that he wanted to lick right off her.

But again he kept his thoughts distracted from his baser instincts with mentally repeating how many digits he had memorized of the mathematical constant pi.

Then those lips said something he didn't catch. "Pardon me?"

"Ye look distracted," Maggie repeated patiently. "I knew my cousins would catch your eye."

The two young women had gone ahead of them to search for berries. "They seem well-bred, but they're not you." She opened her mouth to counter him, but he kept talking. "You've told me more than once that you didn't allow yourself friends, that you could never confide in anyone. Are you including your cousins in that, too?"

She frowned and glanced at the young women, who were chattering happily. "They are my cousins, and I love them, but did I allow them to be close friends? Nay, I could not. But they're generous, lovely women who always tried to include me in their plans."

"I simply don't understand your reluctance. You could have kept quiet about your dreams. Surely women don't tell each other *everything*."

"Ye'd be surprised," she said dryly. She walked at a slow pace, the basket softly bumping her skirts with her uneven stride on the slope of the hillside.

"That sounds like you have experience with friends," he pointed out.

"Nay, I have experience with women who tried to be my friend, who confided in me and tried to draw forth my own deepest thoughts. They wanted me to talk—they wanted to help. But I . . . couldn't."

She suddenly seemed so lonely to him, inside a prison of her own making it was true, but that didn't change how she felt.

"I couldn't risk that I might reveal my dreams," she said solemnly. "Even talking to ye about them makes my stomach hurt."

"You fear I would tell someone?" he said in a soft, husky voice.

"'Tis a fear I've had all my life. When I was ten years old, there was a woman in my village, a healer like Euphemia, but also a seer. She had the people's respect, too, and sometimes when I visited her, I used to imagine what it would be like to be open with my deepest secrets, if everyone knew. Maybe they'd respect me like they did her—like they do Euphemia. But both of those women took a terrible chance by trusting others. Euphemia has been lucky, but the healer in our village? An outsider came, a friend of a clansman who'd heard of her abilities. This woman was desperate for a child and pursued Maeve for days trying to get her to see a child in her future. When finally Maeve saw only a cradle with cobwebs upon it, the woman was furious. She began to poison the minds of any who listen, how Maeve was a witch who could not be trusted."

Owen watched Maggie's expressive face, the sadness and the fear she didn't hide from him. He didn't want her to think he believed in all of this, but could not deny how watching someone accused of witchcraft must have affected her.

"Surely, Maeve's friends and family didn't believe this stranger," he said.

"Nay, but others did, especially those who'd not received the help they thought they'd been due. Eventually, Maeve was driven to flee for her life, leaving behind her family. I never forgot that, Owen. My family was all I had. I didn't want to shame them—I didn't want to leave them. I may not have allowed myself close friends, but I still had the love and support of my clan." Her lips twisted in a wry smile. "Even if I could never let anyone but my brother and mother truly know me."

She'd let her fears isolate her—and yet she'd still become a warm, loving woman instead of someone bitter at the fate she believed she'd been handed. He wanted to know more, but just then Maggie's cousins called for help to reach a bush just off the edge of the path. When he was done, he turned around and found Maggie completely gone. Helen innocently told him that Maggie had earlier mentioned a promise to help her mother. Owen knew it was an excuse, that Maggie had planned to abandon him, but he felt obligated to accompany the McCallum women until their baskets were full. Dorothy and Helen seemed so carefree and innocent, something Maggie had never been allowed to be.

He saw many of his clansmen scattered over the mountainside, and it eased his distracted thoughts to be participating in an event that had been handed down for centuries, perhaps even a millennium. He'd forgotten how it felt to be one with his people, with his land, harsh and rugged though it was.

And then Helen brought another handful of berries for the basket, and she looked so happy and sweet—a McCallum celebrating Lughnasadh with a Duff. It seemed suddenly both strange and wonderful. He and Maggie were helping to make that possible.

And when he found her again, he'd remind her that her life had begun to change, that she had the future of two clans to help mold. She didn't need to hold herself back.

An hour later, at dinner in the great hall, another overflow of food welcomed the berry pickers and those arriving for the horse race. Owen found Maggie with Cat and the Ladies McCallum and Duff, and Maggie gave him a sweet smile with a tinge of the devil in her eyes. Cat looked back and forth between them and tried to hide her amusement.

His mother bade him sit. "Come eat with us, Owen."

"Not if you're going to discuss needlework, Mother."

The two older ladies exchanged a look and a laugh.

He eyed them both, hands on his hips. "You honestly became friends because of needlework?"

Their smiles died and this second glance between them told a more sobering tale.

Lady Aberfoyle gave a deep sigh. "No, it wasn't just needlework, son. I soon realized who better to understand the kind of marriage I had—"

"—than one who had suffered through the same," Lady McCallum said kindly, putting her hand on Lady Aberfoyle's.

Owen found himself glancing helplessly at Maggie. Her eyes had a sheen of tears. Cat bowed her head.

His mother turned to Maggie. "I found it difficult when you arrived here."

Owen stiffened. "Mother—"

"Let Edith speak," Lady McCallum interrupted.

"Please do," Maggie added.

He clenched his jaw and remained silent. He didn't want his mother hurting Maggie any more than she already had. How many people had to mistrust his betrothed before she fled from his household for good?

*You* mistrust *her.*

This voice in his head was beginning to annoy him.

"Thank you for listening, Maggie," Lady Aberfoyle said. "I always knew my son would marry, of course, but I thought she would be an English bride, or at least a wealthy Lowland girl. He spent so much time in England, I just assumed . . ." She sighed. "And then he offered for you, and it was as if all of my recently dead husband's sins were being flung at my feet."

As his mother wiped a tear from the corner of her eye, all Owen could think was that she wanted pity.

"And to focus on myself was a mistake, of course," Lady Aberfoyle continued, "but so often in my life, with a man such as the late earl, if I didn't, no one else would take care of me. And no, Owen, you have always cared for me."

She probably could read his anger and bewilderment from even an eye twitch. Deadly pale, Cat watched their mother soberly.

"But my husband was dead," Lady Aberfoyle continued, "and I thought at last I would be free of the guilt of what I'd had to stand by and watch him do. But Maggie, you were a reminder I could not escape. I love you, Cat," she said, turning to face her daughter, "and I showed it too much. I knew your cousin Riona's parents were neglecting her, and I thought your compassion to her was sweet and inspiring. But your father—your father felt his brother was using his generosity. When it came time to live up to the contract your father had made with the late Laird McCallum, I watched, appalled, as he sent you away, Cat, and misled Riona into taking your place. Until that point, I had no idea he wished to change his mind. From your birth I'd pleaded with him to find another way to peace, to not betroth two children together, leaving them to bear the burden of the clans' expectations." She took a deep shuddering breath. "But did I do anything to stop his manipulation at the end? I did not. I didn't know how. And seeing you here, Maggie, betrothed to my son because he cared more for honor than his father did—it reminded me of all I'd done wrong. It was . . . so difficult to watch the man I'd freely married become more and more dishonorable with every year that passed. But that does not excuse my lack of welcome, as I tried to face everything that had happened. Can you forgive me, child?" she pleaded with Maggie.

No one said anything for a moment. Cat's shoulders shook beneath her bowed head. Lady McCallum still clutched Lady Aberfoyle's hand as if giving her support. Owen remembered that Lady McCallum had had to own up to standing by while her drunken husband abused innocents, committing even worse crimes.

Owen knew what he would have done in their place—but he was a man, used to the freedom of being in command and taking for granted the ability to make his own decisions. He wondered what would have happened if these two women had gone against their husbands in a world that permitted a husband to imprison his wife for no justifiable reason.

And then Maggie hugged his mother. "Of course, my lady. There is little enough for me to forgive."

He was stunned at Maggie's generosity to a woman

who'd treated her badly. Maggie seemed to believe that the past was the past, and that forgiveness enabled people to move on. He'd once asked for the same gift after leading her on when he'd been betrothed to another. But after her graciousness, he'd dismissed her dreams with scorn, and now he'd done it again. Even if he couldn't understand her dreams, he was beginning to see that *she* believed in them, that she honestly was trying to save his life. Her brother seemed too happy and in love to be plotting with her against the Duffs— his own wife's clan.

But that didn't mean Owen could ever accept such visions as the truth, and he wouldn't mislead her.

Lady Aberfoyle patted Maggie gratefully, wiped the tears from her eyes. "Thank you. Now I need to find my niece and apologize to her. This festival is a day of new beginnings, yes?"

Lady McCallum stood up as well, put an arm through her new friend's, and walked slowly with her.

Owen met his sister's wet-eyed gaze.

"Well," Cat said breathlessly, "that was something I never expected." She smiled at Maggie. "And we have your mother to thank, it seems."

"That's still a surprise, even to me," Maggie admitted, accepting the handkerchief Owen offered her.

"You don't have one for your sister, eh?" Cat teased.

"Yes, I do," he said, pulling another out of the sporran at his waist. "I was concerned I might be coming down with a cold."

Maggie and Cat chuckled, and Maggie looked upon him with a tenderness that he should welcome. He'd been countering her every attempt to prove herself a poor bride, with his own proof that she'd be anything but. His strategy was working.

Then why was he so uneasy? Women gave in to their emotions—it didn't mean that a man had to. Emotions just made one vulnerable, when as chief, as earl, he had to be in control of himself at all times.

He needed to eat and leave the hall, be on the back of a horse where no thoughts were involved, just instinct and skill and the bracing need to compete.

# CHAPTER 15

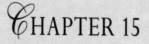

The sun was still lingering above the mountains when the competitors on horseback came thundering down the road toward the castle. Maggie stood just before the stone bridge over the moat, near the finish line in the meadow beyond. Her brother Brendan sat on the half wall, and she kept an arm around his waist. The horses' pounding hooves vibrated right through her, increasing the thrill. For a rare hour, she allowed herself to just enjoy the moment. Lady Aberfoyle's apology had both surprised and pleased her—mostly for Owen's sake. When Maggie had to leave him, she would like to think he and his family understood each other better.

"Hugh's in the lead!" Riona cried, practically jumping up and down.

"Nay, 'tis Owen," Maggie corrected mischievously.

"Hugh," Brendan said as if Maggie were blind.

But in truth, Maggie didn't know who was in the lead, and it really didn't matter to her. What mattered was the excitement of the men controlling their massive mounts. Especially Owen, she thought, feeling a little breathless. He leaned forward over the neck of his gelding; his bare legs beneath his plaid expertly guided the horse to do his bidding. Dozens of men trailed behind him, and more than just Hugh challenged him for the win. As the horses streamed across the final line, Maggie wasn't certain who had won.

But she decided the women had won, for soon the men were stripping off their plaids and following each other into the spring-fed moat, wearing just their shirts. They drenched the sweat from their bodies, and their shirts were clinging in a much-appreciated, if unseemly fashion.

"Oh, my," Cat said, a bit breathlessly, from where they all crowded to gape over the side of the bridge. To Maggie, she added, "We unmarried women can be quite overcome by such displays."

Brendan covered his ears.

Maggie could only grin at her, feeling a bit breathless herself. "Let's wave!" she urged Dorothy and Helen, hoping Owen would look up and notice them.

The two sisters waved, but Owen only captured Maggie's gaze with his own, and any remaining air in her lungs simply vanished. He'd been grinning, a rare sight on his face, but now that grin faded to a look of such intensity, she felt scorched. She had some sort of plan to dissuade this, she knew, but for the life of her, she couldn't remember it.

And then Hugh pushed Owen face-first into the water, breaking the spell.

Two Duff clansmen grabbed hold of Hugh by both arms and yanked him back. Riona cried out, then covered her mouth. Brendan stiffened and leaned forward as if he meant to jump into the water to defend his brother. Maggie tightened her grip around his waist to keep him from interfering. Hugh just kept laughing.

Owen got to his feet, sputtering, and called, "Surely ye cannot fault a man for wishing he'd defeated me?"

And there was that brogue again, Maggie thought with an inner thrill. Did he even realize he'd let down his guard again, been a Scottish chief rather than a British earl?

Hugh was released—at least the men had the decency to look abashed—and Owen clapped him on the back as they sloshed through water and then the reeds growing wild along the embankment. They all found their plaids where they'd left them, swinging them over their shoulders as they began an impressive group march toward the bridge. Fluttering with excitement, the castle women led the big procession into the courtyard.

In the great hall of the main towerhouse, servants headed to the kitchen to prepare for another feast, and all the men dispersed to their rooms to change. Maggie didn't know if Owen wished a hot bath, so she followed him up the stairs and caught him just as he opened the door to his room.

"Owen?" she called. "Should I send some serving boys with the bathing tub?"

He looked into his room, then gestured for her to come closer. Curious, she approached, only to have him take her arm and pull her inside.

"Owen!"

He took both her arms in his big hands and practically lifted her onto her toes. "Maggie, stop putting those poor cousins of yours in my way. I won't be waving to them, leading them on."

Her mouth opened and closed; she knew she should respond, but his sandy hair was dark with water as it brushed his shoulders. Even his eyelashes were spiky with moisture. One long drop slid slowly down his nose, mesmerizing her. His face looked shadowed from the whiskers that had grown during the day.

He gave her a little shake. "Do ye understand me, lass?"

The deep musical Scottish sound of his voice made her give a little internal moan. She didn't even realize she'd made a sound out loud, until he drew her right up against his wet body.

"I—I understand," she managed in a husky voice.

"I think ye need convincing."

And then he was kissing her, putting her back up against the door and pressing his hard, wet body along hers. She moaned and slid her arms around his neck, holding on as if she never wanted him to let go.

This was wicked, leading him on when she wouldn't marry him.

This was dangerous to her own well-being and self-respect.

And she didn't care. She wanted this—she wanted him. She felt herself tumbling into the rising passion as if falling into a deep pond and sinking down, down . . . She lost her breath, and it was glorious. His tongue mated with hers, and she explored his mouth with equal vigor.

He left her mouth to kiss his way down her neck and she tilted her head to give him even greater access. His hands continued to move on her body, from her waist and up her torso to skim the delicate flesh above her cleavage. Every touch made her shiver; the moistness of his tongue tracing along the lace of her décolletage made her moan.

"Your stays are not so tightly laced," he murmured against the top curve of her breast, his hands feeling her waist.

"I kept them loosened . . . in case we ate out in the grass."

"Perfect."

He gave a little tug down and she felt the constriction across her breasts ease. And then his hands were freeing her, her breasts indecently bare above the neckline of her gown. For a moment he lifted his head and kissed her again, while his hands cupped her breasts.

He was chilled from the water, and her skin was so very hot that it made her gasp and jump.

"Forgive me," he said, smiling against her mouth. "Let me try something warmer."

He bent his head and took her hard nipple into his mouth. She bit back a startled cry, shocked and aroused, helpless to look away as he licked and suckled. She felt it outward into every limb of her body, and then inward, deep in her most private places.

She wanted more, and she held his head to her, burying her fingers in the silky thickness of his hair.

When his hands reached beneath her skirt, she knew she'd been waiting for this, to feel so alive and wondrous again.

But it was wrong—she knew it was wrong. She wanted completion for herself, but couldn't offer it to him, not without ruining herself and perhaps getting with child.

"Stop, oh, Owen, we must stop," she pleaded. "I will not be your mistress and I cannot be your wife."

He lifted his head slowly and eyed her. Flustered and terribly sad, she didn't know what emotion he was trying to hide, anger or disgust or sadness. Her skirts fell from his hands, and she reached to cover her aching breasts.

Recklessly, she stumbled on. "I—I've thought of another way to satisfy the contract."

He took a step back from her. "I cannot believe

ye're bringing this up now," he said between clenched teeth.

"But I have to! If ye won't have one of my cousins, then I could marry one of yours."

His brows lowered so ominously she expected storm clouds to gather above the castle and rumble with thunder.

She rushed on. "After all, maybe they won't mind a wife who has difficulty staying thin. Surely ye've noticed, and ye must be so disappointed. It runs in my family, ye know."

She ran out of words and waited for him to berate her over her cousins or her girth, but instead, he suddenly wiped both hands down his face, then showed her an impassive expression with a touch of curiosity. As if he wasn't angry at all.

She thought of the tenderness he'd showed her, the one he so quickly masked, just like he masked most of his deeper emotions. If she married him, it would kill her to know he would have to hide disbelief, disdain, or maybe even pity over her dreams, as if he'd assumed she would have grown out of such childhood fancy. She'd spent her whole life hiding her true self from everyone but her brother and mother, and now she'd offered her secrets, her vulnerability, to him. She didn't want to be different, hadn't wanted to tell him he would die—she didn't *want* him to die. Two tears slipped down her cheeks.

This time his frown showed concern rather than anger. "Maggie—"

But she tugged her clothing into place even as she whirled, opened the door, and fled from him.

MAGGIE avoided Owen as much as she could during the banquet that evening, pleading a headache instead of dancing, because she couldn't bear to be in his arms. He was acting just as politely, giving her the same secret heated looks, as if she hadn't just rejected him—again. Any other man would give up on her for all the trouble she was causing. But not Owen. He was stubborn, and used to getting what he wanted. That was all it could be, she told herself, trying to ignore the little pain in her heart.

She had one more full day with her family, and she intended to enjoy it. After a restless night of little sleep, she spent the day watching a footrace among the children and then among the men, cheering on both her brothers. Cat put up a fuss about women not getting to compete at anything, and soon at least a dozen women—Maggie included—kicked off their shoes and stockings and raced barefoot across the meadow.

It was strange for Maggie to be a part of such an event after a lifetime of reserve, but it certainly felt good to be exhausted and laughing and not think about her problems.

At dinner, the bard professed a long recitation of the

Duff clan history, and Maggie translated for Riona and Cat, who, having been raised in England, were only now just learning their Gaelic.

That evening, Maggie took advantage of their new friendship by sitting down with Lady Aberfoyle and asking about the Duff family history, just as someone might who would be joining the family. Of course, her motive had deeper reasons, and she was able to steer the conversation toward details about Owen's closest male cousins. To her relief many of them were in attendance, and the lady helpfully pointed them out, including two bachelor cousins.

"There you are, Owen!" Lady Aberfoyle suddenly called to someone behind Maggie.

Maggie wanted to wince, then silently reminded herself she'd already told him her plan. She turned and gave him a pleasant smile.

"Maggie is quite ready to join the family now," Lady Aberfoyle said.

"Why specifically now?" Owen said, then raised an eyebrow at Maggie.

"Because she's been so interested in everyone," Lady Aberfoyle said. "I've just been pointing out your various cousins."

"You have?" Owen said with interest. "Then that means I should introduce them to her. Do you mind if I take Maggie away, Mother?"

Wearing a pleased smile, his mother agreed, and Maggie had no choice but to go with Owen.

"Interested in my family, are you?" he asked pleasantly, even as he slid a tight arm around her waist. "The male ones, perchance?"

She didn't confirm nor deny—what was the point? She spent the next half hour meeting various Duffs, all while Owen kept a possessive arm around her. Some she'd already seen in passing and hadn't even realized how closely related to Owen they truly were. She didn't want Owen to think he'd won, so she was eager and interested and asked polite questions of each one. Every so often she caught a glimpse of her mother regarding her dubiously, but Maggie ignored that, too.

Owen's cousins were attractive men—being so closely related to Owen, of course—and one, his second cousin, was an accomplished barrister in Edinburgh. He and Maggie would have the most in common, she knew.

But really—she was hardly going to do anything about finding a new husband right now. She was betrothed to the earl—it was Owen who needed to accept that she wouldn't marry him, to allow her her freedom to save her clan however she could. But he obviously wasn't ready to do that. Their wedding date was growing closer and closer, as he was so fond of pointing out; the banns had been read twice now. Was he honestly going to make her reject him before God, a priest, and everyone they knew, instead of joining with her to find a different solution?

Was he so confident that she was wrong, that he'd willingly risk death?

That night, she prepared for bed, already beginning to mourn the next day's departure of her family. When Kathleen had gone, Maggie pulled the counterpane down and fluffed her pillow—and saw a several pieces of folded paper sticking out from beneath. She froze, remembering the talisman she'd found in her bed ten days ago. Carefully, she pulled it out, opened it, and studied the writing on the first paper in surprise. It looked like her own hand, but something seemed . . . wrong.

She read the first paragraph and froze.

Owen, forgive me. I could not bear to be the cause of such dissent among your clan and disappoint my own people. With me gone, you'll be free to choose the woman you want. I won't suffer long, I promise. Drowning is a quick death.

Maggie gasped aloud and read it again, her hands trembling. She quickly went to the second page, which had a bold messy scrawl with the words:

Go home while you still can.

She slowly sank down on the bed—and hastily stood up again. She hadn't been chased away by fires, an evil talisman, rocks meant to trip her, or the anger of Martin and Gregor, so someone had decided to be far more direct.

*Go home while you still can.*

It was a cowardly act, anonymous taunts to scare her into abandoning the marriage and the contract between their clans.

Or was it not anonymous? Had Gregor or Martin already shown her their contempt, and when their hatred hadn't worked, they'd taken to threats?

She stared at the letter again, trying to think without letting her panic overwhelm her. Someone had copied her handwriting. The only samples were the letters to her family. And she knew they'd received them—at least some of them, because both her mother and Riona had mentioned them. So at least one of her letters had been either borrowed or stolen. Who had the skill to copy such a thing? So far, only two men had shown outright objection to the marriage and were her only suspects so far. It could be anyone, but she couldn't let herself panic over the unknown. She had to rule Gregor and Martin out first. She didn't know if either of the men could write, and that would be the place to start.

She buried the two notes deep in one of her chests, the one with her winter garments, and crawled into bed—after checking it thoroughly for any other unwelcome surprises, and pushing a chest in front of the door. She lay wide awake for a long time and considered if she should tell Owen or not. She'd been threatened, aye, but no one had tried to harm her.

But he needed to know. She'd been honest with him from the beginning, and she wasn't going to start lying now. She'd tell him . . . after her family left. She didn't trust Owen to keep it a secret from them, and all she'd need was *two* furious Highland chiefs keeping her locked up in her room as they looked for an enemy. The threats had been against her—she wasn't about to cower until they went away. However the contract was satisfied, there would be peace between the Duffs and the McCallums. She would see to it, and no one would stop her.

# CHAPTER 16

The next morning in the great hall, Maggie sniffed back her tears as she hugged her family good-bye. Riona and Cat held each other tightly, literally rocking in a fierce hug. Hugh practically lifted Maggie off the ground in a warm embrace.

"I don't like leaving ye like this," he said quietly.

Arms around his neck, she whispered in his ear. "It'll be all right, I've told ye that."

"We'll be back for the wedding," said her mother, not bothering to hide her tears as they clasped hands. "Only twelve days left."

Lady McCallum gazed at Maggie intently, saying even more with her eyes than she could with words, urging Maggie to come up with a solution before then.

To Maggie's surprise, even Brendan gave her a quick hug, then ran to his horse as if embarrassed. The party mounted and rode off, and Maggie watched until she could no longer see them, her chest aching with unshed tears. Owen remained with her, even when his mother and sister returned to the castle.

"Were you tempted to leave with them?" he asked dryly.

She looked up at him. "Not at all. I finish my commitments."

"Unless it's marriage to me."

"I could still be married," she hedged.

His mouth quirked in a faint smile. "Do you really think after last night that any of my cousins would dare cross me by asking to marry you?"

"If you freely give me to one of them, he might."

"Like a gift, as if you're my property?"

"Of course not," she scoffed. "I should have said when ye agree to revise the contract."

"And you said 'one of them.' Randomly. It doesn't matter which one. So love doesn't matter?"

"I didn't say that—*you* did. I'll take the time to know them better."

"And how do you plan to accomplish that without damaging your reputation?"

"I don't know. I'm giving it thought." She began to walk toward the castle.

"I've been patient, Maggie," he called in a low voice.

She paused, looking over her shoulder but not meeting his gaze. "But not open-minded."

She thought of her dream again—she wasn't even certain they were already married in it. What if just planning a ceremony and attending that day was enough to make it all come true?

She should tell him about the letter right now, so they could put their heads together, in case it had something to do with her wedding day. But not until Hugh was far enough away that Owen couldn't send her with him. Tonight.

She continued to walk, and he didn't catch up to her. There was no point in wasting the day, not when Martin had not gone home to the village yet. Maggie first had to find out who was so against uniting their clans that they'd threaten her with death.

She was very careful walking over the bridge, and with thoughts of a suicidal drowning, the water below wasn't soothing or picturesque.

Most of the guests were still lingering over breakfast, and Maggie had no problem spotting Martin Hepburn and his daughter. Maggie forced herself to speak to guests at a table near them first, and to her relief, when Martin saw her so close, he grumbled something to his daughter and left. Maggie excused herself from the one table and went to his.

His daughter was saying good-bye to another couple, red-faced and glancing down the hall to where her father was disappearing outside.

"Good morning," Maggie called to her.

The woman came to a stop, wide-eyed.

"Forgive me," Maggie continued, "but we were never properly introduced."

"Ye're Mistress Maggie," Martin's daughter said, her voice practically a squeak. "His lordship's betrothed."

"And ye're . . ."

"Nellie Hepburn." She lowered her gaze. "My da should not have run off like that. 'Twas impolite."

"I do not mind. I ken 'tis difficult to change the hearts of those who've spent their whole lives thinking one way." She paused. "Are ye willing to give peace between our clans a chance?"

Nellie's big brown eyes went wide. "I'm a woman like you, mistress. We don't want our men dying for what amounts to a matter of pride."

"I'm so glad to hear that. I'd like to help find a way to convince others like your father that I mean well. If I write him a letter, would it help?"

Nellie shook her head. "Mistress, he cannot read."

Ah, just what Maggie needed to know.

"Could ye read my note to him?"

"I wouldn't be able to do more than make out a few of the letters," she said, blushing.

"I'm sorry. Then might I visit ye sometime? Ye live in the village?"

Nellie's expression showed a bit of fear. "I'm not sure that's wise just yet. I promise to bring him to the castle more often so he can see how good ye are for his lordship."

Maggie actually felt herself blush. "I—what a kind thing to say."

"The way the two of ye look at each other . . .'tis very romantic." Now it was Nellie's turn to blush.

Maggie touched the woman's arm. "Thank ye."

"Just the truth, mistress. But please, as for my da. Leave him to me, ye ken?"

"I do."

She watched Nellie hurry away, shoulders hunched, and Maggie felt sorry she'd had to upset the woman so. But if no one in Martin's family could write, then she could cross him off her list.

As for Gregor, Kathleen had mentioned he'd owned a smithy in the colonies. Surely he knew how to write.

LATER that evening, Owen relaxed for what felt like the first time all day. The farewells that morning had been hard for Maggie. He felt relieved himself. He'd been concerned that Maggie would finally confess to her family her refusal to marry, especially after trying to find other eligible Duffs. Her brother would have been forced to attempt to take her home. That wasn't going to happen, and it could very well have been a standoff between the two men. Owen had grown to respect Hugh over the last few days, and hadn't wanted that to happen.

Owen was no longer surprised by the power of his obsession with Maggie. He found himself watching her whenever they were in the same room. She'd surprised him by talking to Martin Hepburn's daughter earlier that day. Owen might have thought it was random, that she was just being polite, but she'd seemed to focus right in on the Hepburns. Strange.

And then this evening, one of his cousins arrived, one who hadn't been in attendance the previous day. When Owen saw Maggie smiling as she spoke to him, Owen had felt such an overwhelming feeling of jealousy and possession, he'd had to stay away from them, lest he overreact. It felt like every part of the refined, logical man he'd once been was being stripped away, bit by bit, as if his ancestors were claiming him back to the Highlands, urging him to take the woman who was his.

When he saw Maggie to her room for bed, she tried to speak to him, but he wasn't in the mood to listen, not with how confused he was feeling. He retreated to his own bedroom and when, not a quarter of an hour later, someone knocked, he opened the door, ready to confront Maggie.

But it was the housekeeper, and she was twisting her hands together uncharacteristically.

He frowned. "Mrs. Robertson, is something wrong?"

"Might I speak with ye, my lord?" she murmured, looking down the hall.

At Maggie's room.

Owen stepped back and she followed him inside. He closed the door and regarded her, folding his arms over his chest. "What is this about?"

She bit her lip, then reached into a hidden pocket in

the folds of her skirt and pulled out a sheet of paper. "I thought I'd left one of Lady Aberfoyle's chests in Mistress Maggie's room, my lord. I was searching for an item she wanted, and I admit I was in hurry, and tossing things this way and that. But . . . I came across this. Oh, my lord, I—I—" And then she bowed her head.

Alarmed, he read:

Owen, forgive me. I could not bear to be the cause of such dissent among your clan and disappoint my own people. With me gone, you'll be free to choose the woman you want. I won't suffer long, I promise. Drowning is a quick death.

He stared at the words, unable to believe what they said. Maggie was so unhappy being forced to marry him that she wished to do herself harm?

A coldness seemed to seize his chest, making it hard to breathe.

"My lord?" Mrs. Robertson said hesitantly. "I'm so sorry."

He nodded, then as if from a distance, heard himself say, "I'll take care of this. I'll see her safe. Do not tell anyone what you have seen."

Mrs. Robertson bobbed her head several times, then shook it, looking panic-stricken, before hurrying away.

He stood still for a moment, unable to move. The thought of a world without Maggie . . . And then the coldness that had frozen him began to crack one painful piece at a time, stabbing him. He'd never imagined how much she'd grown to mean to him, had never imagined the sorrow of knowing she was so terribly unhappy, she'd rather die. He should have let her go with her brother—

But she hadn't asked him. Did even the chance to escape marriage not matter anymore?

He closed his door and walked swiftly to her room. He didn't think about knocking, didn't even know what he would say to her. He just opened the door.

She was wearing naught but her thin nightshift, bent over a chest, clothing dumped on the floor. She cried out when he appeared so suddenly, then put a hand to her chest.

"Och, Owen, why did ye scare me like that?"

She looked so normal, her usual exasperation with him evident, but it didn't help. All the while she'd been insisting she couldn't marry him, she'd been sinking more and more into despair. He'd driven her to this.

When he didn't say anything, she frowned and rose slowly to her feet. "What is it? What's wrong?"

He didn't know what to say or how to explain it. He should ask logical questions and discover the answer. But all he could do was hold up the paper.

"Oh, I was just looking—" Those unusual eyes went wide. "Owen—I didn't write this, I swear to ye. Here's the second part of the note that must have gotten mixed up between the garments."

He just stared at her, then said hoarsely, "I didn't

find it. Mrs. Robertson . . ." He trailed off. Would Maggie lie now that she'd been discovered? When he had the proof right there?

"Oh, Owen," she murmured in a voice far too tender. "I would never take such a cowardly way out. Ye ken I'm a fighter—I've been fighting ye all along. Here, read this one."

He took the paper and had to force his eyes to focus.

Go home while you still can.

"Someone forged my writing," Maggie said grimly. "They just wanted to scare me, I know. I found it last night."

"Last night?" he repeated, with only a faint echo of anger. He was too relieved, too overcome.

"I couldn't show ye this morn," she insisted. "My brother was still too close and ye might have made me leave with him. I was going to show ye earlier tonight, but ye didn't want to talk to me."

"I was . . . angry about my cousins." His anger seemed ridiculous, so minor in the scheme of all that had been revealed to him about how he felt about Maggie.

Suddenly, he captured her face in both hands. "Ye're telling me the truth, lass," he whispered.

She cupped his face in return. "Aye, I swear on God and the Virgin Mary."

And then he was kissing her, her trembling mouth,

her damp cheeks, her fluttering eyelids. He kissed her
forehead, her mouth again, her neck, and then pulled
her so hard into his embrace, he heard the air leaving her lungs with a gasp. She smelled of lavender
and herself, and with his hands he discovered how
soft her back was. He clumsily pulled at the tie of her
long braid, and soon her dark, rippling hair flowed far
down her back.

He was separated from her skin by the sheerest
linen nightshift. No padding hid her delicate waist. He
slid his hands down and cupped her ass, molding her,
then bringing her hard against his hips.

"Maggie," he said against her throat. "Maggie."

She arched against him, as if she, too, couldn't be
close enough.

He didn't know what to touch first. Through her
garment, her skin felt smooth and warm. For the first
time he cupped her breasts unbound, and they filled
his hands.

"I need to feel you, Owen," she whispered, almost
shyly.

And then her hands were at his belt, and somehow his plaid was falling and only his shirt and her
shift separated them. He pulled her back against him
harder, lifting her knee, spreading her thighs, pressing
himself against the soft heat there. She cried out and
clutched him to her, feeling his back and lower, grab-
bing his ass as he'd done to her.

For just a moment they rocked together, his penis

rubbing along the length of her. He felt her knees soften, and then he picked her right up and carried her to the bed. He set her on her feet, and she started to fist the nightshift at her hips, but he stopped her. She looked so suitably worried that he found himself smiling.

"Allow me."

He took the folds in his hands and moved slowly upward, letting the fabric drag along her thighs. He kissed her, head slanted, mouth opened hungrily over hers. She kept her hands on his chest as if she'd fall without his support.

And then he could touch her waist, and his hot hands cupped her there and moved slowly higher, her nightshift draping over his arms. He took her breasts in his hands and for a long minute he played with them, cupping, kneading, gently twisting her nipples, then caressing to soothe them. She didn't seem to be able to take a deep enough breath, and neither could he.

At last he needed to see her, and he drew the nightshift right over her head and stepped back. She stood there, chin lifted, her body slightly trembling. The candles scattered through the room made her body glow, the brightest, most beautiful thing in the shadowy room.

He bent to take her breast deeply into his mouth even as he played with the other one. Her arms went behind and she braced herself on the bed, head dropped back, her dark hair vivid against the pale sheets.

Dropping to one knee, Owen kissed his way down

her soft belly, and then nuzzled at the silky hair of her sex. He thought she would protest, but she only moaned and spread her thighs. She excited him, Maggie did. Bold and unafraid and a match for him in every way. He stroked her with his tongue, then lifted her thigh and went deeper, against the heart of her, where he wanted to be.

She clutched his hair, murmuring his name, her excited pants growing faster. He circled her clitoris with his tongue, then stroked, reaching up to caress her breast. She arched backward as she reached her ultimate pleasure, and he kissed her softly before rising.

Her eyes, blue and green, were half closed with pleasure and satisfaction, but no shame. Then she stared down at his shirt, where it stuck straight out at her hips. He didn't hesitate, only pulled the garment over his head.

But she scooted back on the bed and reached for him. He climbed up and over her on all fours, staring at her hair gloriously tumbled around her shoulders like a dark sun. He settled down between her thighs, kissing her with urgency again. She moved restlessly against him, lifting her knees, clutching his hips hard, and it was as natural as breathing to slide into her. She gave a little gasp, and he stilled.

"Nay, it doesn't hurt much," she said. "It just surprised me."

"Tell me if there's any pain," he whispered against her mouth.

He started moving then, withdrawing until she cried out as if he'd leave her, then surging back inside with the satisfaction of knowing she desired him. He couldn't stop himself, the pleasure taking over his mind, his will. He thrust hard and deep, over and over, knowing he should wait for her to climax again, but unable to. He cried out with the passionate release, shuddering, surging, feeling only her heels against his ass, watching through half-closed eyes as she flung her arms exuberantly wide and looked up at him with such a wicked, delicious smile, none of her reluctance and diffidence there.

She was his, at last, forever.

And then reality came back to him, not with slow, languid pleasure, but with the dawning realization that he might have shown her too much, too much desperation and need, shown her how much he cared, how lost he'd be without her.

He didn't want to be so controlled by his emotions, by a woman. When he gave in like that, that darkness seemed to rise up and possess him. He'd spent his lifetime learning to manipulate his very will, and he'd just surrendered it all to this obsession with a woman who wouldn't marry him.

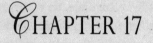

# CHAPTER 17

$S$till joined to Owen so intimately, Maggie saw immediately when he began to withdraw from her—both physically and emotionally. It was his expression first, steadily changing from passion to contentment to wariness and then at last into utter impassivity. Then he left her body, leaving her feeling so very empty, rolled off her and right out of bed. Suddenly, she felt too wanton, too sinful, and she pulled a sheet over her.

She should be used to his behavior. He'd done his best not to allow her a glimpse of his emotions, of his vulnerabilities. When she'd seen his reaction to the suicide letter, she'd felt they'd at last reached a deeper level—she'd known she wasn't just a bargaining tool between two powerful clans. Her love trapped unacknowledged in her heart could be denied no longer, and she'd given herself to him, *made love* with him. She didn't want to regret it, but apparently he did.

He poured water in the basin and washed his face and hands, as if he needed to be free of the scent of her.

Oh, now she was the one who was letting her doubts hold sway, reading too much into a simple act. He'd told her he'd desired her from the beginning. His emotional retreat wasn't about the physical connection between them.

He hadn't drawn on his clothing yet, so perhaps that was a good sign. She could study him at will, at the patterns formed by candle and shadow on every sculpted muscle of his body. He was masculine and overwhelming, and he made her skin heat just by seeing all that splendid . . . man. He had a few small scars just to make things interesting and intriguing.

And then he turned to face her, and she saw that he was aroused again, that he still desired her. She wanted to melt back into the pillows, to draw back the sheets and offer herself to him.

And with her luck, a baby and a wedding ceremony would be the result. Oh, God, had she just guaranteed that she'd *have* to marry him?

She burst into tears.

She saw Owen's shock for only a moment before she had to cover her face and hunch there, growing more and more miserable. She wanted to curl into a little ball and stay hidden for the rest of her life. It was all too much.

"Maggie?"

She felt his hands on her back, and she wanted to

shrug him off, but that would take too much effort. And for a moment, the heat of a human hand felt so comforting.

"Maggie, talk to me. Did I hurt you?"

Even his brogue was gone again. She cried harder.

"I promise you, I did not make love to you to force our wedding."

And now he could read her mind. How could he know parts of her so well, but not trust her? The tears were flowing so fast she had to use the sheet to mop them up. And then he put a handkerchief in her hands, and she blew her nose.

"I c-can't marry ye, Owen, and wonderful though this was, it didn't change my mind. It makes me realize even more powerfully that I won't watch you die."

He said nothing for so long that at last she had to lift her face to him. Through watery eyes, she could read nothing in his expression, nothing at all. Maybe it was better that he couldn't love her. And that made her shoulders shake with sobs, because she loved him, hopelessly, helplessly, pointlessly. If he returned her love, the tragedy of their eventual separation would be even worse.

"Ye need to leave, Owen. I just can't talk about this anymore."

"But we haven't discussed the letter."

"In the morning. And if ye see Mrs. Robertson before I do, please explain about the letter, and ask her to keep quiet about it. And now, I just . . . need to be alone."

And like a child, she rolled beneath the counterpane and turned her back on him. She could hear him dressing. She stiffened as he spoke.

"Lock the door, Maggie. If it makes you feel safer, put a chest in front of it. There's someone in this castle who can't accept peace, regardless of who gets hurt."

"Very well," she mumbled.

It seemed terribly long until the door finally closed. Knowing Owen was right, she turned the key in the lock, then rushed back to bed, crying all over again for what felt like forever, until her head ached and her nose was raw from blowing.

Love and disappointment were so horribly painful. She wished she could be like him, only having to deal with facts.

As she lay there, too tired to even hold to her convictions, her doubts began to taunt her. Could she have interpreted the dream incorrectly? Could Owen be right, that it was only a nightmare? She hadn't had a true dream vision in ten years.

Oh, she could begin to doubt everything now. After all, she'd slept with him when she knew she wouldn't marry him. She'd led him to think her intentions were honorable, when they really weren't.

But he'd led her to think she meant something to him. And she started to sob again.

It had taken a long time for Maggie to fall into an exhausted sleep. When a knock on the door awoke her, she felt bleary-eyed and little rested.

"Who is it?" she croaked.

"Kathleen, mistress. I'd come in, but the door seems to be locked."

Maggie groaned. "Give me a moment."

She sat up, feeling a muscle twinge here and there. Beside her, there was a spot of blood on the sheets. She yanked the counterpane up. She would have to try to remove the stain herself. She didn't think Kathleen would spread her secrets about, but she wasn't taking that chance. No one was going to be able to force her to marry.

After wrapping the dressing gown around her, she opened the door to find Kathleen only the first servant in line. The rest carried in a bathing tub and buckets of hot water.

"I know ye usually bathe at night, mistress, but his lordship reminded me that ye hadn't."

"How kind of him," Maggie said, striving to sound calm.

Very well, it *was* kind of him to remember, she thought grudgingly. And then she looked at all the faces of the young men and boys carrying buckets, all of whom nodded as they passed her, but most did not meet her eyes. How was she ever going to know who wished her gone? Were there young men who'd be angry that they didn't get to try their skills against the enemy they grew up hating? She felt sad and frustrated—and then angry with her weakness. Anyone who did not see the advantage of peace was a fool.

After the tub was filled, another bucket left near at hand for rinsing, Kathleen finished laying out Maggie's clothes and departed.

Maggie practically moaned when she sank into the tub. She was so grateful it had been fashioned for a big man, because she could sink almost to her chin. She let the heat soothe her mildly aching muscles, and wished it could wipe away all her mental anguish, too.

As she was lazily soaping her arms, a knock sounded and the handle turned. Nothing happened.

"Maggie?"

It was Owen's voice, and though she'd known she would have to face him soon, she was a little too pleased to say, "'Tis locked. You may return in half an hour."

There was no answer for a long moment, and then he politely said, "Very well."

Was she actually disappointed? What was wrong with her? He was a man who only wanted her for her body and as a pawn in a feud. He thought she was either a liar or simpleton. And now she had to worry that she was carrying his babe.

And yet she wanted him to walk in on her naked?

She groaned and put her head back on the rim of the tub. She really was a simpleton. A lovesick simpleton. That could be the only explanation.

She had less than a half hour—she'd better hurry.

When he knocked again, precisely on time, Kathleen was still lacing her gown into place.

"Just a moment, my lord," Kathleen called.

"I should have had you write him a note," Maggie said. "Then he would have given us more time." She watched the maid out of the corner of her eye.

"Aye, no matter. I'm about done."

Maggie nodded and tried not to sag with frustration. It was pointless to question Kathleen—surely Gregor could write.

At last, Kathleen opened the door, bobbed a little curtsy to Owen, and departed. Owen shut the door behind him and stood there.

Maggie hadn't known how she'd feel when she saw him again. He was studying her with those dark eyes, and she felt uncomfortably aware of what he'd done to her in the night, the intimate things he'd . . .

Oh, damn, now she was blushing.

"Yes?" she asked, trying to sound cool and unaffected.

And then she realized that he was carrying a tray.

"I brought you breakfast. May I sit down?"

She gestured to the little table near the window, where he proceeded to place individual plates, a bowl of porridge, as well as a platter in the center piled with bacon, salted herring, and fried eggs. It felt strange to have him serving her, but he owed her a lot more than that.

She sat down and placed a napkin across her lap, and watched him do the same. He filled a small bowl with porridge for her, then set a small helping of everything else on her plate, even as she broke open a warm bannock and sniffed appreciatively. They ate silently for several minutes, until at last Owen eyed her.

"You look refreshed this morning. I trust you slept well?"

She sighed. "Not really. I had a difficult time falling asleep."

"I'm sorry."

She wanted to ask him exactly what he was sorry for, but she didn't. The words were an easy thing to say and were seldom meant.

"Before we discuss the letter, I wish to discuss our lovemaking," he said.

Maggie lifted up her head sharply. "Ye cannot mean that."

"I wanted you to know I did not plan it, that I would never deliberately try to trap you into marriage."

"I didn't think ye did."

"I am relieved. But regardless, if there's a child—"

"Then we will discuss it."

"I will not allow a child of mine to be born a bastard," he said firmly.

"I didn't say I would either. But Owen, if we marry, ye could die!"

"We're all going to die. But before I do, I'll have ye to wife."

She closed her eyes. Did he know what he did to her when his brogue peeked out? And why was he so bloody dense?

She took a calming breath. "Let's discuss the letter."

He touched her arm again. "I had a strong reaction to it. I can only imagine how it was for you. You are a composed young woman to have handled that without running for help."

"And what would that have done? I want whoever this is to think he's cowed me, to think he's succeeding. And besides, think ye I've not had terrible information before that I could share with few people?"

He only nodded, took another bite of bacon, and chewed before swallowing. "Is this the first open threat?"

"Aye, 'tis the first threatening me with serious harm, but there've been other issues that have demonstrated how upset this villain is."

"Both fires and the talisman," he said.

She nodded. "I'm assuming it's the same person, although we can't be certain right now. When we were up on the mountain leaving the standing stones and I fell? I'd already traveled that path three times, between accompanying Euphemia and you. Those rocks weren't there before. They were placed right where we came over a crest in the path, and couldn't see them without tripping over them."

He slowly set down his knife. "Why did you not tell me this?"

"It seemed . . . foolish, and there was no way to prove I was correct. But now, with the letter, 'tis no longer just a few things to annoy me. I told ye about what I overheard Gregor say against me—which he's done more than once, I believe." She arched a brow.

"Yes, he did try to talk me out of marrying you. Do you think he's the one who's taken this so far?"

"He's not the only one angry with me, but yesterday I confirmed that Martin Hepburn can't read."

"Ah, I wondered why you were talking to Nellie."

"Ye're not going to ask if I revealed too much?"

"I trust you."

Stunned, she stared at him. It took everything in her not to refute that, because if he trusted her, he'd respect her fears about his death. But she had to admit, Owen had shown a small amount of trust: he hadn't taken control of the investigation, told her not to worry about it and let a man handle it. Her brother probably would have, at least before his marriage to a strong woman.

"And there's Gregor," Maggie finally continued, "he's not from here, not really. He's spent most of his life in the colonies and only heard the stories of the feud. He hasn't experienced the pain of needless death and destruction."

"None of us have, at least between Duff and McCallum, since the marriage contract signed at Cat's birth."

"Then why would he want to resurrect that all over again?"

"I don't know," Owen mused. "And we can't say for certain it's him."

"Nay, we cannot."

He sat back in his chair and took a sip of his ale. "I must admit it's hard for me to believe one of my own people would be so cruel to a woman. I fear what will happen if I don't send you away."

"Ye're not sending me away. I'm not a coward, Owen, and I won't be coddled."

"So you're saying you refuse to back down before this villain and you'll marry me regardless?"

"I'll make sure the contract is satisfied in some manner."

He frowned and spoke coldly. "You're not marrying a cousin of mine. If you're carrying my child—"

"I thought we agreed not to bring that up!"

As if his words had power, she remembered again his naked body on her, in her, the way he set her afire, the way he could make her moan. She kept her gaze on her plate until her thoughts were under control.

"What if I question Kathleen again?" she asked.

She glanced up at him, only to find him gazing pointedly at her cleavage. She cleared her throat.

He looked up and blinked several times. "Forgive me, what did you say?"

"I said I could question Kathleen again."

"No, we don't want her to alert her brother. I had a

chance earlier this morn to talk to my uncle. He says that Gregor has relatives in Ledard, a village not too far from here. Perhaps they know something about Gregor or his parents. I will go and speak to them today."

"I will come with ye," she said solemnly. "Who knows what danger I would be in here without ye to protect me?"

He grimaced. "My uncle is my war chief. I imagine he can keep you safe."

"He's getting old."

He exhaled. "Very well. Can you be ready in an hour? It's several hours' journey."

"I'll ask Mrs. Robertson to see to provisions for us."

He stood up and began to gather their breakfast.

"I'll do that," she said. "You go see to the horses."

He was looking at her with such intensity that her breath caught. She tried to remain composed, but it was difficult. At last he nodded and left her alone, and she could breathe easier again. Somehow she would find a way to deal with him and not let her emotions show.

If he knew she'd fallen in love with him, he'd have even more ways to manipulate her into marriage.

# CHAPTER 18

It was a rare cloudless day in the summer, and the blue sky was like a tent stretching from mountaintop to mountaintop. Maggie breathed deeply once the castle was no longer in sight, and she realized how oppressive it had felt, knowing people hated her being there. She rode easily on the mare's back, and Fergus and another clansman lingered far enough behind Owen and her that if they wanted to talk, they wouldn't be overheard.

"I cannot fathom why you look so content," Owen said, riding beside her.

She squinted at him in the sun. "Because I haven't left that castle in almost three weeks. I feel like I can breathe again."

"You despise my home so much?"

"Ye ken that's not what I mean," she said impatiently. "I feel a rising dread there, Owen, every time ye speak about marrying me."

"If you're so worried about me dying, then you must feel something."

"I don't want your death on my conscience."

He looked straight ahead at that, and his expression smoothed right out. She eyed him curiously. Was he, perhaps, thinking that the chance of him becoming wounded was greater, now that the threats against her were escalating?

"You haven't brought me any books that you're studying lately," Owen said.

Changing the subject. Interesting. "There hasn't been time, what with the festival and my family's visit."

"There are so many things we could discuss. I wanted to tell you about an invention I saw demonstrated in London, a diving bell for breathing under water. They lower it into the water, and when the swimmer stays beneath it, the air is trapped so he can breathe. They even replenish the air with weighted barrels of air sent down from the surface."

"Are ye wishing to breathe under water, Owen?" she asked quietly, feeling the first touch of sympathy for him over Emily's drowning. Had it affected him more than he let on?

He gave her a confused look. "It is simply a fascinating device."

"Emily drowned. And now someone's threatened me with drowning. And ye bring up the diving bell."

"You're reading too much into my curiosity, Maggie." And he faced forward again.

She knew a dismissal when she experienced it. She let him mull her words.

At Ledard, a small collection of stone cottages at the edge of a hill roamed by cattle, Owen tried to keep their arrival low-key, but when they had to ask for Gregor's relatives, word spread. By the time they were heading to a small home on the outskirts, Maggie turned around and saw at least a dozen people gathered together on the central green, talking and watching them. Once she would have made a joke about his celebrity, but she held back now.

Owen dismounted and came to help her, but she slid down before he could. The less touching, the better, she thought. He knocked on the door, and an elderly woman's voice could be heard, calling for patience. It was a long minute before she opened the door, her back hunched beneath a rounded hump, her hand braced on a cane.

"Aye?" she asked in a high-pitched, querulous voice.

"Mrs. Kincaid?"

She put a hand to her ear, and he raised his voice and repeated himself.

"Aye, and who are ye?" She squinted at both of them with interest but not suspicion.

"I'm Owen Duff and this is my betrothed, Maggie."

He left off his fancy title, Maggie saw, and her surname, as well.

"Ye're Himself!" Mrs. Kincaid said in obvious delight. "Come in, come in!"

Owen nodded to Fergus, who waited outside with the horses, then had to duck to enter the single room with its earthen floor. Mrs. Kincaid had them sit down at her wooden table side by side on a bench, and after putting two tankards of ale before them, she took the chair.

"O' course new chiefs like to know their clan," Mrs. Kincaid said, "but to think ye're paying a call on me!"

They each took a sip of ale to be polite.

Owen smiled. "We do have business to discuss, Mrs. Kincaid. I understand you're related to Gregor and Kathleen Duff?"

"Two of my sister's children. They live in the colonies."

Maggie's eyes widened when Owen glanced at her before speaking.

"They're recently returned and have taken up residence at Castle Kinlochard. Kathleen is a maid, and Gregor works in the smithy."

"Ah, his misfortunes followed him, I see."

"Misfortunes?"

Her eyes were still sharp beneath heavily wrinkled eyelids. "So ye don't know much about them?"

"Very little, which is why I'm curious."

"Have they done ye wrong?"

"I don't believe so, but I know little of them and wish to be prepared."

"And ye're not saying why the chief himself would be visitin' an old lady."

Maggie hid a smile, and Owen said nothing.

Mrs. Kincaid sighed. "Weel, I believe in supporting Clan Duff. All I have is the letters I received from the family over the years. Do give them back to me when ye're done."

"Of course I will," Owen said.

After accepting the care of a packet of old yellowed letters tied with string, Owen paused when Mrs. Kincaid laid a hand on his arm.

"Remember that the family suffered for their decision to leave us," the old woman said quietly. "I know not what has happened to them that brings ye here, but they're my sister's children, and I need ye to try to understand them." She looked at Maggie, as if she needed a woman's confirmation.

"We will, ma'am, and thank ye," Maggie said. After the door shut behind them, she whispered to Owen, "Those letters sound intriguing."

"They do, but they must await my business in the village."

Maggie accompanied Owen for an hour spent in Ledard, introducing himself to those who didn't know him and hearing their concerns. Maggie held back, not wanting her McCallum name to be debated. After they left, they traveled a mile or so to reach a meadow beside a stream, some distance from the village, for their midday meal. Maggie offered a wrapped package of beef and cheese to Fergus and the other guard, who went off a distance to see to the horses.

"Ye've got wise men there," Maggie said, as she removed more packages from her saddlebag.

He only nodded, showing little interest in the food but much interest in carefully untying the letters so as not to damage them. There were dates on each, so he read them aloud in order. Many were concerning an important event or tragedy, Mrs. Kincaid's sister's death first, the deaths of the other children, the smithy that their father built which struggled along, then his death and Gregor taking over.

Owen frowned as he studied the final letter.

"What is it?" Maggie asked.

"This last one was written by Kathleen, defending her brother." Owen read silently a moment, then looked up at Maggie. "She's insisting that their Scottish relatives not believe the worst of Gregor, that he had good reason to publicly accuse a local woman of being a witch."

Maggie's mouth sagged open, and suddenly she didn't think she'd even be able to eat another bite. Her worst fear, that she'd be accused of witchcraft . . . and Gregor had done that to someone. Could he somehow know about her dreams, and that was why he was targeting her, why he might have put the talisman in her bed? Was it more than her just being a McCallum?

Owen reached across the blanket and briefly clasped her hand. "Stop. I can see every thought crossing your face. Gregor knows nothing about you."

She nodded, knowing he was probably right, but

her mouth was dry and it was proving difficult to swallow. He handed her a flask of cider and she took a deep swallow. "What else does it say?"

Owen read the words aloud, "'Dear Gregor had good reason to believe this woman a witch. He'd courted her himself and had seen the signs.'"

"She'd probably rejected him, and this was how he repaid her," Maggie said coldly.

Owen nodded. "A logical conclusion. 'This evil woman rallied her family and neighbors against Owen, and his business suffered. I don't know how much longer we can remain here.'" He looked up. "And that's it. They must have made the decision to return to Scotland right after this letter."

"How lucky for us," she said sarcastically. Then she gave Owen a searching glance. "Is this enough to believe he's the one out to frighten me away? It seems his goal is to end the peace between clans, not do me bodily injury."

"It is enough to question him, perhaps even confine him, before bringing it up at the next assembly of gentlemen," Owen said grimly.

Maggie sighed. "I don't know how I'll tell Kathleen. He's the only brother she has left. How many siblings died?"

"Five others."

She hugged herself. "Should I ask her about the witchcraft charge he made?"

"Why? I know it feels personal to you, but I doubt

even more information on the subject will matter to us. It's enough to know he behaved dishonorably to another woman, and came here in desperation. I imagine they thought the childhood they left behind was rosier than the reality."

"I know she said Gregor wasn't happy to be working for someone else."

Owen shrugged. "If you cannot afford to buy a business, you have to save for it somehow."

"I imagine that is the fault of the McCallums, too."

They finished their meal mostly in awkward silence. At last Maggie wrapped the remains and stored them away while Owen tightened the saddle girths. When it came time to help her mount, he put his hands on her waist, she looked up into his eyes, and for just a moment, she wished so many things could be different, that they were just two people looking ahead to marriage, without the complications of clans and enemies both internal and external. Then she heard their two guards talking near the road, and she looked away from Owen and all of her sad what-ifs.

The journey back to the castle was uneventful, with little to discuss. Maggie mostly dwelled on sad thoughts until they were beginning the climb up the final hill before leveling into the meadow surrounding the castle. Suddenly a crack sounded, Maggie felt a whistle of air past her, and her horse reared. Controlling the animal took all her concentration, and by the time she looked up, Fergus and the other guard were already halfway up the hill, their horses taking the incline easily. Owen was in front of her, standing in the stirrups, blocking her with his body as he tried to see into the distance. She saw no telltale sign of blood on his clothing, and tried to relax her galloping heart.

"What happened?" she cried, guiding her horse up beside him.

He pointed and ordered, "That way, hide in the copse of trees. Ride quickly. I'll follow."

She didn't protest, just did as he ordered. Her back itched as if someone was aiming for it. She took a deep breath only when the shadows swallowed her up. She followed a deer path until several trees were between her and the road.

They'd been shot at. It could have been a British patrol or someone from a rival clan, but . . . she knew better. A sense of coldness moved through her, filling her, chilling her.

"Are ye all right?" Owen demanded.

She gave a start, not having even heard him approach. A villain could have come upon her and done anything. She was a fool.

"I'm fine," she said grimly.

Owen leaned toward her and plucked at her sleeve. She stared down at the hole torn through—and the trickle of blood. Her mouth sagged a moment before she said, "I don't even feel a sting."

His warm hand gripped her arm, and he studied it closely. "Just grazed ye. Won't even leave a scar." And then he stared at her with eyes warm with concern and frustration.

"That person couldn't have been aiming at me," she said, her bravado growing fainter.

He grimaced. "Ye've been threatened already."

"Well . . . we have to go see who it is!" she said, and as if sensing her eagerness, the horse gave a little dance sideways.

"My men will return with their report. We'll wait until then."

He kept looking at her arm until she wished to hide it. "Owen, stop. 'Tis nothing."

"It could have been everything," he said solemnly. "I could have lost ye."

She didn't know what to say to that. The Owen she was used to normally revealed nothing in his voice, but for once, she heard regret and sadness.

"I already introduced ye to Dorothy and Helen," she said lightly. "Ye'd be fine."

His brown eyes blazed.

"I was teasing," she said in a weak voice.

"I didn't find it amusing."

By the time the two guards returned, Maggie was glad of it. Owen was frosty with barely restrained temper, and she understood that he hated feeling helpless. Worse yet, the two men could report nothing. The gunman had slipped away by the time they made it up the hill. On the final mile home, Owen and the other two surrounded her, and even back within the castle walls, she didn't feel safe. The gunman might have come from here, she realized bleakly.

Owen dismounted at the stables and marched toward the smithy. She wanted to hurry after him, but Fergus stepped in front of her, while the other man followed Owen.

"Mistress Maggie, we have our orders," Fergus said apologetically.

She watched, practically holding her breath, as Owen faced down Gregor, who was working over the fire, long tongs in his gloved hands and a glowing horseshoe at the end. All it would take was a thrust and Owen would be scarred for life.

But Gregor lowered the tongs and spoke to Owen, then slammed the tongs back into the fire and gestured with both hands. Several people near the smithy were openly listening, but Owen and Gregor weren't garnering too much attention beyond that. At last Gregor walked away beside the guard, taking long, angry strides.

Owen returned to Maggie. "It is done."

"What is done?" she demanded. "What did he say?"

"That he is innocent, of course. Yet he'd just begun to work at the smithy not an hour before, and he did not think anyone could vouch for him. I did agree to look into the matter of witnesses, so he agreed to a fair hearing before the next assembly. Until then, he will be under guard within his own room in the barracks."

Her stiff shoulders relaxed a bit. "I guess that is fair. But what shall I say to Kathleen?"

"Allow me to handle it. I am her chief."

Maggie wanted to protest, but didn't. He *was* the chief. Or did she simply not want to be the one to tell Kathleen that her only remaining sibling could face a terrible punishment if his guilt was decided?

"Now can you be at ease, Maggie?" Owen asked. "The wedding is only ten days away. Your family will be safe when they arrive."

She was glad for that. But his words made her wonder—did Gregor's capture change how she felt about marrying Owen? She wanted her family to be safe—but she wanted Owen to be safe, too. The thought that he might not die was an ache in her chest that made her eyes water with hope.

By supper, there were whispers all through the great hall, but Owen had forbidden either his two guards or the smithy from discussing what had happened, in case Gregor was innocent. But Owen seemed positive he was not, and his confidence mildly eased Maggie, even when Kathleen did not make an appearance, and Mrs. Robertson came to help her prepare for bed and change the tiny bandage on her arm. Maggie wouldn't even need it in the morning. For once, the housekeeper's poorly hidden disapproval seemed absent, as if Owen had revealed what Gregor had done. Maggie accepted the woman's help, but didn't discuss anything herself and let Mrs. Robertson leave disappointed.

Maggie's confused thoughts settled on the most important one: Could she marry Owen now? And could she live with the risk that she might be wrong?

But she didn't have long to wait before her decision became undeniable.

For only the second time in ten years, she had a vivid dream. She was awake, sitting in Owen's room, looking out the window upon the newly budding trees of spring. Her hands rested protectively on her very swollen stomach, and she experienced the most incredible feeling of tenderness and joy and anticipation.

Maggie sat up in bed with a gasp, wide awake in a dark room, with the moon outside the window the only light. She put a hand to her stomach in amazement and wonder. She was with child. Soon there would be a babe in her arms, nursing at her breast, looking to her for guidance and protection. The ache of love was surprisingly deep, and it brought tears to her eyes.

Keeping her hand tight to her stomach, she whispered, "I'll do what's best for ye, little one. I'll keep ye safe and happy."

OWEN drank a mug of ale and stared out the window at the courtyard below. It was just past dawn, men were in the training yard working, guards were patrolling the battlements looking out on the countryside—but the smithy was absent a worker.

Everything inside Owen tightened into a twisted

mass of anger, revenge—and through it all, the overwhelming sensation of relief. He could have lost
Maggie. When that gunshot had rung across the
mountain and he'd seen the spot of blood on her sleeve,
the surprise and fear in her expression, his vaunted
sense of dispassion and control had been obliterated.
Someone had threatened the life of his future wife. She
was an innocent, a woman being used to bring peace
to two clans—she didn't deserve to risk her life for it.

And he couldn't lose her. The thought of his life
without the rare grace of her smile was unfathomable.
The challenge of matching wits with her brought true
satisfaction. He was falling in love with her, and there
was nothing he could do about it—

But protect her. The primitive need overrode all his
thoughts of himself as a civilized man.

The only credible person who'd made any threats
against her was Gregor. When Owen had first seen
him in the smithy after the gunshot, it had taken an
extreme act of will not to pummel him into the ground
right there, to demand his vengeance like the days of
old, where he could have met his enemy on the field
and destroyed him in combat.

But he wasn't a warrior knight—he was the chief
of the Clan Duff and he had to rule his people with
impartial justice—even though a cowardly worm like
Gregor, who would shoot an innocent woman, didn't
deserve fairness.

But bringing the case against Gregor before the assembly of gentlemen was the correct thing to do. It was his duty to keep the law for the clan, and his right to sentence a man for attempted murder, but even in his bloodlust, he wanted the fact to be undisputable. He wanted Gregor to confess.

And Gregor hadn't. He'd been unable to name a witness who'd seen him within the castle before his shift in the smithy. And he hadn't denied that he was against the uniting of the two clans. But he claimed he had not fired a musket at Maggie, that he'd never shoot a woman.

Owen wanted a confession, not a protestation of innocence, he thought, taking another swig of ale. He wanted to know that the right man paid for the crime. For years, he had watched his father hand out punishments with little care for the truth. He'd been a dictator, a man who believed in the superiority and power of his title, and thought everyone else beneath him. Owen had been determined to be different, to bring justice to his clan and display fairness.

Now he felt as if the need for revenge was eating away his humanity. He'd spent his adult life combating his emotions, dealing in logic and science because it made sense, inspired nothing but pride and wonder and satisfaction. It was disheartening to realize that underneath, he could feel bloodthirsty because of a threat to his mate, as if man had not advanced in thousands of years, regardless of the ability to understand the planets or create new machines to aid mankind.

There was a knock on the door, and Owen turned his head. "Come in."

Maggie entered, then leaned back against the closed door and regarded him warily. Such an expression actually disheartened him. Had he thought a threat to her life would make her confess her love and accept his protection? No, he knew her too well. She was independent, determined to have her own way even if it made no sense.

To his surprise, she hadn't even dressed for the day, was still wearing her dressing gown. He forced his mind not to go to what lay just beneath, so close at hand. If he'd thought taking Maggie's virginity would ease his obsession with her, he'd been completely wrong. He wanted her even more, and forcing himself to regard her dispassionately took great effort.

He arched a brow. "I thought after yesterday you would allow yourself to rest longer."

She shook her head. "We need to have a discussion and it can't wait."

She approached him and stood at his side, staring out the window. He wanted to put his arm around her, but hesitated, then felt exasperated with himself. He slid his arm around her waist, and to his surprise, she leaned her head against his shoulder and sighed. Such a small surrender from a woman like Maggie should have appeased him, but it didn't.

"What is worrying you?" he asked quietly. "Gregor is confined. I promise he will never hurt you again. Is your arm sore?"

She shook her head almost impatiently. "'Twas barely a scratch. Nay, I am glad to know Gregor will pay for what he's tried to do—not that I understand it, even now. But . . . that isn't what I came here for. You need to know that I am with child."

She said it so matter-of-factly that he almost didn't understand the significance. And then he took her upper arms in his hands and stared into her face.

"With child?" he echoed, searching her eyes as if only seeing her emotions would have meaning. And then he realized a painful truth. "How can you know that? A woman has to miss her menses, and it's only been days. Can you truly call yourself 'late' without waiting for a more appropriate length of time to pass?"

She sighed and shrugged off his hands. "Sometimes you exhaust me, Owen. Nay, I've not even missed my womanly time yet."

He frowned. "I don't understand."

She put a hand on her stomach. "I dreamed of my advanced pregnancy come next spring. I know I will be having a child."

She'd dreamed. Of course she'd dreamed, he thought. He knew better than to question her about it, whatever he felt. He wanted her as his wife; he wanted a child—and if her belief made it happen, so much the better.

And then he could see their babe in her arms, and the surge of tenderness and love was daunting.

"Then we shall marry as quickly as possible," he said, feeling not one bit guilty to use her beliefs to persuade her.

She watched him with suspicion. "'Twas that easy to convince ye I spoke the truth? Ye suddenly believe in my dreams?"

"What do you want me to say, Maggie? I like having the truth from you. I want no secrets between us."

"And ye want us to marry, and this is the perfect excuse."

"I don't need an excuse to marry you, although it seems you do."

She glanced away, a blush of guilt rising. "Aye, this pregnancy changes things for me. I won't have our child a bastard, as ye said. And with Gregor now being held for the crime against me . . . 'tis time to accept my fate."

"Such a ringing, romantic endorsement of your own wedding," he said dryly.

Her face only reddened more before she sighed. "I'm sorry, Owen. Nothing has ever been easy for us. How can ye expect me to proceed with joyous abandon? I've never had a dream that didn't come true. I'm frightened for ye. But there's a child coming, and I have to trust that I've been shown one path for ye, with the chance to change it. I hope we have. I pray we have," she added fervently.

He cupped her face with both hands. "I may not have said it before, but your concern for me moves me. Ye don't care about my title or my lands—"

"Of course I do—they're what will help bring peace to both our clans."

He grimaced. "Ye know what I mean, lass. From the beginning of our betrothal, ye've been worried for me."

He brushed his thumb along her lower lip. He would marry this woman; she'd share his bed and his life. It was daunting and overwhelming and he couldn't think about how he'd changed because of her. But he knew he wanted her. She carried their future within her. He leaned down and kissed her. She seemed stiff for a long moment, until with a low moan she sighed and leaned into him, sliding her arms about his waist.

# 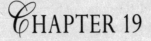HAPTER 19

Inside her heart, Maggie knew she'd surrendered to her love of Owen weeks ago, and now she surrendered her very life to him. She would be his. If she'd hoped for an impassioned declaration of love, it had been within only a little corner of herself, a sad little corner that had to accept the fact that with an arranged marriage to a man like Owen, she had to take her blessings where she found them. She would never have a great love, but he wanted her, and she would learn to be content with that.

Because she wanted him, with a desperation that frightened her. She wanted the impossible—she wanted his love, she wanted a future with him, and she didn't know if she could have those things.

But oh, when his kiss deepened into one of hunger, when he pulled her so close to his body that she could feel the pounding of his heart near to hers—she simply melted. Her flesh burned to experience the pleasure he'd given her just two days ago. She reveled in the feel of his hands sliding down her back, cupping her backside, pulling her firmly against him. They kissed for a long, sweet moment, exploring and tasting. He would be her husband, the father of her child. He would have a powerful, important place in her life. She would just have to find a way to accept him for who he was, even if he couldn't accept her the same way.

She shivered when he parted her dressing gown and it fell from her shoulders. He didn't touch, just looked at the way the fabric skimmed her body. He lifted the nightshift over her head, leaving her bare to him in the morning light, then he put his hand on her flat belly and stared into her eyes. Was he looking for the truth? Or could he simply believe her? Her eyes misted as she prayed they would find happiness as parents.

And then he pulled off his own garments so quickly it made her smile.

"I like that smile," he murmured. "It is all too rare."

But her smile faded when she looked down his body, admiring the way his broad chest tapered into narrow hips. She let herself touch him, skimming her hands over smooth, hard muscles, brushing his nipples as he'd done to her. She could feel his flesh shiver as if her touch excited him. And that excited her. She let her caresses move lower, across the ridges of his stomach. As his breathing increased, she felt a powerful sense of wonder that she could affect him so. And then she clasped his erection in her hand and he shuddered. It was hard and thick and smooth, and she explored it with great interest.

"Though I'm enjoying this, lass, I won't be able to stand it for long," he said hoarsely. "Your touch is far too—"

Then he broke off with a gasp as she reached lower, to caress the round sacs below. He liked that, too, she realized. She would have a lifetime to learn everything about him.

She hoped. Oh, she hated that little voice of worry deep in her mind that wouldn't leave her.

But she forgot all of that as Owen's hands began to caress her at the same time, one hand lingered at her nipples, the other moving between her legs to slide along her newly moist flesh. As they touched each other, neither looked away, and it was incredibly moving to know unabashedly what they could make each other feel, to acknowledge, if only with their eyes, the power of their connection.

And then with a groan, Owen moved backward, pulling her with him as he sat upon the bed. He lifted her onto his lap to straddle him.

He leaned back on his elbows, his expression eager. "Guide me inside of you."

This new position intrigued her, and though she felt awkward about how to accomplish it, she came up on her knees, took him into her hand, and slid him along the depth of her. It made her shudder, and when he suddenly took her hips in his big hands and pulled down, sheathing himself deep inside her, she gasped.

"Am I hurting ye?" he asked, his body frozen in place, but with a restrained sense of urgency as if he really wanted to be moving.

She shook her head, her awareness centered inward, on how good he felt filling her. "Can I move?"

"Please God, aye," he ground out.

She braced her hands on his chest and leaned over to say, "I'll conduct my own little experiment and ye can analyze the results."

His chuckle was mixed with a groan as she lifted herself up a bit, then sank back. The friction felt so good she did it again, and soon she was enthusiastically riding him, striving to find what felt best. He caressed her breasts, and slid his fingers wickedly between her thighs, and soon she was panting, her head thrown back with exaltation as she found her ultimate pleasure. As if he'd been waiting just for her, Owen took her hips in his hands and arched to thrust himself inside her and join her in fulfillment.

Maggie collapsed forward to rest her head on his chest. She could hear the thundering of his heart gradually slow down, feeling a sense of peace steal over her as he ran his fingers gently through her hair.

"So you're truly my betrothed now," he murmured.

She nodded, and let her breath out on a long sigh. Silently, she sent forth another prayer that she was making the right decision, that in her selfish need to have her child legitimate, she wasn't somehow sending Owen to his death.

Suddenly her world turned upside down as he rolled her onto her back. And then he was thrusting inside her again, a slow buildup into speed, and all she could do was go along for the ride and let him take her over the edge.

An hour later, when Maggie called for Kathleen to help her dress, the maid arrived in a far more subdued manner than she'd ever shown before. Her complexion was pale, her eyes downcast, and Maggie experienced a pang of sadness and even guilt, though she'd done nothing wrong.

She put a hand on Kathleen's shoulder. "I'm so sorry about your brother."

Kathleen nodded. "Thank ye, mistress."

"Is there anything I can do?"

Kathleen finally searched Maggie's eyes as if looking for answers. At last she shook her head. "I cannot believe my brother guilty of this, but I'm content to know that the assembly will listen to his words. I will find witnesses for him."

Maggie nodded, and when Kathleen began to unlace her gown, she debated asking about the charge of witchcraft that Gregor had made against a woman in the colonies. But what was Kathleen going to do—incriminate her brother? So Maggie said nothing.

Nine days sped by in a rush of business, from planning the wedding with Cat to working with Mrs. Robertson to learning the methods of the household. Now that Maggie had accepted her role as mistress, she would not shirk it.

And it gave her a good reason to avoid Owen as much as she could. She was frightened of the power of her feelings for him, and felt vulnerable knowing he did not feel the same way. She couldn't let herself openly love him, couldn't give him that power over her. She knew that without being in love, someday he might grow bored with her, and she was afraid of how crushed she'd be to see him try to hide his disinterest. She stayed away from his bedroom, and asked the same of him. She wanted at least something of their wedding night to feel special, and if that was a renewal of exploring the pleasures of their bodies, then she would accept that.

When her family arrived the day before the ceremony, she felt some trepidation. But she'd warned her brother by letter what had been going on, so that he could provide a strong escort, and would be wary within the walls of Castle Kinlochard. Brendan; Hugh; his wife, Riona; and their mother arrived late in the evening. Maggie had a quiet supper sent to their dressing room and joined them for a talk.

Hugh ate with his usual hearty appetite, and Riona would have joined him, but she obviously saw the concerned looks Lady McCallum couldn't hide.

Maggie ignored it all and talked with excitement about the food that would be served at the banquet afterward and the flowers she'd planned to decorate the church with. Brendan fell asleep and Hugh carried him to his bedroom, and on his return gave Maggie a look. She was boring him to tears, she knew, but it was for the best. She was hoping Hugh hadn't informed his wife about Gregor's threats against Maggie.

"I can't take any more of this," Riona said at last, rising to her feet and beginning to pace. "Maggie, aren't you frightened that this man—what's his name?" she asked her husband.

"Gregor," Hugh said as he sat back and eyed Maggie.

"That this Gregor had such hatred hidden within him?"

Maggie let out a frustrated breath. "Hugh, ye were supposed to keep this a secret. I didn't want anyone worried for nothing."

"Ye'll find out soon enough, sister dear, that there are few secrets in a marriage."

"Few!" Riona echoed, rounding on him.

He put both hands up, smiling. "I was teasing."

Riona rolled her eyes, then reached to take Maggie's hand. "Were you not scared? I heard there was a fire, and threatening words, and then a gunshot!"

Maggie frowned at her brother, who only shrugged. She said, "It no longer matters, because the man is under guard now."

Her mother was watching her very carefully, but said nothing.

Riona turned back to Hugh. "And this is all right with you?"

"Of course it's not all right," Hugh said. "I am disturbed that my own sister would keep these things from me the last time we were here. But I also know she thought she was doing what was best. I sometimes pity poor Owen," he said, almost as an aside.

"I had to keep silent," Maggie insisted. "I didn't want ye here, where ye could be hurt. As for me, I had Owen's protection."

"And he did a crack job at that, I see," Hugh said dryly.

"I am alive and well and about to be married."

"And ye seem so happy about that." His voice took on a note of sarcasm.

She took a deep breath. "I *am* happy. This will be a good marriage."

"Does he love ye?" Hugh shot back.

She hesitated. "I don't know. I want to believe it will happen, but he's a man who doesn't show his emotions—unlike you, brother dear, who shows more emotions than are necessary."

Hugh only grinned, and Riona looked from her husband to Maggie with confusion.

"Then I'll show ye another emotion, Maggie," Hugh said, his smile fading. "Empathy. I sense a difference in ye, and I see ye holding your belly as if in protection."

Maggie stiffened, then dropped her hand, trying not to blush with guilt.

Lady Aberfoyle's expression turned from shock to happiness to worry, all in the blink of an eye. "Margaret, ye're with child?"

"I—I think so," she admitted. "'Tis too soon to ken for certain—"

"Then our children will grow up together!" Riona cried happily, as if forgetting that her fears had begun this conversation.

"Ye're pregnant, too?" Maggie asked, allowing delight to raise her spirits.

Riona grinned and nodded, and they both hugged. Maggie saw her brother watching with fond satisfaction, as if he'd set everything up himself. And in a way he had, kidnapping the wrong bride and setting in motion the conflict that even now interfered between Owen and her.

As for Maggie's admission of pregnancy, no one looked embarrassed or ashamed, for in the Highlands, a child was welcomed, and often sealed the bond between the mother and father. In fact, Hugh looked downright relieved.

Maggie gave him a light swat on the shoulder. "Stop that! In England, ye'd be calling Owen out for dishonoring me instead of looking like ye're thrilled to be an uncle. Am I not right, Riona?"

"Yes, she's right," Riona admitted.

"But we aren't in England," Hugh said easily. "We're in the Highlands, and what started out as a betrothal to end a feud has changed into one where the two of ye cannot keep your hands off each other. I am only sorry to know there are still ignorant people who don't want peace." And then he scowled. "Ye're certain ye've got the right man locked up?"

"The evidence against him is mounting," Maggie said. "And nothing has happened to me since he's been confined." She touched her stomach again. "And I've been shown a dream that I was with child—it seems I'm meant to marry Owen."

Maggie thought she'd calmed and comforted her family enough, but her mother followed her to her room when it was time for them all to retire.

Maggie welcomed her with a smile. "I'm afraid I don't need the wedding-night explanation from the mother of the bride."

Lady McCallum winced. "I cannot claim I'm unhappy about that. I've heard 'tis an awkward conversation. But things must be going better between ye if ye're carrying his babe."

"Better, aye." Maggie sagged onto the edge of the bed, where her mother joined her. "But . . . he doesn't love me, Mathair; he cannot believe in me."

"How do ye ken he cannot love ye? Just because he hasn't said the words yet? He's a man, and sometimes sentimentality is a difficult thing to admit."

Maggie shrugged. She wanted to believe that, but . . . "Oh, he wants me, and has no problem showing *those* emotions," she said wryly, once again touching her stomach. "He was happy that the revelation of the baby changed my mind about the marriage."

"I thought Gregor's capture did that?" Lady McCallum asked uneasily.

"It did. But Mathair, Gregor professes his innocence, still. I guess only a complete admission of guilt will truly satisfy me. What if—what if I marry Owen and—" She broke off as her throat became too full to speak.

"Ye do love him," her mother said, sympathy gleaming in her eyes.

Maggie nodded. "But how can he ever love me if he doesn't believe in my dreams?"

"If he respects ye—and I think he does, because he didn't force ye to marry immediately—then love should follow, my lass. Ye've already committed to this marriage. Commit to believing that Owen has feelings he doesn't know how to express. Commit to a happy future, where Gregor can never bother ye again."

Maggie nodded, quickly wiping away a solitary tear. "Look at me. I never thought I'd be crying on the eve of my wedding."

"Perhaps it only proves the depth of your emotion. I have faith in ye. And I have faith in Owen. He didn't have to propose to ye; he could have taken our prized land and left us with no way to earn coin in these difficult times. He has honor."

Maggie nodded again, then accepted her mother's hug and held on longer than necessary. Then her mother kissed her forehead and left.

Maggie was alone, wondering for the thousandth time if she was doing the right thing.

# CHAPTER 20

Maggie tried to enjoy her wedding day, but every moment was steeped in a creeping sense of rising fear. Owen had surprised her by having the seamstresses make a new gown—the one she'd been wearing in her dream. She'd stared at it as Kathleen had held it up, and horror was a nausea that seemed to rise from her belly and into her throat. In the end, she'd stood a little too close to the fire, and Kathleen had had to toss the pitcher of water at the hem to combat any flames. Maggie felt guilty, and promised Kathleen they'd repair the gown for the next big assembly or festival—but she wasn't going to wear it on her wedding day.

If Owen recognized the green silk gown she'd worn the night he first officially welcomed her to the castle, he hadn't said a thing when she reached his side in the family chapel. Maggie was still shaken that he was alive and smiling at her, but she could not get over the feeling that her dream could unfold any moment. She barely noticed the fresh flowers in vases, or the way the rare sun shone through the windows with beams of light. Owen's gentlemen and their wives faded into the background. His sister Cat and uncle Harold were simply backdrops near the altar, waiting to stand at their sides.

Maggie could only look at Owen, at the pride that lingered in his faint smile as he took her hand from Hugh. They were in the chapel, which hadn't been in her dream. They were honestly getting married. She even managed to relax a bit, and her voice didn't shake too much when she repeated her vows.

And then it was done, and Owen was kissing her, and people were cheering. Maggie tried to remember that she was doing this for peace and to save lives and to give her baby a name. And she was doing it for love, even if he couldn't reciprocate. Could her love be enough for the both of them?

The wedding feast was full of food and gaiety, poetry and songs. The more hours passed, the better Maggie felt. Her mother broke the traditional oatcake over her head for good luck. And Owen kept touching Maggie, whether it be her hand or her arm, or her thigh beneath the table. They'd barely kissed these last few days, and even she was growing more excited about the wedding night than worried. The day was almost over. Had she truly succeeded in keeping Owen safe?

Kathleen came to her at the dais. Though subdued and thinner since her brother's confinement, she'd lost her pallor and had seemed to put on an optimistic attitude. Maggie hoped for the girl's sake that Gregor's punishment wouldn't be too severe.

Now Kathleen leaned over and spoke into Maggie's ear to be heard over the pipes. "Lady Aberfoyle—"

Though Maggie had heard the honorific through the day, it still sounded strange. At least she was Maggie McCallum, and had no need to take Owen's clan name for her own. She would consider it, of course, if it helped keep the peace.

"There seems to be a disturbance among the weavers in the woman room," Kathleen finished, then added apologetically, "Ye said as the new mistress of the castle, ye wished to be told such things."

"Of course, Kathleen, thank ye. A disturbance?"

"I do believe an argument is growin' worse."

"Very well, I'll go settle things right now."

Women were weaving during her wedding banquet? It seemed very strange. Maggie didn't bother to tell Owen she was leaving for something so small. In fact, she didn't even see him in the crowd. But she headed up the spiral staircase to the next floor, rushing past both her and Owen's rooms, even as she hoped she would find the argument already amicably settled. It was her wedding day, after all!

OWEN noticed Maggie had left the hall, but it wasn't until he received the note from Kathleen that he thought anything about it. Maggie wrote that she wanted to meet him in his room in private. Did she wish to avoid the traditional friendly escort to their bedroom? He liked his wife's daring. And he was a little drunk, too.

*His wife*. Those two words had taken on a new meaning. Fergus tried to follow him upstairs, and Owen stretched two arms across the width of the corridor to stop him.

"It's my wedding night, Fergus," Owen patiently explained.

Even the tips of Fergus's ears reddened. "Aye, my lord, but—"

"But nothing. My wife awaits. Stay here and enjoy yourself."

Owen was practically whistling as he took the stairs two at a time. The corridor had grown darker, but torches were lit at intervals. He opened up his door, anticipating seeing Maggie naked in his bed, the candlelight illuminating her like a painting come to life.

But there was no light on at all, which was strange. And then something hard hit him in the head. He stumbled forward to his knees, dazed with the pain, then felt a sharp stab in his back. With instinct, he arched backward and grabbed, catching his fingers in hair as he fell. On the floor, he twisted and grabbed the assailant's thin ankle, but a kick caught him across the jaw and he lost his hold.

As he began to lose consciousness, he swore he could smell Maggie's perfume. The door slammed shut and he was alone—too alone. He tried to get up on his hands and knees but reeled with dizziness and the throb of pain in his back. He didn't know how badly he was bleeding, but he couldn't risk simply hoping for help. He crawled the rest of the way to the door, and though it felt a mile above him, he reached the handle and managed to open it. He collapsed near the threshold, the torches weaving as he stared at them from between half-closed eyes. He wasn't certain how long he lay there.

"Owen!"

His uncle's rumbling voice had an urgency Owen had never heard before.

"Who did this to ye, lad?" Harold demanded.

"A . . . woman." Owen lifted his trembling hand, and he thought he saw strands of hair caught between his fingers.

As if he was falling farther and farther away, he could hear a woman scream.

MAGGIE couldn't seem to stop screaming as she stood in the doorway and saw Owen lying in his own blood. She felt frozen and brittle, as if she could be broken in half. She had done everything to avoid this wedding, had thought Gregor's capture would save Owen, and it all had led to him bleeding just as she'd foreseen. Fate had cruelly taunted her, but hadn't allowed her to change a thing.

Someone had her by the arms and was shaking her, but she stared past at Owen on the floor, face white as death, eyelids fluttering.

"Fergus, send for the physician!" Harold shouted past her.

He let her alone then, and she staggered forward and dropped to her knees beside Owen. She pulled him across her lap, straining, and then Harold was helping her.

"Put your hands on the wound," she cried. "Stop the bleeding!"

As Harold did as she commanded, she rocked Owen as his head bobbed lifelessly on her shoulder, his arms trailing like a puppet whose strings had been cut.

"Don't die," she whispered into his hair, pressing kisses there, too. "Don't die, please don't die."

And then people rushed into the room and pulled Owen away from her. She screamed at the loss, needing to be with him if it was his final moment. But Harold had her again, holding her by the arm so tightly she felt bruised.

"The physician will see to him," he said sternly.

Maggie blinked up at him. "Physician—? There isn't one in the castle. Euphemia—"

"Owen sent for him from Edinburgh, wanted him here for the ceremony, though I didn't know why." Gruffly, he added, "Thank God."

Maggie stared at Owen lying unconscious on his stomach, Fergus helping the physician cut the garments from Owen's back. Owen had sent for the physician because of her dream, as if he honestly believed her. She didn't realize she was crying until Harold pressed a handkerchief into her hand.

"Ye shouldn't be here, lass," he said.

"I won't leave him."

He couldn't die—God wouldn't allow him to die, not when Owen had just proven that he trusted her.

She and Harold stood arm-in-arm for a moment, watching, and Harold spoke thickly, "I couldn't find the words to tell him how impressed I was about his studies, how seriously he took them, how he wanted to help his clan."

"Ye can tell him when he wakes up," Maggie insisted.

Fergus was lighting candles and lanterns all about the room. Harold suddenly left her and bent to something on the floor. Maggie couldn't look, worried the pool of darkening blood would make her even more nauseous than she'd been these last few mornings with their babe.

Their babe.

Harold rose slowly to his feet, then turned a ferocious look on Maggie, holding out items in his hand. "This is a McCallum dirk. I recognize the pattern on the hilt."

She stared at it, blinking. "I—I—" Why would a member of her clan want her husband dead? It didn't make sense.

"And this letter. 'Tis from your own hand," Harold accused.

His expression grew so ugly she recoiled. "My hand? Let me see it."

He wouldn't let her hold it, as if she might rip it to pieces. She felt cold and prickly inside, like something terrible was beginning to happen. But she forced herself to study the letter, then raised her head and said with conviction. "I didn't write that."

Harold scoffed without words at her protest, their shared worry for Owen gone as he looked at her with disdain.

Someone had forged her writing before, to scare her. This time it implicated her. But Gregor was still confined—her brother had checked just before the wedding. Had Gregor been innocent all along, with the true villain waiting for them to relax their guard? Or was there a second conspirator?

"Why would I lure Owen here to hurt him?" she demanded, knowing her future depended on convincing the Duff war chief of her innocence. "I love him, I married him."

"Ye're a McCallum *forced* to marry him," Harold responded coldly. "Owen told me about your reluctance—he even laughed about it, as if he thought your protests amusing."

She flinched, but knew Owen might have displayed such pride when she first refused to marry him.

"And what is this?" Harold demanded.

Without releasing her arm, he bent and picked up something that had been next to the puddle of blood.

He held it up, and Maggie could see a broken hair comb. Recognizing it, she felt for the one in her hair, but it was gone.

"Is it yours?" he demanded.

"I don't know. If it is, I was here with Owen—it could have fallen off as I lifted him so you could see to his back."

Harold seemed to grind his teeth together, but he said nothing more. She met his gaze defiantly, with conviction.

He pushed her toward Fergus. "Take her to her chamber and keep her there."

"I'm not leaving Owen," she cried, ducking Fergus and stepping closer to the bed. "You can watch over me, Fergus, but I can't leave him. I won't leave him." Her voice broke.

The physician eyed her briefly, then returned to his work with a needle, while Mrs. Robertson dabbed at the blood to keep the wound visible. Maggie hadn't even seen the woman enter, but at least she gave Maggie a reassuring look, as if now that Maggie had won her good regard, she could not so easily lose it.

Maggie turned back to Harold. "Do ye not think it suspicious that all this time, someone seemed determined to hurt me, that they even shot at me—I didn't shoot myself!—and now I'm suddenly a suspect in Owen's attack?"

"Ye could have accomplices," Harold said woodenly. "And perhaps your accomplice was trying to shoot Owen, not you. It will all be discussed when he awakens."

"And he'll confirm I'm telling the truth," she insisted.

Fergus stood beside her, obviously hesitant to touch her.

Harold let out a breath. "Very well, remain here, and Fergus, make sure she stays in that chair." He pointed to one beside the bed.

Maggie obediently sat down in it.

"I'm going to see to the McCallums," Harold told Fergus.

"What do you mean?" Maggie started to rise, but Fergus put a hand on her shoulder and kept her there.

"I'm going to put your family under guard in their rooms—for their own protection," Harold pointed out. "If people believe ye did this—"

"And they only will if ye insist on telling them such a ridiculous story," Maggie said.

"Regardless, when people are angry and afraid, they turn on those they've long regarded as the enemy."

"Are ye speaking of your own actions?" she asked coldly.

Harold eyed her, then spoke more evenly. "I'm following the clues, the McCallum dirk, the letter in your own hand—"

"It's not my hand," she insisted.

"People could well believe that now that ye have Owen's trust and his money, you, a McCallum, want him dead. And before he lost consciousness, Owen said his assailant was a woman."

"He did?" Maggie said in surprise. "Ye didn't say that before." A woman?

Then Owen groaned, and she couldn't think about anything else. She leaned forward to take his hand, where it hung off the end of the bed. "Doctor?" she said tentatively.

The older man straightened from where he'd been washing his hands in a basin. He had kind eyes above a stern gray beard.

"I don't believe the dirk penetrated any major organs," the physician said, glancing from her to Harold. "If the wound doesn't inflame, he should live."

Maggie let out a shaky breath and said quietly to Owen, "Did ye hear that? Ye're going to live. But ye've got to fight, Owen. Ye have to fight for our babe."

She didn't know if he heard her; he didn't squeeze her hand, but she wanted to believe that his fingers moved just a little within hers. And with this small bit of hope, she began to think about who could have done this.

OWEN slowly opened his eyes, the throbbing of his head inducing nausea. He closed his eyes to control himself, then tried again. The first face he saw was Maggie's, relaxed in sleep but for the frown line between her eyes. She slumped on a chair, her hand resting on the bed next to him. Maggie. His wife.

He was awake, he was alive, and lying on his stomach. He mentally moved through the aches in his body, knowing his head hurt, and then lower, where pain stabbed him in the back when he tried to turn.

And then he remembered actually being stabbed.

"Owen, lad?"

At his uncle's voice, Maggie jerked upright, her gaze going right to Owen. He watched hope suffuse her expression, saw tears of gladness shine in her eyes.

"Owen, oh, Owen," she whispered, reaching to touch his forehead.

To Owen's surprise, Fergus grabbed her arm and pulled it away. He frowned up at his bodyguard. "What is going on?" he demanded, his voice a croak. He cleared his throat. "Fergus, release your countess."

Instead of listening to him, Fergus shot a glance at Harold, who gave a short nod.

Maggie dropped to her knees beside the bed and touched his face. "Owen, ye made it through the night. I was so afraid. Ye're warm, but not overly feverish. How do ye feel?"

"Like I've been trampled by a horse," he grumbled. He lowered his voice. "What is going on?"

"What is going on," Harold began, "is that ye claimed a woman attacked ye, and I found a McCallum dirk beside ye and a note from Maggie insisting that ye meet her in your room."

"Uncle," Owen began.

Harold put up a hand. "A maid even saw Maggie rushing from the room before ye were found."

"I was rushing *toward* the woman room," Maggie insisted tiredly. "Ye pass this door to reach it. I was told there was a disturbance there, and obviously I'd only been lured from the great hall. No one was there at all. When I came back, I saw ye lying in a pool of blood, just like . . ." She trailed off, and this time, twin tears fell slowly down her cheeks. She leaned forward then, kissed his hand, and whispered, "But ye'd sent for the physician, Owen. Ye believed me."

Owen hadn't been able to get her conviction about her dreams out of his mind. He'd told himself he was only sending for the physician as a precaution. Apparently, he'd help save his own life, he thought wryly. Nay, Maggie had saved his life. She'd been trying to save it all along. He smiled at her, and she smiled back. He didn't know what sort of gift she had, but he could not deny the truth of it. And that realization suddenly overwhelmed him, as he thought of all the ways he'd denied her, humiliated her, subjugated his own conscience. But he couldn't let himself think of that now, not when she was still in danger.

Maggie didn't look at Harold, only continued to run her hand through Owen's hair. When he winced, she cried out.

"Oh, ye have a bump, Owen," she said with worry. "Ye were hit from behind."

Owen slowly unfolded the fingers of his left hand, still clenched together. "I caught her hair."

It was not the dark brown of Maggie's, but reddish blond.

Maggie didn't look surprised, but sad and worried. "I've been thinking, Owen, and I believe we were considering the wrong sibling. Kathleen was the one who lured me from the hall. She had easy access to my handwriting."

"She's the one who gave me the letter from ye," Owen said. "And Uncle, when ye speak to Kathleen, have her show ye her ankle. I caught it hard, and there'd be a bruise."

Without Owen even making a suggestion, Maggie lifted her skirts to reveal her delicate, unblemished ankles. "Do ye think she's been working with her brother from the beginning?"

Owen shrugged, then grimaced at the shot of pain. "We won't know until we question them both."

"They wanted to incite clan warfare," Maggie said grimly. "If ye'd believed I tried to kill ye, ye might have imprisoned my brother, and the McCallums would have come in force." She shuddered. "There'd be no end to the feud. I still need to know why!"

"I'll find the lass and bring her here," Harold said, nodding to Owen as he left the room.

Fergus backed toward the door and stood there, looking abashed. "My lady," he began.

"It's all right, Fergus," she said. "Ye were protecting my husband. Now could ye send someone to fetch broth for our patient, and also send word to my family that I am well and will come to see them soon? I do agree with Harold, that they should remain secluded until we've apprehended the right person."

She glanced at Owen, who smiled before closing his eyes. He liked the sound of her giving orders with such confidence and pride. He found himself gradually drifting into a doze, still feeling her hand resting on his.

When the door opened, he simply listened and trusted Maggie to deal with anything.

Harold said, "I found Mrs. Robertson unconscious and Kathleen gone."

Maggie gasped and Owen opened his eyes.

"Oh, that poor woman," she said. "Will she be all right?"

"After a few minutes, I was able to awaken her," Harold said. "She showed me the writing paper, ink, and pen she'd found in Kathleen's things before the wedding, assumed they were stolen, and was going to report it to ye afterwards."

"We don't know where Kathleen is now?" Maggie asked.

"I'm searching the castle."

Nodding, Maggie turned to Owen. "Would ye mind if I go to my family? They'll be frantic with worry."

Though he tried to remain awake, their voices began to fade away. Something was wrong—he could tell by Maggie's voice, by . . . something. But he couldn't stop the long slide his consciousness seemed to take down a deep well.

*Maggie, don't go.*

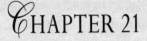

# CHAPTER 21

Maggie did not go to her family's rooms, but grabbed a cloak to disguise herself. Now that word had been given to search for Kathleen, it was easy enough to take the servants' staircase at the rear of the tower-house and no one bothered her. Once she was in the courtyard, still awash in the gray shadows of dawn, she went to the barracks, where Gregor was being confined in his own room.

A guard nodded respectfully to her, and she was able to gesture him farther down the hall, so she could speak in private to Gregor. A little slot had been cut into the door, probably for ease of passing in trays of food, and she opened it.

When Gregor saw her, he came nearer at once, then raised both hands when she stiffened.

"I mean ye no harm, mistress, but somethin' is terribly wrong with Kathleen."

She almost gaped at him. "What are ye saying?"

Gregor rubbed his hands over his unshaven face. "I don't know what to do. I know I've made no friend of ye, but if I send the guards, somethin' worse will happen to Kathleen, I know it. She's the only sister I have left, but she looked . . . wild when she came to me. Go after her, mistress. She said somethin' crazy, that her task was complete and there would never be peace. I fear she's goin' to harm herself."

"Where did she go?"

"The loch. She talked about water like it would ease her soul. Please, mistress!"

Maggie motioned to the guard to return, then ran back down the stairs and out into the courtyard. She saw that the gates remained open, that everyone still assumed that with Gregor confined, and with the wedding banquet guests going to and fro between the castle and village, there'd been no need to close down the defenses.

Maggie slipped through the gatehouse and across the stone bridge. The sun had yet to rise above the mountains, and tendrils of fog hovered over the moat and curled down the road she followed. It was an ominous sign, she thought, shivering.

She walked as quickly as she could, but it still took what had to be a quarter of an hour before she reached the loch, where the fog seemed to hover over the surface in patches.

In the distance, she saw the boat still moored, and a lone woman setting something inside. Her light reddish blond hair stuck out against the darkness of her gown. Maggie knew she couldn't get there in time, but began to run anyway.

It was too late; Kathleen pushed away from rocky edge with an oar and began to row. By the time Maggie reached the water, Kathleen's boat was at least twenty yards from shore, with fog draping around it. If Maggie tried to swim, she'd only sink with all the clothing she was wearing.

"Come back, Kathleen! Gregor is so worried about ye!"

To Maggie's horror, Kathleen picked up a rock and tucked it down inside her loose bodice, wearing a satisfied and calm smile all the while. Gregor had been right about his sister's plans. Maggie raced to the other boats, only to find holes bashed in them. Maggie had been in such a rush to confront the woman before she could get away, so worried she'd be stopped, that only Gregor knew her plans. Would he send help—and would it be on time? Once again, she'd acted without enough forethought, just as Owen had accused her.

"Kathleen, talk to me. Tell me what happened and why ye're so angry with me."

"I didn't want to be angry with ye," Kathleen said, her tone casual and almost chatty, even as she put another rock in her bodice. "Ye were just a victim of this foolish contract between two old men. At first Gregor thought we could make everyone angry with ye. I was willin' to let him try. I even helped. Remember that ball gown during the welcomin' banquet? Och, I knew ye'd make a bad impression in such finery."

Maggie well remembered how she'd felt, looking so fancy when most were hardworking simple clansmen.

"But Himself—he was agog with that gown, and I was angry, even though ye were puttin' off marriage and my plan was workin'. Ye should have been frightened off by that talisman. But then ye started diggin' into my brother's past, hurtin' him. Ye started to fall in love with his lordship, and I knew ye'd eventually give in and marry him. I couldn't have that," she explained, her eyes wide with sincerity. "It took me some time to realize I couldn't just kill ye—although I did try. I was so angry when ye went to my aunt. And then I realized how much better it would be if I made it look like ye killed his lordship. It would ruin ye and yer clan."

"But why, Kathleen?" Maggie hoped by keeping her talking, someone would come by soon and be able to help. Yet the boat was drifting farther away every moment, the fog's eerie tendrils wrapping themselves around Kathleen's skirt now, moving higher, as if it would soon take her for its own. "Why do ye hate McCallums so much? Ye spent most of your life away from Scotland."

Kathleen's eyes suddenly seemed to blaze, and the hatred in her voice sent Maggie back a step. "The McCallums are the reason we lost everythin'! Ye stole my father's cattle, made him lose our cottage, our land."

Maggie knew what kind of a man her father had

been—if he'd ordered cattle thieving, it would have happened. It also could have been in retaliation for reiving by the Duffs. There was no way to know the truth. But Kathleen wouldn't care about the truth, not anymore.

"I could have killed ye any time," Kathleen continued, her voice back into that awful singsong sound, "but I wanted ye to suffer as ye made us suffer. Do ye ken what it's like to see your brother lose his life's work? Do ye ken what it's like to be just a little girl on a big boat to America, with my mother dyin' beside me? No one found me for hours and I laid there as she got cold, so cold."

Her voice trailed off, and her eyes had a wild, faraway look. The boat rocked beneath her, and she flung her arms wide to steady herself.

Maggie covered her mouth with one hand, horrified by what Kathleen had suffered. It must have changed her, destroyed her.

"Kathleen, come back," Maggie beseeched. "Let the Duffs help ye; let your brother help ye."

"I'm done here. They'll never trust ye now without me to blame everythin' on. The Duffs will triumph over the McCallums."

"Kathleen!"

But the woman stepped overboard and sank with barely a splash, leaving only a few bubbles to pop on the surface.

Maggie waded into the water, screaming the maid's name. By the time the cold water hit her waist, she felt it pull at her skirts, threatening to drag her under, to drown her. Had Kathleen somehow known Owen's first betrothed had died by drowning? Nay, how could she have? Yet she'd threatened Maggie with drowning, and then gone through with it herself.

Maggie heard voices, shouting, and then clansmen passed her to wade out toward the boat and eventually swim.

"She's under water!" Maggie yelled, and watched as they all began to dive. She stumbled into a hole and went down on one knee. The cold water seeped into her clothing, shuddered across her skin. Sodden, she struggled to get to her feet, gagging on a deep gulp of water.

And then Harold had her by the arms, lifting her upright, holding her against him as she coughed. After he helped her to shore, they both watched as the men continued the search.

"Was she trying to get away?" Harold asked quietly.

Maggie shook her head. "She—she put rocks in her clothes and killed herself."

The boat continued to drift. It took some time before they found Kathleen's body. Only when they brought her to the surface, white and lifeless, did Maggie turn and retch onto the ground. And then Harold wrapped her shoulders within a big arm and led her away to the horses.

OWEN ate breakfast quickly, ravenously, knowing he had to be strong for Maggie. It was Gregor who'd told his guard what had happened, that Maggie had gone to stop Kathleen. Harold had followed Maggie to the loch, but as yet, had sent no word back. Owen couldn't lie in his bed, knowing she was out there, alone against a killer. He demanded his shirt and plaid.

"My lord!" Fergus cried, both hands before him as if he'd push Owen back down, but didn't dare lay hands on him.

"My wife is in danger," Owen said angrily, tossing the blankets aside. The stitches in his back burned with each movement but he barely noticed it. "Now help me don my shirt or by God—"

Fergus found one in a nearby chest, and helped it over Owen's head. Lifting his arms was surprisingly painful, but he didn't let that stop him. While he breathed heavily, Fergus laid out his plaid and belt on the bed. When it was ready, Owen lay down upon it and belted it around him. Fergus helped him don his stockings and boots like he was a child. As Owen rose unsteadily and walked past Fergus, the bodyguard grabbed the ends of the plaid and threw it up over his shoulder.

"Do ye want the brooch, my lord?"

The free ends slipped down to his waist and, frustrated, Owen permitted Fergus to clasp the excess in place with the brooch. Owen thought he'd walk all the way to the barracks, but he realized that wasn't going to happen. He sat in his big thronelike chair on the dais in the great hall, sent everyone away, and told Fergus to bring Gregor to him.

But before that could happen, Harold entered the far double doors, and to Owen's utter relief, he held Maggie by the arm. His wife looked white with strain and grief, but she was alive and apparently unharmed.

"Maggie!"

When he shouted her name, her head came up. Their gazes met, and all the love and relief he felt practically unmanned him. And then she was running toward him, and he rose to meet her. She came into his arms, hard against his body, and he did his best not to stagger. She was soaked and shivering.

Burying his face into her neck, he kept murmuring her name. She was crying softly, and it was some moments before he could understand the words.

"I should have known . . . I should have realized . . ."

And then more quiet words of regret and guilt.

He took her arms and gave her a little shake, until she looked up at him with wet, dripping eyes.

"Maggie, she tried to kill ye, and she could have succeeded."

"She tried to kill ye, too, and blame it on me," Maggie said, her voice hoarse. "But . . . such terrible things happened to her."

"Tell me."

He sank back in his chair, drawing her onto his lap. Mrs. Robertson handed him a blanket, and he wrapped it around Maggie. He saw when the Mc-

Callums entered but they stood back and listened as Maggie recounted her talk with Gregor, the man's fear, Kathleen's crazy confession just before killing herself. Lady McCallum and Riona held on to each other with silent weeping, then reached toward Cat when she arrived and drew her into their embrace. Hugh looked grim and full of frustrated anger. Owen knew just how he felt.

Owen kissed Maggie's tearstained face. "Hush, lass, let it go. She was warped by what happened to her family. Ye did nothing to her, yet she couldn't see that."

"I know, but . . ."

And then Gregor was brought into the hall between two guards, Harold following behind.

Gregor took one look at Maggie and realized the truth, collapsing to his knees with a cry of grief. "She's dead?"

Maggie nodded, her face spasming with sorrow.

"It's my fault, my fault," he cried over and over. "She thought to avenge us, to rescue me, but I couldn't— couldn't—"

"What did she say to ye?" Owen demanded.

"It's not what she said, it's what I didn't do." Gregor threw his hands wide. "I didn't protect her. I spoke of my rage at fate and blamed the McCallums. I blamed everyone but me and my stupid pride and my temper. I lost my business in the colonies when I couldn't have the woman I wanted. I tried to punish her with my wild accusations and instead I impoverished my sister. And when I realized ye'd made peace with the McCallums, who'd been the cause of our flight from Scotland—" He broke off when he saw the chief of the McCallums himself. He hung his head and it was difficult to hear his words as he admitted, "I set the fires. I told my sister what I'd done. I was so angry. I had no idea she'd take it farther." He collapsed onto his hands and knees, head hanging, and sobbed.

"Let him go, Owen," Maggie whispered, taking his hand in hers. "Let him find his fate somewhere else. He's a broken man."

"If ye wish it, lass. Now come with me and let me take care of ye."

MAGGIE felt so exhausted, it was as if she was removed from herself. She hugged her family, both old and new, and then allowed Owen to lead her away, back to the room they would now share. Every trace of blood was gone, but she knew it would be a long time before it was erased from her memories, her very soul. He'd almost died.

"Go back to bed," she suddenly said, worried that so much exertion was too much for him.

"Nay, I'll sit here and be with ye. I'm no infant to lie there and drool."

She finally gave a shaky smile, even as he slowly sank into a chair with a sigh. Once again, he pulled her onto his knee.

"Owen—"

"Enough of your worry, woman. I'll touch ye as I want. Ye're my wife and I didn't even have my wedding night."

She never thought she'd smile again, but she did so, even as she allowed him to tuck her head beneath his chin. They sat that way for several long minutes while she told herself all was well. Owen was safe and whole. She shuddered and pressed herself even closer to him.

"I believe in ye, Maggie," he said after a while, his voice a rumble in his ribs beneath her ear. "Why did ye not wait for me to make things right?"

"I couldn't," she whispered. "I knew she'd get away, and it was my fault I didn't see how twisted she truly was. She almost killed ye, Owen. I love ye so much, it was as if she stabbed me, too. All that blood. I thought—I thought—"

She felt his gentle hand tilt up her chin, and she saw through eyes blurred with tears that he was regarding her with sweet tenderness.

"I love ye, too, Maggie," he said quietly, "more than I ever thought possible."

She drew in a breath, searching his face with desperate eyes, listening to the beloved brogue of Scotland in his voice. "Ye . . . love me?"

"I do. I don't deserve your love, but I'm humbled that ye offer it."

Maggie's eyes filled with glad tears. "Our love can be the start of a new life, where we celebrate the ways we've changed. *You've* changed. Ye sent for the physician!"

A corner of his mouth twitched.

"Ye could say ye were taking care of all possibilities," she said, "but to me, it felt like ye *believed* in me."

"I do, lass, I do. I may never be able to explain or prove the things that've happened to ye, but it doesn't matter. Maybe someday ye'll tell me about your dreams of our childhood."

"And that's not looking for proof?" she chided.

He reared his head back. "Nay, it's about needing to know everything about ye and experiencing again this connection we've had since before we even knew each other."

She leaned up and kissed him, trying to show all her feelings because words alone didn't seem enough.

"Maggie," he whispered against her mouth, then kissed her cheeks and forehead. "Maggie, it scares me how much I love ye. When I knew ye'd left to confront a madwoman on my behalf, it was as if I'd been stabbed again. I can't lose ye. I can't lose your smile and your wit, and the way each of life's experiences is something new to be understood and embraced. Ye tried to protect me, even when it meant risking your life. Your loyalty to your clan was something I never doubted, but you, Maggie, everything ye are—" He broke off, then bowed his head until their foreheads touched. "Ye humble me, lass."

She was crying again, but this time she was smiling, too. "Oh, Owen, how could I have known what we could share? If I'd had a dream about *this*, I'd have followed ye to England and back until I made ye see that what we have is—is—"

"Like magic," he whispered against her lips.

She carefully put her arms around his neck and held on. "Aye, like magic, and I promise that we'll never let it die. I never let myself get too close to anyone, afraid to reveal myself. But you and your family and your household have shown me I've been wrong. I've made good friends here, and I count your sister as the most important friend yet. I won't stand on the outside any more, like a coward. I love ye, Owen."

"I love ye, too, Maggie. I can't hold back my emotions anymore because they spill out of me every time I see your face. Let me show ye how I feel." He began to stand and move toward the bed.

"Nay, that won't be happening." She planted her feet on the floor and refused to be budged.

"But we missed our wedding night," he said with indignation.

She chuckled. "Lucky ye are that we already had it, and it was so powerful that we made a babe. Now go lie down and recover."

"Woman, I'll have ye know—"

"I didn't say ye'd be recovering all alone in that big bed."

He blinked at her. "Well then. I do believe I'll need to be recovering all day long."

Laughing, she took his hand and led him to their marriage bed, which she planned to put to good use for many years to come. Just not today.

# EPILOGUE

That night, safe within her husband's arms, Maggie dreamed. Their future came vividly to life, the five children she would bear, a mix of girls and boys. She saw Owen giving lectures in Edinburgh, saw herself at his side, discussing their research, involving their children, teaching a love of learning and science that would extend for generations and produce great minds who solved scientific mysteries that had once seemed like only superstition or magic.

But it was their obvious love and respect for each other that molded their children, that provided the safety and security for exploration of the mind and of the soul.

And when Maggie awoke, her head pillowed on Owen's broad shoulder, she smiled a secretive smile, and told herself this was one dream she could show him by living it rather than foretelling it. Although maybe she'd tell him their first child would be a boy . . .

# AVONBOOKS

*The Diamond Standard*
*of Romance*

*Visit* AVONROMANCE.COM

Come celebrate 75 years of Avon Books
as each month we look toward the future
and celebrate the past!

Join us online for more information about our
75th anniversary e-book promotions,
author events and reader activities.
A full year of new voices and classic stories.
All created by the very best writers of romantic fiction.

*Diamonds Always*
*Sparkle, Shimmer, and Shine!*